GERTRUDE

GERTRUDE

A NOVEL by Hassan Najmi

translated from the Arabic by ROGER ALLEN

Interlink Books

An imprint of Interlink Publishing Group, Inc.
Northampton, Massachusetts

First published in 2014 by

INTERLINK BOOKS
An imprint of Interlink Publishing Group, Inc.
46 Crosby Street, Northampton, Massachusetts 01060
www.interlinkbooks.com

Library of Congress Cataloging-in-Publication Data

Najmi, Hasan.
[Jirtrud. English]
Gertrude : a novel / by Hassan Najmi ; translated from the Arabic by Roger Allen. -- First American edition.
    p. cm.
ISBN 978-1-56656-971-2 -- ISBN 978-1-56656-945-3
1. Tour guides (Persons)--Morocco--Fiction. 2. Stein, Gertrude, 1874-1946--Fiction. 3. Toklas, Alice B.--Fiction. 4. Women authors--Fiction. 5. Americans--Morocco--Fiction. I. Allen, Roger, 1942- II. Title.
PJ7852.A5337J5813 2013
892.7'36--dc23
                                2013023660

Printed and bound in the United States of America

10 9 8 7 6 5 4 3 2 1

To request our complete 48-page, full-color catalog, please call us toll free at 1-800-238-LINK, visit our website at www.interlinkbooks.com, or send us an e-mail: info@interlinkbooks.com

In memory of my friend Sargon Boulos, the poet.

And for Muhammad al-`Alami.

And to the memory of that young Native American woman who talks to her Moroccan friend on a Seattle night as they are returning from a nightclub. She points with her finger: "There used to be a tall green tree here," she says, "but they cut it down to put all this cement in its place!"

And for Muhammad Badish as well.

CONTENTS

Gertrude was a remarkable person. All she had to do was enter a room in order to make it feel full even if it were actually empty. She had a complete understanding of painting. She bought some of my canvasses when no one else in the world wanted them.

Pablo Picasso

I met Gertrude only once. I did not like her because she insisted on imposing her own dominant personality on me and everyone around her.

Anaïs Nin, *Diaries*, Part II

...At that time we had been in Tangiers for ten days, during that first trip to Spain when so much happened that was important to Gertrude Stein.

We had taken on a guide, Mohammed, and he had taken a fancy to us. He became a pleasant companion rather than a guide. We used to take long walks together, and he would take us to see his cousins' wonderfully clean Arab middle class home and drink tea. We enjoyed it all. He also told us all about politics. He had been educated in Moulay Hafid's palace and knew everything that was happening. He told us just how much money Moulay Hafid would take to abdicate and just when he would be ready to do so. We liked these stories and also enjoyed all Mohammed's stories, which always ended up with "and when you come back there will be street cars, and then we won't have to walk. That'll be nice."

Later in Spain we read in newspapers that it had all happened exactly as Mohammed had predicted, but we paid no further attention. Once in talking about our only visit to Morocco we told Monsieur Marchand this story. "Yes," he said, "that's diplomacy for you! You two were probably the only non-Arabs in the world who realized what the French government wanted so desperately to know. But you had found out quite by accident, and to you it was of no importance."[1]

[1] Translator's note: In the Arabic version of the novel, this text is included in its original English form, and I have not made any changes to the text or its punctuation. The author of this novel notes that it comes "from the French translation of Gertrude Stein's biography, *The Autobiography of Alice B. Toklas*, Paris: Gallimard, 1934, pg. 173." In fact, the Arabic version begins on the seventh line of the printed English page. Before it we read: "There were several French families there, the French consul, Monsieur Marchand, with a charming Italian wife whom we soon came to know well. It was he who was very much amused at a story we had to tell him of Morocco. He had been attached to the French residence at Tangiers at the moment the French induced Moulai Hafid, the then sultan of Morocco, to abdicate."

1. MUHAMMAD

I was afraid that when I got there I would find him dead.

Fear ran ahead of me as I hurried to him. Truth to tell, the phone call I had received from the hospital administration made things sound urgent. I leapt down the stairs and made straight for my car, parked on the street. I made use of all my modest driving skills to get there as fast as possible, forgetting—a really bad habit of mine—to fasten the seat belt or even to check first to see if the car's documents were in the glove compartment.

Through the window in his hospital room I could see that the sky was ash-grey. I had never in my life seen clouds quite so dark, seemingly suspended on high from the universe's ceiling. His breathing was fitful and constricted, emerging as a series of terrible rattles. I looked over at his bed, and he beckoned me with a mere flick of a finger on his right hand. Head lowered, I moved hesitantly toward him. He would always prefer to talk to me as though he were confiding a major secret; that was even the case when we met in the evening on the sidewalk of the Café Paris. He would always lower his voice, pull me toward him by putting his arm around my head, and talk to me about things that he apparently did not want to share with anyone else.

Annoying though it may have been, that is the way he used to talk to me about the Parisian phase in his life and about the fruitful years he had spent with her there—by whom I mean Gertrude, and also Picasso, Matisse, Braque, Modigliani,

Apollinaire, Jean Cocteau, Hemingway, Scott Fitzgerald, Max Jacob…and others. Needless to say, I believed none of it, all those tiny secrets that he did not want other customers at the café to hear. In spite of that, I always went along with him and respected the obvious enjoyment he got out of talking. Most of the time he was the one doing the talking, offering words of inspiration, direction, counsel, and admonition, voicing his opinions at times and objecting at others. The crowning moment on each occasion may have come when he started talking about her—Gertrude, of course, and her friend Alice—and his fulsome memories of the time he had spent with them both. That would prompt a series of winks, jabs, comments, and self-deprecating sarcasm. All the while he would seem like an ancient warrior, but one who had never in his life engaged in any real conflict or dispute. He used to have a whole series of stories and allusions to offer about her, as part of which he would refer to letters, none of which we had ever read, and pictures of which we never saw the slightest trace.

It was a small square-shaped room on the third floor of the hospital wing for heart and coronary patients. The ceiling was low, and the entire room was only large enough for the patient's bed, a white iron chair, and a metal table, with instruments, milk products, and a notepad and pen on it. However, there was a large window that looked out on the back of the hospital, with an expanse of yellowing grass and a dilapidated wall beyond which you could make out the poles and wires of the train tracks. You could also see the old customs building with a non-working clock at the very top of the tower, jutting up almost to the base of the dark cloud cover.

I raised his pillow a bit to make him more comfortable. He immediately started talking. It was actually the first time I had ever seen him unwilling to wait; he was acting like someone who had to leave in a hurry.

I did not pay sufficient attention to what he was saying, and in fact saying with all the insistence of someone who just wants to talk and is keen to find the right words to suit the occasion. I thought he was going off on one of his rambling tangents again, or else that I was listening to the kind of expressions that normally come flooding out in rasps when someone is close to death. At first I was in a complete panic, but then I managed to pull myself together and show a degree of resolve.

"Don't laugh at what I've told you," I heard him say at the end of his bitter remarks. "I hereby consign to you my trust. You have given me your word."

"I'm asking you," he went on, "to turn my memory into your own garb, to go the whole way"—here he coughed—"the one I hoped would be my own way. Do you understand?"

Needless to say, I did not understand. Such was the seriousness of the situation: with him close to death, I was in no way laughing at him or what he was trying to confide in me. Feeling sorry for him, I hurriedly put all the papers, clippings, and faded photographs into my leather briefcase and left. It was my intention to let our mutual friends know about gravity of the situation and to contact everyone I knew to prepare for the funeral. He had given clear instructions that the ceremony was to be as modest as possible; he wanted the Marchand Cemetery to be his final resting place "when the call comes," as he would continually tell me. Thankfully the doctor had given me advance warning.

As I drove there, I burst into tears.

This time they did as I asked, which for me was unusual. I was surprised to see myself in tears. Here was a lonely friend, someone with no family or relatives to contact, provoking the kind of tears reserved for a father. For the very first time, as far as I could remember, I was crying without the tears getting out of hand. As I drove the car and looked out the window at the rows of buildings spreading out like mushrooms, I found that I could not forget either that final phrase he had used or the fractured tone in his voice as he whispered in my ear with that impeccable Arabic that he knew so well and relished.

"I don't want everything else to die along with my pain," he had said. "I've borne a good deal of it on my own and lived my life in seconds and hours, not just days, months, and years. Now I can't write it all down as I had hoped. I'm beaten, so it's your job to score a victory for your brother!"

He had told me his own remarkable story over and over again, with ever-advancing old age and fading memory playing their usual role in scrambling the information. Every time he repeated the story to me, he would be adding and omitting some of the details. I used to regard the whole thing as mere entertainment; some of the details might be true, but a lot of it seemed to be the typical imaginings and memories of an old man—a time when people of advanced age like to tell endless stories about their past. Even though I knew him and had kept his company for some twenty years or more, I could never be certain about the exact color of his almond-colored eyes even when I was looking directly at them. I would listen closely to what he was saying and trust him—this time at least. So then, it wasn't just a story or a figment of his imagination. It was a blazing segment of his own life!

He seemed more serious than ever before and showed a determination that brooked no doubts. He was not just out to convince me; this time he wanted me to take on his whole story. He handed me personal documents with his veined, spot-marked hands that shook as he did so, as though he were playing a betting game with his final documents. I planted a warm kiss on his forehead which was already turning cold—a shaykh and his disciple. Then a delayed apology, like a scene from the tape of a dreadful old Egyptian movie in black-and-white.

Muhammad had spent his entire life as if he were never going to die. In the final months he was convinced that he was going to live a further phase in his life. At no time did you even imagine that he had lived as long as he should. I have to admit that this enthusiasm amazed me, such a burning desire to live in spite of how little life, in all its insouciance, seemed to offer.

So where did such hidden energy come from, I kept asking myself.

He was someone whose entire body was encapsulated in his heart; that was where his strength was, and his source of happiness as well. It may well be that he had no idea of where to put his heart when he needed to find a secure spot for it. He had clearly made a mistake in realizing only very, very late that his heart had started consuming him and his lungs could no longer get enough fresh air. Even so, people—myself specifically, but others as well—will often overinterpret things; they want to give everything a meaning in spite of the fact that not everything necessarily has one. Many things on earth happen purely by chance, with no reference to mind or even the absence of heart…for even a minute or a minute and a half. And yet we are constantly overlooking and forgetting things or simply do not know.

That's the way things are all the time, even though we may try to come up with all sorts of meanings. Life is its own self, and on occasion it aspires to turn into a gypsy, preferring to be neglectful, to become a child again, strip down, turn off the mental clock, and skulk aimlessly about. We're often wrong when we imagine that everything has to have rules, systems, and principles, and at the same time forget that spontaneity, childhood, and madness all operate on a different kind of logic, one that has more in common with poetry and life itself. That is why I have always tried to understand and comprehend things, especially when observing a friend who follows his heart and turns away from the common herd.

Here I have to say that it was only in this spirit that I conducted myself with Muhammad. I did not behave the way some of the friends in our group did, although at this point I am not going to say who they were. With him, specifically, they were like savage dogs and never took him seriously enough. Everything he did, every single part of him, they treated as a huge joke, even his clothes, his cap, the way he combed his hair, his expressions, his face, his wrinkles, his curved eyebrows, and the slight curvature of his shoulders. There was no way to escape such cruel remarks, and he really suffered in the midst of a herd of nasty pigs. It could well be that, as time went by, he began to collapse under the sheer weight of these poisonous comments without even being aware of the repercussions and damage they were causing.

Here I can make the claim that Muhammad would not have been dying (or, at least, not so easily) if he himself had not come to the conclusion that death alone had become his one means of escape—"the only genuinely feasible truth," as he regularly told us all.

It may be that he had finally stumbled on the one condition he had been searching for in order to be rid of the pain and his sense of chronic failure. Maybe he only died because he had to, either because of his own excessive involvement in life or else because a man will prefer to die when life is no longer fulfilling. Dying will be the sole reason or, to put it all simply, because "the call has come."

It is only now that I can appreciate the profundity in that short sentence he once shared with me when he was talking about Gertrude, his American friend whom he could never stop talking about: "When we go to someone else and they reject us, we have to know how to get back to our own selves."

It is my conviction that he never learned how to do that. Ever since his first encounter with Gertrude in Tangier, he had waited a while, but he had never seen her again. When he finally gave up or decided that she might have completely forgotten him, he made up his mind to travel. It was almost as though his purpose in going to see her in Paris, where she was living, was only to confirm his own despair. Truth to tell, he never told us everything about her, and that made him seem a bit ambiguous. He never encouraged anyone to check on the authenticity of his memories. It is true that I may well have been the only one who felt that he was actually repressing a good deal of private pain, patiently and quietly hiding and tolerating a large concealed burden. However, none of us were able to share with him the pain he was enduring. Now I know for sure, without a shadow of doubt, what I did not know before; after all, time can teach people things they have not learned before.

Personally, I was not aware early on what was implied by his insistence on choosing me specifically as the person to tell things to and to keep telling them to; names, faces, expressions, and distant places would all be repeated in my presence. Was he in a panic about the possibility of everything being forgotten and erased from memory? For someone who has only the bare threads of his life left to him, could anything be more cruel than to see all traces disappear? Perhaps he was passing on to us (to me, actually, although I was not aware of the fact) strands of memory threatened with oblivion through indifference and neglect. I did not much heed the level of attention he paid to me or his excessive confidence in my purported abilities. It did not even occur to me that he needed me to help him to return to his own self so that I would not come to some kind of compromise with his memory. What is certain is that it was a memory that was torturing him, while at the same time he regarded it as both wonderful and tender.

He may have been beset by feelings of regret. There was no nostalgia in the normal sense of the word, but he may have had the obscure feeling of nostalgia that poets have, the kind where such feelings belong to neither past nor future!

His only desire was to recover his sense of pride, but, simply stated, he did not have the necessary resources to do so. He was like someone who wanted to traverse the ice-sea using burning words, but the words let him down! For that reason Muhammad was always on fire in his desires and yet suspended in his ideas—until, that is, all of a sudden he abruptly came across someone close by who could share the task with him. It was partly illumination and partly guesswork—I don't know which was the more prominent—that led him to me. He did his level best to cram his own horizons into mine, but at first I turned away, since I was neither interested nor eager. We did not have enough common interests. My own aspirations lay elsewhere, and I was not prepared to try crossing a chasm when I had no idea how deep it was.

Originally I had stalled him politely with promises, and as a result I found myself suddenly forced to honor them. What promises, you may ask? I do not know exactly, but they may have involved getting close to the light in spite of an early sensation that my wings would get burned. Deep down I was, and maybe still am, suffering from the same symptoms as most of my generation—a desire to get away from memories of the past and a clear sense of aggravation toward the previous generation who continually threw the past in our faces every time we opened our mouths. I never realized, nor did my contemporaries, that the people who had been clinging to the past—talking endlessly about it and repeating themselves—have a particular reason for doing so, but we members of the younger generation do not give it any credence. Perhaps we too have a reason for behaving that way, but we are not sure of the precise reason either!

I cannot recall exactly when he broached the subject with me for the first time, neither the day nor the month, although I do remember that it was a year and a half or so before his death. During one of his clearer moments he launched into a fervent request that I compose his memoirs for him. I had previously been delighted to hear that he had in fact some personal memoirs that needed editing—at least, that was my understanding. But then he told me that they were not available as a manuscript but existed solely as a silent archive within him. What he was asking me to do in fact was to transfer that archive to written form. It was at this point that I told him I was a poet at the start of a career; I had no idea how to write a biography. True enough, I told him, I have both written and published things; people had been able to read some of the poems and free-prose pieces I had produced. However, none of that qualified me for undertaking such a major task as this one. For his part he expressed the opinion that his complete trust in me was the basis of his request, in addition to which he thought that the little poetry I had already published showed "an outstanding narrative quality," to quote his own words.

That statement astonished me and made me ask myself not merely about his insistent request but also about what I might write and how I might operate. I will confess that I had my doubts about his sincerity. People will sometimes heap praise on something you have written in prose form as a way of criticizing your poetry! He must have realized what I was thinking to myself, because I can recall now that he went further.

"Okay then," he said. "No one else is going to write about my life. It's you and only you! Don't compose conservatively like poets. Yes, you're a poet, but you know how to tell a story as well."

In spite of that, I still felt worried about moving so far away from the kind of things I do best. I am only good about writing things about myself. I balked at the idea of suddenly turning myself into a "slave" and becoming a pen for hire! My poetry had always been a symbol of innocence, so how could I possibly turn it in a trice into something akin to a crime weapon? With those thoughts in mind, I declined his request.

He still refused to lower his arms; every so often he would resume his request. Recently he had tried to assure me that the book would be mine and would carry my personal signature; all he would be providing was the work's materials. I got the feeling that what he wanted was to see his secret safely placed into a book; that was all. He had made up his mind that I was the one to do it, either because he trusted me or my writings or for some other reason. I have no idea which. I still hesitated, made nice remarks, and offered excuses; for a while I may even have given him the impression that he had failed. As it is, I think I made a mistake to a certain extent. If only I had moved beyond my delaying tactics and come to my senses. His live testimony would have been bound to lessen the burden of the project, instead of the kind of thing that I am trying to do now. But events in life are judged according to the way they work out, so it is inevitable that there will be failures, erasures, missteps, forgetfulness, separation, absence, and avoidance, all in the cause of seeing the writing process brought to fruition.

The worry about my pen being for hire is not the only reason for my dilatory behavior. There is also the fact that I was much less bothered about the life story of Ba-Muhammad al-Jabali. When he was much older and time had caught up with him, everyone simply called him either Muhammad or Ba-Muhammad. Actually I was so uninterested that I never bothered to ask him who had chosen his professional name, "the man from Tangier," as he was universally known. He used to describe himself as "a retired writer" or "formerly a writer," with the claim that earlier in life he had indeed written literature. Everyone continued to regard him as a member of the "literary family," someone to be reckoned with. Those people would consort with him, and he with them. He used to share his opinions, experiences, and advice with them, but he was also known as a painter and on occasion a sculptor as well, although, in this latter case, many people regarded him as "lacking talent" or "lacking an esthetic flair." I myself have been unable to determine the exact nature of this perceived lack, something that was regularly mentioned every time the subject of sculpture came up.

I never heard anyone among his Tangier friends describe his paintings or sculpture in complimentary terms. That was in spite of the fact that, as friends of his, we would regularly do the right thing by turning up at his private exhibitions and praising his contributions at public exhibits. We used to write short reviews as well, and general impressions, all out of a feeling that he deserved some publicity and because we were convinced that selling his artistic works was his only source of income. In fact, we only knew him for his paintings and sculptures; we never read anything he wrote. In any discussion of his literary side we made do with his own reminiscences about himself and his former reputation as a writer who had decided for some reason or other to stop writing. Some student research papers still mentioned his name in their bibliographies and made passing mention of "his literary past" even though his earliest output was so limited. To tell the truth, we all used to imagine a past for him or invent a personal account—exactly as we do for ourselves.

But now that Muhammad is dead, I can see how far he went wrong in his life. That said, I never thought he made the wrong decision when he decided to involve a young writer like me in his biography. From one point of view, he must have persuaded himself over and over again that it was not yet the right time for memories, even though he could watch as the years passed swiftly by. From another viewpoint he maintained his dogged trust in me, almost as though he were watching in a clear sky as a gleaming star approached his own constellation. Did he select me to fulfill his desire to write about his life because he was utterly convinced that I would not hurt him in any way? That I would not toy with his feelings and scoff at the hallowed memories that he loved to relate? Was it that, or just the lucky guess of a man with experience?

I get the impression that at the time the idea of taking on the project of writing about his life seemed like something fairly minor, the kind of fleeting thought that soon disappears without trace. Clearly everyone gets the idea at some point that inside them there's a book about their own life, especially when they read books about other people's lives that really impress them. But, once confronted with life's never-ending compulsions, they soon forget about the idea and discard it. However, Muhammad was obsessed with the idea, as though it were an object clutched in his hand rather than simply an idea lurking in his mind. He made it abundantly clear that inside him he had this cogent force that kept the idea both in his mind and on his tongue.

The whole goal was totally remote from any aspiration for eternity; the sarcastic smile he would give at the very suggestion made that clear enough. But, whenever he felt sad or angry, he would tell me that he had traversed the twentieth century. As far as he was concerned, it was all time that had been wasted. He would tell me that he had lived with no hope in either life or death, a thought that always motivated his feelings and one he repeated whenever anyone was listening. In spite of that, he had no desire to turn his biography into a reformulation of the kind of destiny that he would like to have had. When the questions became too much, I surprised him with one of my own. We were sitting distractedly one evening at the Café Paris in Tangier. Did he want me to get some revenge for him, to write on his behalf and take revenge on a past I had never lived and a woman I had never even known—the woman he had loved while she had rid herself of him? It was as though I had given a name to a nasty feeling that he himself refused to acknowledge.

It was curious how angry he became.

"You're talking," he said, "so you can say whatever you like, as though talk is just something to say…"

"No, no," I interrupted. "It's said that way so that people can listen to it!"

Signs of approaching death were already visible on his face—a slight flicker of some previous internal feeling or else an apparent readiness to depart. Needless to say, no one spotted it at the time; it is only now, amid the welter of these fresh preparations, that I sense that in those final months of our friendship I was observing him in a particular way, the full import of which I did not realize at the time. It was just like looking at someone for a last time, anticipating that you will never see him again—as though death the butterfly had alighted on his shoulder but none of us could see it, and he himself was unable to feel the soft and gentle impact it had on him.

As I retain my happy memories of him and recall his face and its features and his own memories, I feel that we were two travelers passing along the way; they did not know each other and only met by chance on an express train. One of the two told his life story to the other and then left.

2. THE HOSPITAL

As he lay there in the hospital under the bed sheets, he looked like human wreckage in its terminal solitude. For several minutes I felt as though I were standing over the fragments of a smashed vase. It was as though he had felt himself falling, but, when he could not resist the secret forces that were pulling him down, he had performed a farewell dance on his own and then withdrawn into silence. A curtain seemed to have been lowered around him, enveloping him in its folds, and he had now headed back to the womb whence he came.

The nurse stood meekly by his deathbed, collecting his belongings and putting them all in a plastic bag. She folded his clothes neatly, put them in his suitcase, and handed it to me. I signed a receipt for them, avoiding as far as possible the series of questions she asked me about his origins, family, life, and friends…and all the things he still owned!

I stared at his features—the face of the corpse he had now become. It felt as though I were doing my level best to store them in my memory before they vanished forever. Even though he was actually dead, to me he still looked self-assured. What caught my eye was the broad smile on his lips. So here was death giving him a welcoming smile, and he was reciprocating with an even bigger one. While he was still alive, his facial expression had never shown the kind of clear indication that it was doing now. More often than not, his face would look frozen, without revealing any particular significance. To be sure his jaw muscles would regularly show when he was feeling tense inside. I may be exaggerating a bit here, but, truth to tell, I had never really appreciated the real meaning of death until Muhammad died in my presence, in fact in my arms.

It had only been a short while earlier that Muhammad had been here with us, going over his will again and making sure that I was committed.

So what exactly is death? Swift departure? Postponed regret? A huge white eraser that creates a void for which tears are no compensation? The only compensation is actually silence, which transforms into oblivion, something that in itself is simply a crack in the memory—small at first perhaps, but growing ever larger as the days roll by.

Is it true that time, which erases everything, does not do so with memories? I do not think so. It is merely an expression used by grave-diggers to enhance the market for marble. For memories to remain alive, their owner has also to remain alive. But, once he has died, it seems that the only reason is so that he can remind other people that he was once a living person. And that is all there is to it.

No person or thing ever managed to upset me as much as Muhammad's sudden and shocking death. I have no idea why the death of one friend may affect us so much more than that of another, even though in both cases we all receive the same news. Could it be that the degree of closeness in life is mirrored in that of death as well? Or could it be that the context in which we hear the news manages to create an additional level of shock and loss, one that is intense in some cases but cooler and less exceptional in others? So why was I so shocked by Muhammad's death? He was not the same age as I, nor had we shared the mass of things that contemporaries normally share. A feeling of regret perhaps, or of a period of time I had not known how to fully exploit? An accumulation of absences, a sense I had that I was gradually but relentlessly burying parts of my own body? Or was it simply Muhammad himself—with his particular temperament, his moods, his experiences, his love, his dreams, his illusions, his memories, his fancies, and the isolated nature of both his life and death—was he the one who made me feel so incredibly sad when he died?

In addition I should not forget what he told me that very noon when I was listening to his final words.

"The film, *Abu Hassan*," he gasped. "Finish it. The scenario's not finished yet!"

I was fully aware of the agonized feelings of someone so close to death when he was not able to write about his life the way he had wanted. I had no choice but to play along and give him an assurance that I had never offered before to either his memory or his memoirs. I promised myself to do all I could to read the personal papers he had left me and think seriously about his biography. Even so, I tried to convince myself that it might have to be a biography that at the very least could cover our lives together at the sidewalk café in a cosmopolitan city whose fabled legend was gradually shattering and dissolving before our very eyes each day. But then forgetfulness, sloth, and rejection are sometimes the result of accelerated circumstances, although they are not necessarily visible as part of our inner selves.

From the time of my final encounter with him, or, to be precise, with his remains as we buried them in a grave on the edge of the Marchand Cemetery, I chose to distance myself from soirées at the Café Paris and the circle of sidewalk friends. I did not even pause to think exactly why and how this decision came about, one that kept me away from familiar surroundings that a short while earlier I had come to regard as an integral part of my life and my very being. Was it a way of avoiding the need to confront the void left by Muhammad's death, or simply other pressing obligations and the force of circumstances, especially my involvement in the school strike and its consequences?

I was heavily involved in the strike; almost everyone else was as well, whether due to the worsening financial situation that we all faced, a matter of honor and audacity (as I insist was the case with me), or else sheer exploitation, that being a factor regularly used by professional educators who used to regard (and maybe still do) every strike call as the proclamation of yet another vacation. Such decisions would have little or nothing to do with any justification for the strike itself, so much so that you might find four or five different union cards in the pockets of some of their educators, with each organization calling for a minor or major walkout, whether successful or not. In any case, the person concerned would always come out on strike.

But then audacity comes at a cost. It took only a short time, from one night to the next noon, for me to find myself as a teacher out of a job; I do not like saying that I was fired (not wishing to repeat what the authorities have to say on the subject). There is no need at this point to mention the arrests, imprisonment, and trials of strikers that took place at the time. I was surprised when the newspapers talked about me with some admiration—not exactly about me personally, but rather about "the people who had decided to take an action that was guaranteed by the country's constitution. Even so, the authorities chose to humiliate them and withdrew their right of protest." Unlike others, I did not have the honor of being jailed, but I was one of the people who were fired from their teaching jobs. My own government chose to be rid of me so that I could start using my own words with a precision that suits me.

In such circumstances my whole life changed, and I changed with it. If Muhammad had been alive at that particular point, he would certainly have known how to impact my self-esteem as an "organic intellectual!" (That very phrase makes me chuckle now). I can visualize him now, sitting at his usual place in the café and putting his index finger on various parts of his head as a way of showing that he is thinking or trying to remember something. Clutching my arm, he would give a wink with one eye to attract his interlocutors' attention and use his hands and fingers to make gestures that would lend the necessary weight to his remarks.

"So now you've finally done it!" he would be saying. "How often have I warned you not to get involved in fights where the parameters aren't clear?! I've told you time and again that you don't need to commit yourself. Let your poetry do it for you in its own particular fashion!"

That is the way Muhammad was with me—and others too. He never felt happy about glossing over situations or indulging in cartoonish acts of heroism. He would always look at things from a different perspective, and time after time his point of view turned out to be right on the mark. Because that was the way he was, he soon became the anchor of our gatherings, one of the major monuments of Tangier and manifestations of its oral landscape. His advanced age was no impediment when it came to sitting down with aspiring writers and chatting with them about innovative trends. He would hardly ever abandon his woolen coat or white shirt, and yet he always managed to look neat and tidy and to convey a youthful spirit. Controversy was his primary métier, and he had a particular talent for nonplussing his jokester foes during our nightly soirées in the La Bricola Café by the shore, the Ritz Restaurant, the al-Hafa Café, or the usual spot on the sidewalk by Café Paris. He had a gentle kind of sarcasm that he aimed at his victims, something that always showed his broad experience, wisdom, and perceptive abilities.

There was one occasion when Sa`id S., a short-story writer of our generation who was very proud of the number of books he had published, managed to get him worked up. He had regarded Muhammad as being "a virtual writer," since not only had he not published as many books, but he had actually not published anything at all. Muhammad let out a malevolent laugh by way of preparation for what was to come.

"God Almighty," he said, "only ever wrote and published three heavenly books, all of which changed the world and mankind. But you're like a rabbit, churning out books every year than no one bothers to read!"

And that is the way it was with any young person who tried to best him. I can personally recall the way he once led me on when we first got to know each other. I had been interrupting too much and maybe not allowing him enough chance to speak. As it happens, talking was one of his particular gifts, something that allowed him to dominate conversations.

"You're still young," he told me, "so learn how to keep quiet and listen to other people. Just look at God. He knows what your fate is, and yet He remains silent and says nothing!"

That made everyone chuckle with laughter.

"But He's not always going to stay silent!" he went on.

Gradually his expressions and verbal comments crept into the things we wrote. If he had wanted, he could have written and published loads of stories, but he made do with telling them out loud, proudly and joyfully. The people who transferred them into textual form were his friends, his general coterie, and even French, Spanish, or American visitors to Tangier. I can say for sure that a number of my colleagues, young writers of stories, regularly included in their own compositions ideas, jokes, and situations culled from his instinctive sense of storytelling. You might say that he became an oral storyteller who knew how to narrate the world and things; it was as though inside him there was a kind of disused typewriter or publication machine. I have no idea how it all worked.

For all of us his Tangerine aura was by no means normal. Wherever he happened to be, he would cast his shadow and leave a trace behind. I was always captivated by the way he talked and the comments he used to make, and by his silences as well. I have to admit that all of us young writers—I, at least—were haunted by his presence; he became part of us. We started using some of the funny nicknames that he gave us all, repeating his expressions, and invoking his ideas in discussions. We would add aspects of his personality to the features that we were writing about. I loved him, had a deep respect for his habits, and paid close attention to his various moods. Even so I never fully believed the things he told me about his past and the memories he shared with me. For example, I did not believe that he had been a friend of an American woman writer who, he said, was "Hemingway's spiritual teacher"! Nor that one of our (forgive me for saying so) failed, neglected, forgotten, and lost artists in North Africa was a friend of Matisse, Picasso, Georges Braque, De Launay, Juan Gris, and Amedeo Modigliani. It goes without saying that I completely dismissed the notion that he knew Guillaume Apollinaire personally and had shaken hands with Pierre Reverdy, that he was acquainted with Hemingway and Anaïs Nin and had met Scott Fitzgerald, not to mention others as well, many, many more....

To be sure, in my own mind the legends associated with those figures loom very large indeed, and yet I find it difficult to put them into the same picture, the same scenario as my Tangerine friend, Muhammad. Even so I teased him a lot while we were sitting next to each other, exchanging memories.

"So then," I would say, "I'm looking at the eyes that saw Matisse and Picasso close-up, not to mention the bandaged soldier's head of Apollinaire!"

He liked the expression and looked delighted. When I said that I was looking at the eyes that had gazed on the completely naked body of an American woman, he guffawed. This statement of mine was intended to reflect the lewd and scandalous references that he was forever making to Gertrude.

As far as we were concerned, his relationship with Gertrude was shrouded in ambiguity. We could never deal with it as a genuine memory or part of a past that he had actually lived. Instead it was just a story. The body of that fat American woman seemed to dominate every sensory outlet he possessed, even though everyone regarded it as simply a story. He lived in a perpetual Parisian mist, even when Paris itself was thousands of kilometers away and Tangier swaggered on its modest way under the clear blue sky.

We may have had Muhammad with us in Tangier, with him seeing us and we him, and yet his sails were set for some far distant sea. His memories were close neither to him nor to us, nor did his lexicon reside anywhere near ours. When he addressed us, it was with the aid of another language, other words, other rituals, and other images, almost as though he were relying on a memory filled with people other than us. As I see things now, he would be looking at the chairs we were sitting on and imagining that we were not there. Instead it would be his own far distant specters who would be sitting on them. We failed to understand a good deal of what he was saying, and he did not seem all that eager to grasp a lot of what we had to say. It was as though we were talking to each other from behind a thick pane of glass or sitting on two sides of an abyss that separated us, so that one side could not hear the other.

During all those years the thing that caused Muhammad so much pain was the private time that kept him far removed from other people in Tangier. We would often wound him (and here I am talking about some of his friends, not necessarily about myself), and yet those wounds were not obvious bodily ones, but rather hurts that affected various parts of his very soul. At the very end neither he nor his doctors acknowledged what was the wound that bled the most, the fatal thrust perhaps. Who knows?

Maybe I exaggerated my associations, especially since the news of his death now seems so remote. It may also be the case that I now view my Tangier memories in bitter retrospect, having left it some time ago—in fact ever since that strike that unions still term "historic." I certainly agree with that verdict, at least with regard to the major impact that the history of that particular day had on people. But it may well be the wound inflicted on him by Gertrude that caused more pain, leaving a deeper scar inside him, one that led to his demise.

The profound, silent pain that Muhammad felt was not a secret to anyone. There was no other explanation for the way he stopped writing altogether. At this point I can even suggest that it was actually the pain that he was leaving behind.

I can just imagine that look, the very first look that a young man from the Maghrib—and from a particular background—directed at an American woman living in Europe, in Paris to be precise, and an aristocratic woman at that. I completely understand the confrontation between what might appear to be "higher" and "lower" in terms of culture and connections, the kind of thing to make a young man rub his hands in glee, to rediscover his own face in front of the woman, his temperature rising. Wetting his lips, his eyes would have a special gleam and his star would shine brighter. Muhammad never spoke about it, but I know that it is the case. Everyone knows it, whether by dint of sheer habit or else because of the enormous gap between East and West where almost everything keeps them apart, except, of course, for wars, explosions, and arms seizures!

Even today I still tear up whenever I remember him, when I am walking along the streets in Rabat and spot someone who looks like him or is sporting a beret like the one he used to wear— most particularly when I see the rare old men like him who cling to life with a strange relish, just the way he did. People like him really felt a need to live life even more fully; they absolutely refused to surrender their youth, and had to stay alive. How often did he insist on hiding his actual age (he was over seventy, maybe even older) under the cover of a much younger person—displays of strength, gathering the vestiges of his thinning hair into a ponytail, wearing white corduroy suits or colored summer shirts, sporting fancy berets, using the very latest style of spectacles, and donning multicolored neckties? He would always have a leather briefcase under his arm and use gold pens and expensive notebooks to write down ideas and observations and compose certain manuscripts!

Right up till today I can still feel that final touch of his hand, that moment when he had told me everything he wanted to say. He fell silent for a moment, and his eyes opened wide, as though he could see a strand of shrouded internal images. In that white cloud of death, did he recall, I wonder, the face of Gertrude, someone whom he loved so dearly before that love was severed and suddenly dissolved in blood—all of which led him to resist it? Or did the face of Bakhta loom before his eyes, his cousin who had grown up, matured, and married while he was away—thus becoming and remaining for the rest of his life yet another wound in his heart? As he lay there dying, maybe he recalled any number of faces, moments, and places, but then maybe he did not remember anything or anyone at all. When death comes to someone who is not expecting it, it deprives him of the possibility of whatever little pleasure can be gleaned from the memories accumulated in his soul's store-room. He leaves the world, as though he had never seen or lived anything—as though he had never been!

3. ANOTHER LIFELINE

"I'll write your life story, Abu Muhammad," I told him, "so rest assured."

But, as though I had said that only out of courtesy, I never wrote anything, the story neither of his life nor of his death. Truth to tell, I was not lying to him in any basic way; it was just that I was reassuring a friend on his deathbed, someone who needed a final word of release. So, as far as I can tell, I was going along with his wishes, just a few gentle words demanded by the situation and necessity. To be more precise, I have never lied in my entire life, whether to other people or to myself. I can never remember telling a lie, by which I mean those black lies which are intended to mislead, deceive, or cause people harm. But when it comes to those little white lies, gentle and sincere, which are usually intended to lighten pain, calm fears, or mend a rift of some kind, well, I may have told a lot of those, and with relish, honesty, and love.

I will freely admit that, as the years and distractions piled up and my mind was preoccupied with many other things and different people—especially my recent move to Rabat and my involvement in journalism—my new profession, I thought very little about my old friend, or about reviewing his personal history and writing it down as I had promised and pledged to do.

His specter continued to haunt me for many years. The obligation I felt was intense enough to make me feel ashamed of myself and my writing hand. For years I would contemplate my hand and its continuing reticence, that left hand of mine drenched in sweat, with its five nails carelessly clipped, a pen-less, shaking hand with its bumps and clear lines, its white empty palm, its sun-tanned top, its green-colored veins standing out—that hand of mine that now quivers like a brown glove hung out to dry on a clothesline. Again and again I ask the same irritating question: "How can such a hand not fulfill its promises and lighten the burden of memory?"

I must tell you that once in a while I have tried to fulfill my promise and set to work at intervals writing something about Muhammad and Tangier and our marginal experiences there. I still did not give any credence to his Parisian fantasies and the American love of his life. His image continued to occupy a modest place in my mind, as it had when he was still alive. But I never plucked up enough courage to continue and never did it.

There are things that happen, faces that pass us by, and books we read that at that specific moment may not arouse our attention enough. But later on we suddenly find ourselves quoting and thinking about them again, and much more seriously. They soon take over our vision and commandeer all our attention, leading us to assimilate ourselves to their horizons. With us they embark upon a new friendship, new conversations, as though they are reestablishing their presence inside us or their sudden and much desired return has led us to rediscover our own selves.

Such things happen to me and to countless others as well.

That is what may be happening to me once again now with this itching desire I feel for Muhammad of Tangier and his legacy. One frigid December night when Rabat went to bed early—that being normal with an administrative capital city that exudes a sense of despair—I took out the sheaf of papers that I had putting off reading for ages. I had been waiting for the time and mood to be right, but neither situation had actually yet occurred. The plastic folder that Muhammad had handed to me was still inside the safe that was full of my own files, papers, important private documents, and a good deal of long since irrelevant materials, although once in a while I would remember to check that at least it was still there. True enough, that safe, chiseled into the thick wall, was a place where nothing could ever get lost, but at the same time it was a location where anything could be forgotten. I knew that the papers were there, but my new career in journalism in Rabat kept me detached.

I cleared the dining table, spread out the papers, and sat down to look more closely, sift through them all, and start reading. I was alone inside the wide-open lounge of our apartment on the fourth floor; the children were asleep, and my wife had also gone to sleep in our cold bed. I hated getting into that bed, as though I had to share it with a corpse. Papers, papers, and more papers: newspaper stories, unfinished fragments of manuscript; bits and pieces, ideas, sentences, isolated words with no context; names, calligraphy drawn in pencil or in different colored pens. His script was his own, the elaborate Maghribi script with its neat letters, its beautiful spontaneous patterning, and its regular print, that he had been accustomed to using ever since he had worked as a dragoman at the Sultan's court, then in the public prosecutor's office in Tangier. All that was before his departure for France, a journey resulting from the cogent attraction of a remote and elusive daydream.

I was thunderstruck by what I was reading; I could feel myself getting more and more excited. It made me recall the famous boxes and cases in the history of literature. Once their owners had died, these papers were left with ignorant widows or else stupid children who, like dumb mules, had no conception of the worth of what their parent had left to them. Sometimes the papers would be consigned to unknown locations and damp, musty basements. I remembered, for example, what happened to Arthur Rimbaud's box of papers, Fernando Pessoa's, and the famous box of Paul Valery's papers. I thought too about other similar boxes that would usually contain the record of a life of writing, secret relationships, official identity documents, intimate pictures, private correspondence, postcards, incomplete writing projects, others partially finished, and yet others that would still be in the form of isolated ideas and short sentences. Suitcases discovered by accident, still smeared with sweat marks or even blood stains, or else tripped over close to shattered bodies or bloated corpses belonging to major writers whose lives collapsed in silence, leaving them to die in oblivion. The fingers on their hands finally surrendered their treasures, to be snatched up by ignorant heirs or wily, rapacious document hunters, people who know very well how to convert the poverty of departed writers into a freshly minted legend that will bring in gold and hard currency. Needless to say, I am not claiming that the documents and papers I am now holding rise to the same level as the famous examples I have just cited or have such exceptional value. However, for me at least, they are certainly a major symbolic treasure, not least because I have started to find a number of references to myself, our many friends, Tangier, and other references that Muhammad made to himself, Gertrude, Alice Toklas, Picasso, and others; to Paris, the Côte d'Azur, the Rhone Valley region, and other places as well.

Once again I found my eyes flooding with tears. How dearly I loved this profound old man whom I had betrayed by keeping him waiting for so very long! I can see him now, breathing beneath the earth; he is anxious and sad, jolted out of his reverie. As I turn in his direction, he looks distracted and flustered.

"Don't be hard on me," I told him. "I've never forgotten you, but I've often forgotten myself! However, here I am back again, for both you and myself!"

With a hand gesture he knew full well, I reassured him, but made it clear that at this point I was just making preparations.

When a writer is not writing, he will resort to another aspect of his personality in order to fill the gap, the void, the erasure. He can then return to his writing, not only better but also ready for more.

It felt like some kind of reverie, daydream, afternoon nap, or even a Hollywood film where the scenes are slowed down. There he stood in my field of vision, looking just like a specter at the very end of a long corridor:

"Finally, Abu Muhammad," I said, "I've realized how things really were. Your friend Gertrude was neither an illusion nor an ordinary woman. But then, when it comes down to it, Abu Muhammad, you weren't easy either!"

I watched as he gave a gesture with his left hand and felt a kind of internal release. At this stage in my life I have exhausted my entire supply of farewells, so I smiled contentedly and opened my eyes as wide as possible to make sure that I was not asleep; either that, or I actually was sleeping but someone was close enough that I had to wake up. Just then, all those details, scenes, and repeated moments came flooding back, as though a photograph album had suddenly been opened and an enormous supply of black-and-white pictures had come tumbling out. There we all were, talking, laughing, hugging, all outside the Café Paris on the sidewalk. Along with other friends we would be drinking, eating, reading, writing, and dancing. There were others on the beach at Malabata, at a musical evening in the village of Jahjuka, attending an evening of flamenco dancing at the Cervantes Theater. There was one of Muhammad clapping alongside the Spanish guitar player and kissing the Spanish dancer on the cheek, and another of him wearing a dinner jacket at one of his exhibit openings.

How beautiful Tangier was!

Muhammad represented one aspect of the city all on his own, in spite of the pain that the city managed to nurture, something that would often make him feel frustrated and alarmed. Tangier did not always manage to live up to the legend you find in books, written documents, and media outlets. In Tangier things were adopted quickly and simply: verdicts on people were always ready, and any interpretation brooked no revision, correction, or apology. People looked on Muhammad as someone who did not know how to live; as far as they were concerned, he was someone from the mountains who had lost his way in life, descending from Jabal al-`Alam to Tangier in an attempt to forge a fresh, phony life that he had never lived out of another one that was lost and in tatters. It may have been something he had read about in books or seen in films, so he had started to transform himself to suit it.

"But the American writer remembered both Tangier and him in the book…"

"But the only unknown person from Tangier whom she mentioned was someone named Muhammad…"

"Yeah, in Tangier, there was just this geezer, Muhammad. Great, a guy from Tangier called Muhammad!!"

"So, not him, then!"… "No, it is him, I told you!"…"No, no, my dear…"

It was all as though lofty Tangier never stinted its children when it came to a modicum of humility, by which I imply those nasty feelings that do not emerge from cracks in walls and crevices in the ground, but rather ooze out of human pores that are psychologically damaged. That explains why Muhammad regularly scoffed at pig-headed people and pretended not even to recognize the word "denial." In spite of it all, he had refused to give in.

I have no idea what my own career would have looked like if I had stayed in Tangier after Muhammad died and I was dismissed from my teaching job. It was my experience as a writer that saved me, along with support from some friends in Rabat who helped me get temporary employment with the press. Even so, my situation was still worrying, like someone whose head has just managed to escape the guillotine only to find itself in the slaughter house! In time I came to discover that this new profession of mine was not simply some passing trade; instead it had become part of my blood and very being. In Rabat I discovered nests of depravity and snake pits, and, most especially, how easy it is to slip up.

The transfer process from Tangier to Rabat was not merely a geographical shift or moving south on a map, from Cap Spartel to the mouth of the River Abu Riqraq on the ocean. Instead it involved a movement in chronological space, one that traversed hosts of people and a whole thermometer of moods. In Rabat you are under daily observation: your clothes, the way you walk, what you have to say. In Rabat you are not yourself; instead you are the way others see you or need to see you. You are not yourself; you are other people!

Tangier on the other hand is open, multifarious, many cities in one. It has to it something of Alexandria, Beirut, Athens, Venice, and San Francisco. Rabat is a closed city, resembling only itself, like some ancient city buried under the sands, a poisoned, self-destructive city. In Rabat you have to fight other people and fight yourself simply in order to live; you must isolate other people and even yourself in order to live. There is something about the air in Rabat that makes you feel as if you have gone downhill from the top of the map to the bottom, almost falling into an abyss from which you look out with an expression on your face that invokes the kind of sympathy aroused by the dog in Goya's famous painting.

Rabat is not Tangier; it is stingy and domesticated. In Tangier, on the other hand, people's moods intermingle, and the spirit of open-heartedness has always matured over time. You cannot live in Rabat the way you can in Tangier…without anything, by which I imply with money or without. In Tangier a little bit of cash is enough to meet all your needs, whereas in Rabat money is just for show. That may be what makes people in Rabat pant and heave in quest of money and the power that breeds and protects it. If it were not for the circumstances and coincidences that govern people's destinies, I would never have come to Rabat. Anyone who comes to that city cannot avoid arriving on the run, rushing after some illusory notion of advancement.

"Rabat is the last Morisco city you have!"

That is what my new American friend, Lydia, said to me when she noticed how far the countryside has affected Moroccan cities with their Andalusian features, with Rabat as the only one left. By now Andalusia is just a focus of nostalgia, of memory, a metaphor! What is even worse is that people look on it as a kind of ghetto. Just look at the way traditional Rabat families close in on themselves, the way they behave. But, at any rate, that is another story.

This mention of Lydia means that I have forgotten something. I had been invited to an evening discussion at the American Cultural Center in Rabat; it was just a few months before it was closed, and the Americans made do with just one center in Casablanca, as is the case now. In the library vestibule I was delighted to meet, quite by chance, a childhood friend of mine, Mustafa al-Sallami, who works there. It was a wonderful opportunity to look back and remember an old friendship from days long past. These days I am sufficiently old that I do not need to embark on new relationships or friendships; I have more than enough names and faces at my disposal that make it possible for me to look back all the time, discard unneeded ones, and remove any number of names, addresses, and phone numbers from my diary. Even so, I felt a special kind of warmth in renewing a friendship which would never have been severed were it not for the fact that our paths had moved in different directions.

As you can imagine in such a situation, we were delighted to see each other. Our meetings became more frequent, and we would regularly have extensive phone conversations. It was inevitable that I would want to exploit the experience of a former English teacher at the American Center, someone who was now focusing on administration after getting advanced degrees in communications and public relations. As I fully realized, al-Sallami was a public relations person without even needing the training in it. As a child he had been able to make friends quickly, and, as he grew older, he could influence and establish ties with everyone, particularly our contemporaries in preparatory school. There was something magic about him that made everyone accept him and seek him out. Everyone loved and admired him; he was always neatly dressed, polite, and reliable. All the preliminaries of the life that I shared with him suggested that he was going to be a highly successful entrepreneur, but, once we had gone our separate ways, I had no idea what happened to him. His initial inclinations were toward science, and that took him to Casablanca for his secondary education, while my own interests were more literary, and that led me to the distant city of Settat. That is how we went our separate ways at that time.

Now here was Mustafa, face gleaming, never missing the five daily prayers, as the characteristic brown callous on his forehead made clear. His stolid seriousness no longer allowed me to ask him about memories of the past. But now I was seriously interested in Gertrude Stein, and from the outset he confessed to me that he did not know that American writer; her name meant nothing to him. He asked me to wait a bit until he could ask an American colleague whom he knew to be much more involved with American literature. I realized that he was referring to an information attaché at the American Embassy where al-Sallami was working as a translator specifically responsible for following events in the Moroccan press.

Thus it was thanks to al-Sallami, but also to the degree of curiosity that my moral commitment to Muhammad from Tangier and his friend Gertrude had aroused, that I made the acquaintance of this female American diplomat. That is the way Muhammad managed things during his lifetime. Even after his death, it would seem, he still managed to bring people's destinies together, establish relationships, and forge new friendships. I think he must have acquired this lovely habit—introducing one person to another—from his earlier relationship with Gertrude during his time in France. It could have been the leisure time he had after leaving her (or her leaving him)—letting her grow old there in Paris while he aged on the other coast of the Mediterranean—that encouraged him to load other people's hearts with an outpouring of friendship and the sheer warmth of human contact.

I was walking along the street and passed by a public telephone. I decided to give al-Sallami a call and see if his American colleague knew anything about Gertrude. Could she maybe provide me with some leads? I was thrilled by his response, particularly when he told me that the topic delighted her; she would be ready to see me in her office whenever I wanted. I expressed my desire to see her as soon as possible. It was the very next day that, rubbing my hands with anticipation, I went to her office.

I had never been to the American Embassy on Tariq ibn Ziyad Street. All the Information and Cultural Offices were housed in an annex on Belfreij Street. A security man at the outside gate advised me to enter through the back door. It was as though I were discovering the place for the very first time, even though I had seen it many times. The entire embassy looked like a fortified military barracks on the top of a hill overlooking the Abu Riqraq Valley. A large flag fluttered in the breeze, higher than all the flags on neighboring embassies, and communications antennas thrust their masts, wires, and concave dishes up toward the sky. The exterior cement wall was surrounded by black iron railings, and there were additional cement barriers and public and private guard barricades on the inside. I submitted to a short, polite search, then they took me to a brightly lit hall, with pictures of the American president and photographs of scenic views and life in the United States on the walls. I could see the back garden of the embassy, the place that many of my colleagues had described after being invited to the Fourth of July celebrations every year. That was an occasion that no one would want to miss—government personalities, members of the opposition, entrepreneurs, businessmen and media, reporters of every conceivable kind, and all aficionados of parties, whisky, and cognac in Morocco's capital city.

In the outside corridor leading to her office, Miss Lydia Altman was standing waiting for me; they had told her that I had arrived on time. She shook my hand warmly, as though we had met somewhere before. Once inside she introduced me in turn to all her female colleagues, who greeted me with enthusiasm. One of them offered me a cold hand; she did not stand up like the others and barely raised her eyes from the computer. I was eager not to appear flustered, and she greeted me politely. Lydia invited me to sit in her neat office, but for a moment I remained standing—my hands clasped to my chest, not sure where I should sit.

"Please take a seat," Lydia said. "Why are you still standing?"

With that we began our first chat about Gertrude. Oh my, how well Lydia knew her! I did my best to explain to her my involvement in this research and that the reason for my increasing interest in this American writer was the fulfillment of a pledge I had made to a friend who was now dead. She uttered a sympathetic "I'm sorry!"

She promised me some books by Gertrude and about her, and even some photographs of her; she even said that somewhere in the library she might be able to locate a voice recording of Gertrude. I was totally taken by the sheer magic of this moment, with the mature, olive-complexioned woman sitting in front of me completely open and unselfconscious…like two friends sharing everything. Her French was slow and captivating, with a special accent. Needless to say, we did not only talk about Gertrude. There were other items of interest as well: Gertrude, Muhammad, Rabat and Tangier, the Mediterranean, Spain, Andalusia, the Moriscos, Islam, Morocco, America, free exchange, and emigration. We then talked about American literature: *Leaves of Grass* by Walt Whitman, Faulkner, Ginsberg, Kerouac, Gregory Corso, Ferlinghetti, Paul Auster, Toni Morrison, Hollywood, McDonalds, everything. We agreed about a lot, and disagreed about just as much. She quickly found out how to get me worked up, in every sense of the word, while for my part I learned how to ask and answer questions and maintain a balance.

"But what do you really know about the country?" I asked her. "Diplomats only know what they want to know! There's a kind of virtual form that they carry around inside their heads. They fill it up with cautious answers which they pick up orally…"

In my opinion a genuinely profound knowledge of people cannot come by filling out a number of questions posed on a prepackaged form, the ones put together by diplomatic institutes.

"In fact we actually know more about your country than you do…"

That is how we allowed ourselves to meander around a number of subjects, one thing leading on to another…

We both invoked a number of ways of showing our admiration for each other, but there were also some indications of equivocation. I told her she was beautiful and open-minded, but she was standing on the wrong side, the side of her country. She in turn told me that I was convincing when I was being objective, but once in a while I would slip when talking only for myself. I told her that for me the most important thing was to convince her, whether just a bit or completely. She replied that I had managed to convince myself, but she had just been listening.

"I've been convinced by some of what you've told me," I responded with a smile.

"No," she said, "you haven't been convinced. You've just given way a little!" She moved her head coyly. "As I've discovered," she said, "you're a writer and poet. So why are you talking like a politician?"

This criticism surprised me.

"True enough," I replied, as though already prepared with an answer, "I'm a poet, but that doesn't mean I can divorce myself from events."

As I was standing up to leave, she asked if I had any translated texts of my poetry that she could read. She suggested that we meet again about the books and continue our discussion of Gertrude. I thanked her profusely and, without really meaning to do so, I slightly enhanced what I had intended to say.

"You've been very warm with me," I said, "and I'm grateful."

What she now said surprised me. "How do you know I'm warm?" she asked. "We've never slept together!"

I hurried to leave. In my panic, it felt as though I had run away.

When I told al-Sallami about this first meeting of ours, he said she was a nice woman who loved our country and its people. He also told me that she was very frank and forthright; her modesty, simplicity, and frankness endeared her to everyone in the embassy. It was only the ambassador himself who did not feel the same admiration, even though he was convinced of her competence. Al-Sallami went on to tell me that she liked joking a lot and steadfastly refused to behave like a traditional diplomat.

"Rely on her completely," he told me. "You're not going to find anyone better to help you with the book."

So my conversations with Lydia continued. She made me photocopied copies of pages and pages about Gertrude from American encyclopedias dealing with famous people, along with whole chapters from books. She gave me a copy of Gertrude's novel *Three Lives*, in English and in French translation, and other books about her and Alice Toklas. Among them, *The Third Rose* caught my eye, as did *The Charmed Circle: Gertrude Stein and Company* and *Everybody Who Was Anybody*. She also collected for me various pictures of Gertrude and photocopies of books, articles, and encyclopedias.

Gradually I started pulling away from the shore, sinking in, and immersing myself. Lydia managed to take me further than I had expected. I could almost smell Gertrude's breath, so close did I feel to her, to her origins, to her family history, to her spirit, her writings, her education, her friendships, and her travels. Muhammad from Tangier now became simply one point in a vast, surging sea of Gertrude. I started to understand what it was that had hit Muhammad, that simple mountain boy who had touched an electric body and got his fingers burned. He had ventured into a very deep location and brought his eyes close to walls on fire with the revolutions of entirely new colorations. When he emerged, he was no longer viewing the world the way he had done before. He had forever lost his previous worldview; it was as though he had lost his own eyes. At first Muhammad's language and writing style had been simple, but he had been buffeted by a swirling psychological force that had impacted the very English language itself with a new fervor.

Doctor Lydia and the books and photocopies she had ready for me gave me back the names of people and places and other details that had been missing. I can see that at this point I should admit that I had done my best to write down the little information Muhammad had told us or me personally while we were sitting on the sidewalk by the Café Paris; I would try to record as much as I could remember. Needless to say, a number of things simply vanished into thin air as soon as they were said. I found it hard to even recall the names of people he met in Café Paris, names he would remember and then give me a short sentence about them based on things that someone or other had told him. Now Lydia is refilling my memory, or at least part of it, with things that had almost been obliterated. She has adopted my crazy project as partly her own, and had started researching, checking, and looking for background information in the libraries on her computer. Every day she brought me information that amazed me and filled in a huge numbers of gaps.

From this point on, it was as though I had suddenly become bewitched, as though Gertrude had become my friend. At times I found it hard to distinguish between Lydia and Gertrude. Had the American affliction enveloped me too? With such feelings in mind I started finding excuses for my old friend; I no longer felt sorry for him or made light of his suffering as I had frequently done before, belittling him with a studied insouciance. We have to take into account the kinds of feelings that our Tangerine colleague had as he read the autobiography of a writer with whom he had lived but who mentions him only in passing; she does not even give his full name. True enough. That famous American woman, fleshy and arrogant as she was, was not to be handed over to any old passerby. She was devoted exclusively to herself, and that was it. The whole of creation, it seemed, was astir inside her, but things were different where Muhammad was concerned. He was not any old passerby, moving past her or she past him only in order at the end to leave him consigned to oblivion.

No, he was a part of her life, residing there and, more specifically, in her body.

Of course, he was not a man of great repute, but she may have been the one who extinguished him early on. He may well have been aware of the very fate which all young men suffered who crossed Gertrude's path as she did theirs. He too tried his hand early at writing and even painting; he certainly had the talent and maturity for it. So he may well have been shocked and hurt when she ignored him. When he died in my arms, he may well have still been feeling the residual pain from those few, bald, dry, trivial, and cold sentences that Gertrude devoted to him in her autobiography written in the name of Alice Toklas. All of which implies that I can now state that he was right to think of taking revenge on behalf of his memory and rewriting his own account of life with this American woman, specifically noting what she should have written. But he had failed to do so. Maybe the fact that he had not written anything for so long stopped him doing it—either that, or else frustration and a fear of failure. It could also have been sheer weakness or his own modest attainments. I do not know and cannot be absolutely certain about it.

It is not always possible to write, to find that everything is ready when you want it to be or in easy reach whenever you decide to get started. Writing is never as easily accessible as a lot of people imagine it to be. It is not just a matter of bringing some pieces of white paper and pens to a table and setting some time aside; above all else, it is a kind of spiritual chemistry, bodily disposition. Writing may be possible when you are approaching something from a particular direction but suddenly you desist, free yourself, and escape when you find yourself compelled to accept what memory is dictating; it may also come completely fresh whenever spontaneity, humility, and love are available, but then it will all vanish in a trice when a spirit of revenge on a person, place, or memory manages to infiltrate our internal selves.

As he told me about the failure of his life project, about the closed secret he had kept locked up for ages before revealing it to me, he had the feeling that I was not the kind of person who could abandon him with regard to his personal problem. His instincts undoubtedly told him that I was never going to consign him to oblivion. I would retrace his steps ever since he had left Morocco to pursue the vestiges of his private pleasure, only to return with a deep wound, as though he were coming home from a war in a distant land where he had tilted at a windmill.

Many were the times when he spoke to me in private so that I could penetrate to the very essence of the question, and yet for a while I found myself affected by the general atmosphere of disregard that enveloped him. I never really noticed the way he tried to stop himself trembling whenever he was talking to me about Gertrude. He was almost trying to write down his own autobiography, using only his lips, eyes, wrinkles on his forehead, and hand gestures. He used to say that writing all the chapters of his book involved his whole heart, the tone of his voice, and his unexplained tremors—his entire body, in fact. Being a member of a frustrated generation, I had grown up to despise talk, so a good deal of what he had to say escaped me. But now here I am some time later, trying to recuperate what I can.

As time went by, my task involved more intense research, collecting data and sorting them into piles, as though I were preparing a doctoral dissertation. It was one of the things that Lydia taught me to do when she began to share her expertise with me. Now I was no longer the only person reading the book of Muhammad, which still had no actual words in it. We started reading together or, more accurately, trying to write it together. Whenever we met—in a club, a gathering, or one of the breakfast sessions with the ambassador that were usually organized by the embassy for the press—we would discover a venue for exchanging new information about our long-time topic:

"Where are you with your friend Gertrude?" she would ask, and I would respond, "Do you have anything new about her?"

Gertrude turned into an open cooperation project between us, to such an extent that I started having doubts about the relationship and myself.

Lydia's face gave you no clues about her age, but she seemed to be under fifty. She had a round face, a coppery light-brown complexion, and a broad, generous bosom—a woman full of life, from the American South. She seemed to be fond of jokes, and was full of fun and wit; her senses were as fiery as coals, although she often preferred silence and liked discussions to be brief. In spite of her calm expression, she did not give the impression of nurturing a calm inner self. I noticed, for example, that she was more interested than I was in what may have occurred between Muhammad and Gertrude in order to turn a relationship that was so intense for many years into one that collapsed and broke apart in an instant. She told me that we would have to do some more digging in diaries and correspondence.

"You'll need a full-scale archeological dig to find out," she told me.

She advised me to wait a while till she could find a way of communicating with the archives at Yale University, the Bancroft Library at Berkeley, and the Harry Ransom Research Center for the Arts and Humanities in Texas which, so she told me, had been presented with a gift by a collector of rare literary manuscripts, the American fox known as Carlton Lake. It contained dozens of letters, postcards, personal documents, and manuscripts linked to Gertrude.

"Who knows?" she said. "There might be a snippet or more to fill a gap or make up for something that is missing in your information."

In a gentle tone she recited a line from T.S. Eliot's "The Wasteland," which she did her best to translate into French, albeit with considerable difficulty: "'*These fragments I have shored against my ruins!*'"

It was toward the end of the couscous dinner at our friend al-Sallami's house in the Atlantic district. Some of Mustafa and Lydia's friends from work were there: Martin, Susan, Sam, David, Julia, Jerry, and Angelina. Lydia, the little devil, craftily asked me a question.

"Tell me," she asked, "what was it about Gertrude that made your friend Muhammad start a relationship with her? Something really weird! He must have had some kind of destructive instinct inside him to fall in love with such a masculine woman!"

"I can't say for sure," I replied, "but it may have been the same reason that led Picasso to attach himself to her, to Apollinaire, and no doubt to others as well. We can never explain for certain why exactly a man loves a woman or indeed why a woman finds in a particular man things she cannot find in other men."

At this party there was a lot of talk and laughter. We were all guffawing as we listened to Mustafa.

"Truth to tell," he commented in his usual fashion, "we don't choose the woman we're going to live with. It's fate that descends all of a sudden on a man. Either it becomes a crown, or else it smashes his skull to pieces!"

Lydia now picked up on the conversation to remind me that my friend Muhammad was a Mediterranean type, just as Picasso was Spanish and Apollinaire was French but of Italian extraction—as we all know.

Before we all thanked al-Sallami's wife for the delicious couscous and left, Lydia and her embassy assistant, Susan, told me that the embassy personnel had put my name forward as a correspondent to make a trip to America as part of an international visitors program.

"If you're selected and received in Washington," she said, "it'll be a terrific opportunity to learn more about your great rival."

I was delighted by this proposal. In the car on the way home, Julia and her husband, Martin, gave me a clearer idea about the program and whetted my appetite for this much anticipated journey. Needless to say, I really wanted to go.

My conversations with Lydia began to become more awkward. When we met, we no longer exchanged new information, but merely brought to a close a discussion that we had not finished in our previous meeting.

"I forgot to mention when you asked me…" I would say.

"In fact the conversation led me far away, and I never finished the thought. What I wanted to say was…"

I looked hard at her, and she gave a jolt. It was as though she could no longer hide from me the tremor in her glances. For the first time I felt the presence of a woman in my life, a woman who was closely linked to me, who thought and speculated the way I did.

I knew that the moment had blossomed, and it would not be long before we were going to her home to finish our discussion. I am on my way there now, on the other side of Rabat. I have thought everything over. One should not be swept away so easily with the very first onrush; I need to pause for a moment to find out where to put my feet. What concerns me first and foremost is to be convincing, open, and ready for any and every possible discussion. In such contexts the best thing is never to get into difficulties with an idea or express a point of view. Diplomats are extremely cautious and observant, and, in the case of female diplomats, the Americans are the best. So there's no need to hurry things. There may be more time later and more opportunities to continue our close relationship, and yet my heart is telling me that the phase during which ideas and behaviors can be selected is already at an end. Lydia has moved on to a higher octave on her musical scale.

I passed through the outside gate to the villa, then proceeded along the long pathway through the garden. When I reached the door to the lounge, the maidservant went ahead of me. Lydia was standing there waiting. No doubt she had decided from the very outset to preserve the necessary courtesies of the meeting and the respect due her office. She had not opened the door herself and was not displaying any haste or breech of the usual protocol inside the house. She invited me to sit on the cane chair and immediately noticed that I looked uncomfortable about her dog that clearly wanted to sit down beside me. When I told her that

I was not used to having dogs around, she reassured me. She was obviously quite used to having it around; not only that, but she also had a cat (I don't know if it was male or female) that stretched out on the white-fringed wool carpet and the cushions scattered around. So I sat down where she indicated, and she lounged opposite me, with the kind of expression in her eyes that promised a whole new horizon.

I did a rapid sweep of the room. It was a lounge opening on to the garden, furnished in the American style: cane chairs where we were sitting, and on the other side leather chairs; an inclining table like the ones used by architects; a carefully lit library with expensive books on art, architecture, and American life, as well as others about Morocco—its ancient cities, mountains, deserts, traditional crafts, and women's jewelry. On the walls were paintings, some originals, other copies; some of them were American, but others were by Moroccan artists, some of our major ones.

"You have a very valuable collection here," I said, "particularly the originals by the French artist Majorelle and some of our own artists now dead, al-Sharqawi, al-Gharbawi, and al-Qasimi." She told me that they all belonged to the embassy and the house was not her own.

"If you prefer," she said by way of correction, "it's my house as long as I'm in Rabat. But when I leave your country, I'll have to find another house. Let me tell you that I'm like a wandering cloud, with no real home on earth."

The thought saddened me, and I apologized for raising things that might be painful.

"Oh no," she replied, "it's only natural. You need to ask the questions, and I'm supposed to answer them!"

Like any business meeting, she let me know what the evening agenda was to be. We would have something to drink first, then move to the dining room; dinner was ready. During that time we would talk about whatever we wanted and resolve our differences quietly. She made it clear that, as far as she was concerned, I was talking only as a representative of my people and homeland and that I too had to recognize that fact. This did not imply in any way that a person could not have his own personal opinion, even when it came to his people and homeland. I tried to explain to her that what mattered to me was that our discussions should be objective. In the long run, sound opinions would crystallize only in the context of a particular people's culture and its general parameters. An individual's disposition cannot be a personal opinion, but such an opinion does not have to wrap itself up as an official policy. This is one of the mistakes that American diplomats make: when there's a mistake and it happens to be an American one, they can never look at it from a distance; instead they obfuscate and justify everything short of Hell itself.

While we were having drinks, we talked at length, then she moved over to a corner and sat at the piano to play for a bit. She told me she had not played it for months and was exercising her fingers in my honor. Tonight she had drunk the best possible glass and was feeling the kind of security she had been missing for ages. She tried to get me to share with her in the musical phrases and light pieces she was playing for me—Schumann, Liszt, and Brahms. Life, she told me, seemed nicer, purer, and that much more replete when she was playing the piano. She reminded me of Condoleezza Rice: "Oh dear! Do you know that she plays the piano as well?"

Oh yes, and I have a particular craving for those brown legs of hers which I saw once in an illustrated French magazine. Just imagine a luscious woman like her playing music and starting wars! I do not know how a body like hers can distinguish simultaneously between piano playing and the whiz of bullets. Lydia told me that "Condi" had never forgotten the way the American South had exploded and the killing of the southern black girls, one of whom was a friend of hers. So her childhood had its own painful memories. But let's forget that topic. I have no desire to ruin our evening with "Condi" and the world's bloodthirsty inclinations!

For a moment I just sat there quietly in the soft light, listening to the music that infiltrated my pores like droplets of silent rain. Then we moved over to the table and continued our conversation. It was obvious that she preferred the way I listened to her associations as she recalled her childhood and its unknown distant roots in Africa, her merit scholarship to Harvard, her father who had died, her mother, now single, living in Albuquerque, New Mexico, and various family and relatives living all over the United States. She asked me not to be too introspective and to talk about myself a bit. She enjoyed a lot of what I had to tell her, even though I knew full well that I am no good at talking about myself.

Conversation at soirées like this one can often serve as a stimulus for the participants. I asked her why she was still unmarried.

"Is there a dating club I can go to in your country?" she asks with a laugh.

"I'm sorry, I'm just interested in knowing…"

She told me that she had been working for ages in that grey-colored barracks, directed by men and with men under her supervision, but they were all so conservative. No one was ever open or opened up to anyone else!

"And what about the Moroccans with you in the embassy?"

"Their greatest ambition is to give you the impression that they're completely upright and honorable, it's as though they've all been castrated. My situation's weird, and I have had an impossible love."

She then told me bit by bit about a fierce love she had had, one that had ended just as fiercely. He was a superficial American type, so she told me, who had been a drain on her life for a long time. It had started during her college years in Boston, then working in Washington and New York. When their relationship was on the rocks and she had decided to tell him that she wanted to split, she had received an offer from the State Department to work in the Middle East as press attaché at the American Embassy in Damascus. Just then she heard that he had died in a car accident on the Brooklyn Bridge, the causes of which were entirely unclear.

"I'll tell you frankly," she said. "I thought long and hard about it all. I came to regret my unclear feelings about him. I kept asking myself if he had realized the way my feelings about him had changed, and his death had been a kind of suicide."

As she looked at me, I could see tears glistening in her eyes. She was talking to me, and yet she looked away for a moment to gather up her thoughts and distant memories, like a visible reflection of some internal light that escapes from a heart or the crevices of a fractured spirit. I made ready to leave.

"It's time for me to go," I said.

"Where are you going?" she asked. "You didn't tell me you would have to leave!"

I noticed that her glistening eyes were now brimming with tears. She said nothing more, as though to leave me the choice as to whether to go or stay. For a few moments, I was at a loss and just stood there. What was I supposed to do?

I allowed myself to stretch my hand behind her back and rub her shoulder in a friendly and sympathetic way that seemed genuine to me. In fact, I did feel responsible for having raised some obviously painful memories. Just then, however, I got the sense that my hand movements were not entirely innocent. It was as though Lydia were waiting for some kind of gesture like this, because she turned and embraced me. At first I tried to make it look as though she simply needed some support in order to be rid of her distress and the tears she was shedding, but she embraced me even harder, put her arms around me, and kissed me on both cheeks the way nursemaids do. Without waiting for my reaction, she suddenly put her lips on mine (actually it was not exactly sudden, because I had rearranged my position to make it all easier). So, for the first time, what happened happened, and there is no need for words to describe it.

4. ARRIVAL IN PARIS

He could still recall that moment when he left the Tangier port. It was very early in the morning, and the light was still very faint.

"You have the address now, don't you?" Gertrude had said to him. "You can come to Paris whenever you want, Muhammad. My invitation will still be open."

With that she put her mouth close to his ear so that Alice Toklas, who was standing next to her, could not hear the few, rapid words Gertrude said to this handsome young Tangerine boy who had managed to fascinate them both for several days. Muhammad stared fixedly at Gertrude; perhaps he wanted to make sure that her offer was genuine, his fear being that she was just being polite. After that, he shrugged his shoulders and stretched his eyebrows and lips, as though to say "I don't know." But deep down he had realized that it was a genuine invitation, an impression that was only amplified by what she had whispered in his ear. It may well have been at that very moment that he made up his mind. From then on, it was only a question of time.

The same port, the same early morning, and perhaps the same faint light as well. But it was another departure, one that he would never forget. For a long time he had gazed at the two stretches of sea, where the Mediterranean and the Atlantic come together, Gibraltar looming through the fog on the far shore. Just moments before the ship at anchor set sail for Marseille he had rushed up the boarding-ladder in case he felt any sudden regret that might make him give in to his feelings and turn back. To prevent himself from reversing his decision, he would need to discount everything he was leaving behind him, except, that is, for Bakhta, his cousin, the woman he had thought of marrying—he dreamed of spending the rest of his life in her embrace. Apart from her, there was nothing that merited either regret or sorrow. He would remember many things, of course: lots of friends at work and in the city, Tangier itself, its extended clean shoreline, his table at the Café Paris, cane shacks on the Malabata shore, his tiny library, and some of his personal possessions, few though they were.

It had been perhaps out of sheer despair that Muhammad terminated his official position and his administrative privileges forever. This is exactly what happens when someone jumps into a void from the top of a high mountain or walks along the top of a high wall in a state of panic, totally unable to walk normally. Anyone who did not know Muhammad from up close as we all did—if only in the final quarter of his life—will suggest that he must have had a touch of madness to do what he did, running away across the sea to the north and storming off like a bull that has managed to cut its rope and rush away.

Anyone who had worked first in the Sultan's palace, then as a dragoman in the Public Prosecutor's office in Tangier, had no need to take off like that and venture into the unknown. We know that he had previously traveled to France, Spain, and England on embassy trips and had spent time in Marseille as part of a Moroccan educational mission. We know too that, when that student mission returned to Morocco, it was to discover that the things they had learned were of no use in the new environment following the Sultan's death and the accession of a new ruler. The students had to get rid of their European clothes and put on traditional jallabas and cloaks. They were almost buried alive, an official position turned into a mere cover for the total collapse of wonderful dreams.

We can of course try to replicate the state of Muhammad's mind when he decided to leave, but we can never be certain of anything. In such circumstances the person involved may not be aware of the deep-seated reasons for making a decision that will change the course of his life. In fact no one can claim that, when he did what he did, he was either angry, in despair, crazy, or stupid. Other people may decide to give it names or divide it into categories as a matter of "fact." They will never let you live in peace if you do not give way and accept the fact that you fit into a certain box, are tied to a readily available formulaic description or label. What matters in this case is that Muhammad made up his mind to travel far away. In accordance with his wishes the boat took him to Marseille; he spent three days and nights on the boat, organizing his memory and picturing the new horizons that might be opening in front of him. As he reviewed his options, he asked himself what he would be losing and gaining, and how he could live an entirely different kind of life with relatively few losses, or even none. At any rate, he would not be arriving in Paris with no monetary reserves or devoid of everything.

So, from the boat to the train, and from Marseille to Paris. He knew where he was going. He remembered the address; in fact he had learned it by heart. In life there exist certain addresses, numbers, and coordinates that are never forgotten or should not be, especially when they are closely tied to our lives or we link them closely to our major reveries and daydreams. From the Gare Austerlitz the fiacre traversed a number of streets, Boulevard Raspail near the Odéon Square, Rue de Vaugirard, Rue de Medicis, after which the coachman drove his passengers in the direction of Rue Guynemer and Rue de Fleurus.

"You're just a few steps from your address, Moroccan. Say hello to your lover!"

That is what the coachman jokingly told him and accompanied him all the way to the door.

Muhammad took his suitcase, briefcase, and khaki holdall off the carriage. As he stared at the numbers on the apartments and shops, he had a strange feeling. Was he afraid that he would not be able to read a simple number like 27 or that he might make a mistake and not see it, as often happens when one's eyesight fails? It was simply a feeling with no clear parameters, nothing that might have been predictable. After just a dozen meters or so he found himself standing in front of a high blue notice-board on which was written clearly in white letters "Rue de Fleurus," right at the head of the street which gave on to the Luxembourg Gardens. Relaxing a bit, he walked confidently across another small junction between Rue de Fleurus and Rue Madame and made his way toward the anticipated house number, as though it were a number in a horse race. Finally, there he was, there was the building where Gertrude Stein and her group had settled in the ground-floor apartment, the wide lower level. There was a large portal, a shaded entryway, and above it an architectural design at the top of which was the name of the French architect, G. Pasquier, who had done the design for the building and supervised its construction in 1894.

It was an enormous building made of marble, looking out on to a small side street and a back view giving on to a courtyard and garden. It was in the ground floor that Gertrude had her apartment, with its living quarters on one side, its studio that Gertrude had turned into her artistic salon, and a room upstairs that Gertrude had told him about, set up as a reserve space for guests passing through.

When Muhammad opened the door, neither Gertrude nor Alice was there; it was some other woman. She gave him a piercing look that scared him.

"Is Gertrude here, Madame?" he asked. He almost asked her if she was the housemaid, Hélène, about whom she had heard everything, thanks to Alice's constant chatter in Tangier, but then he heard Alice's voice asking who it was at the door. Just then her head and curved nose came poking out. No doubt she had been expecting him; there was no sign of the slightest surprise or shock. Muhammad guessed that his last letter to Gertrude had laid the groundwork for his anticipated arrival.

They exchanged greetings and pleasantries, and Muhammad put down his bags. Alice invited him to sit on a couch and rest a bit while Gertrude came down from her room on the floor above (it was not exactly a whole floor, but rather a room somewhat higher in the building's design, similar to a duplex). Hélène was the one who kept up the chatter with Muhammad and Alice. Hélène was their wonderful French maid, nice, efficient, and practical about everything, and patient too, but not superficially jolly. Alice talked to him for a while, then paused for breath.

"Ah well," she continued with a sigh. "Hélène's been with us for nine years, but unfortunately she's going to leave us. Her husband's decided that she should not be working for other people from now on, so she has to do as he wishes."

This decision had made Gertrude very unhappy, Alice went on. She genuinely loved Hélène; she talked about her to everyone and even wrote about her in some of the stories she published. As you know, Alice said, she still mentions her and even talks about her to everyone on her trips abroad when the occasion permits. But the poor woman has no idea about the way the world works or what goes on all around her. Imagine, she thinks that there are no writers or painters in America.

"Why is that?" Muhammad asked her.

Alice's reply was that Americans are always coming to Paris to learn how to write and paint.

"So what do Americans do in their own country?" Alice had asked her.

"Most of them are dentists!" she replied with total conviction.

Gertrude came slowly downstairs, preceded by the smell of

bath salts. She walked slowly toward Muhammad, upright and proud like a marble statue torn from its pedestal and moving with an uncharacteristically light step. Muhammad beamed and held out his hands in preparation for an embrace. They hugged and kissed each other on the cheeks. He realized that she had not actually been in her room, but rather having a bath or shower.

"Well, Muhammad," she said, "you've taken a while to come to us! How are you? How was the journey? I'm sure Alice has started telling you about the servants. That's her number-one topic, and she never stops. It's always servants and cooking!"

He took a look at the epic body, which demanded complete attention, at her almost circular face, and at the hair on her head, carefully arranged to look like a royal crown. Her little white dog, Basket, was playing around her legs. It was then that he noticed how clear her forehead was, although her eyelids looked a bit puffy, maybe from lack of sleep. They sat down again opposite each other. Alice kept sneaking hostile glances at them, with her short hair tied back and a solitary curl dangling in front of her black eyes, a sharp nose, and the slightest trace of a moustache on her upper lip.

Hélène now brought in a coffee tray and started filling the colored cups. It was clear that the smooth china cups had faces and shapes from Picasso's ceramic works on them. When the pleasant maidservant leaned over to pour him a cup, she looked straight into his eyes.

"Good heavens, Monsieur," she said, "how weird it is that you've come all the way from over there, that dark continent!"

Gertrude burst into laughter. "Where on earth did you get that stupid idea, Hélène?" she asked disapprovingly.

Muhammad now intervened to save the poor woman from any further embarrassment. "Let her ask, and then she'll find out! Actually it's a very bright continent. Do you realize that? It gives light to the world."

"True enough." Gertrude went on. "It's all light, Hélène!"

After one cup of coffee, Gertrude stood up to go out, as though she had a previous engagement. She took Basket with her and invited Muhammad to join her. It was time for the spoiled little dog's walk.

"So," she asked him as they were at the crossroads leading to Boulevard du Montparnasse, "what do you have to tell me…after such a long absence?"

It was as though he did not take the question as seriously as he should.

"There's not much worth telling," he replied off the cuff, almost without thinking.

This cold response seemed to shock her, because she stopped and turned toward him as though to block his path.

"If that's the way you're going to reply to my questions," she said in an artificially assertive tone, "then we obviously need to go our own ways at the top of this street."

He immediately became very aware of quite how sensitive the situation was. He apologetically started telling her about everything—that is, after he had talked briefly about himself. He noticed that she was interested in everything that he talked about, but was also concerned about details. Then she took the initiative; she was the one who kept talking, especially about herself. A lot of things had happened, and there were a lot of faces, names, trips, places, books, pictures, projects, and ideas. To him she sounded like a one-person workshop. He did not conceal from her his feeling that she was an exceptionally valuable person, since by now he was convinced that she was someone who liked to be appreciated. On the way back to the house he talked about her while she surrendered herself to the rhythm of his celebratory phrases.

"You've traveled a long way," she said as they exchanged rapid compliments.

"All for you," he replied, fully aware of how to invoke the feminine moment. "All for you and a wonderful opportunity. You deserve nothing less."

"It's wonderful that you've come," she said joyfully. "So, here we go!"

Paris's trees were huddled under a late winter drizzle which seemed reluctant to leave and kept gnawing at the final days of spring. Muhammad was not used to the biting cold that kept enveloping the entire city; it had hit him as soon as he got out of the train and left the station, loaded down with his suitcase, briefcase, and personal effects all wrapped in paper. Fortunately, his woolen overcoat was up to the job, both when he arrived and now that he was staying close to Gertrude. She was listening to him as he talked about the garrulous French carriage driver who gave him the impression of being able to drive his two horses using only his chatter and the sound of his voice; he did not need his whip, which he used only to point at things but never on his horses. All the way from the Gare Austerlitz, he had not stopped talking to his passengers, passersby, itinerant peddlers, and bar owners. When he found no one to talk to, he would go back and chat to one of his horses.

"Come on, you loafer!" he would say, "don't put the whole load on your fellow-horse!"

Then he would go back to chatting with his passengers, telling them the everyday stories about his two horses and his passengers. He was a remarkable personality, much given to joking and wit. Wherever he stopped, he would never forget which of his passengers needed to get down.

"You with the spectacles," he would say. "Here's your stop!"

"Madame," he would say at another turning, "you know where your house is better than I do. Here's where you get off, and don't forget the meat and vegetables!"

Back in the house Gertrude sat on her bench close to the radiator, while Alice carried on with her preferred topic of conversation about maidservants. She could hardly stop herself even when Muhammad made an effort to complement her efforts with little questions so as to steer the conversation in different directions and pass the time of day. While this was going on, he started taking things out of his suitcase and rolls of baggage. All the gifts he had brought were characteristic of his homeland: jewelry, old bracelets, rings, silver and agate necklaces; the best craftsmanship of tradesmen and of the Amazigh in the South of Morocco—in Tiznit, Taroudant, and Marrakesh, in the tiny villages and earthen kasbahs on the edge of the High Atlas Mountains: circular silver and metal boxes for women to keep things in, candelabras of various shapes and sizes in ceramic and marble; beautifully crafted colored candles, glistening pieces of rock to be placed for decoration in glass cases, on side tables, or on top of wood-burning stoves; miniatures of camels carved out of juniper and Maghribi daggers used as wall decorations inside houses now that they were no longer needed in minor tribal conflicts and ancient family feuds. Muhammad had also brought tea utensils: a beautiful silver teapot, a palm-leaf basket, and a set of decorated Hayati cups. There were also some colorful silk fabrics and embroidered covers that could be used for tables and desks. Apart from all that, there was an amazing carpet, with such fine stitching that it would be difficult for anyone with weak eyes to conceive of making such a thing. Muhammad also produced an array of special spices that contribute to the sheer magic of Moroccan cuisine, along with some perfume essences...and a few other minor items and purchases that inspired all due amazement and admiration. Everyone inside the house got to look at this treasure trove of gifts, but, as we can well imagine and anticipate, the largest number of presents, as well as the most beautiful and expensive, went to Gertrude. Everyone expressed their gratitude, but Alice ploughed on with her chatter about maidservants.

"There'll always be good servants," she said, "but even so they all have their faults."

"My dear Alice," Gertrude commented, "they would never work with you from the start if they didn't have faults."

She turned toward Muhammad as though he were somehow interested in the subject of maidservants.

"In fact, Muhammad," she said, "there's nothing worse than having a servant come into your house. They actually enter your entire life, and then suddenly one day they up and leave you without there being the slightest reason for doing so!"

Muhammad surrendered to the multiple associations connected with the history of maidservants in the apartment at 27 Rue de Fleurus.

Thanks in large part to Alice's recollections on the topic, it did not take long for Muhammad to work out that over the years the house had gone through a number of transformations, so much so that it had become a virtual crossroads for many maidservants and their various stories. There was Celestina, the Swiss-Italian, whose aunt was the concierge in the building next door. She had left because she had no experience in cooking, specifically omelettes, which were a required part of Gertrude's diet.

"You know how Gertrude is," Alice told Muhammad. "The only thing she asks maidservants about is her required daily dish: Are you any good at cooking omelettes?"

Then came another one, named Maria Lasgourges, but she could not do the chores in the big apartment because she was so old. Another Maria followed, also Swiss, Maria Entis.

"Do you remember her, Gertrude? She didn't last long and left us to get married."

The two women chuckled at that as they recalled the servant with a glass eye. Gertrude mentioned that she'd used her in one of her stories and given her the name "Muggie Moll." Her husband was a gendarme who was always being transferred from one region to another without being allowed to take his family members with him. Alice also mentioned another servant who had been very neat, named Jeanne.

"You can remember her, can't you, Gertrude?"

Gertrude had looked particularly distressed about Jeanne. She had been forced to leave when she became mentally ill and kept having hallucinations about clouds and marriage.

The conversation now turned to another maid named Jeanne who had left her job for no reason. The two women had gone out looking for her, and the bicycle repairman on the street who had brought her to their attention told them both that she had been suffering from profound depression. She was a mother with a little girl.

"She was so sweet," Gertrude interrupted, "with a pretty ribbon in her hair," and then went on, "She was a wonderful cook. A woman's all about cooking!" She looked over at Muhammad. "Even more important was her voice. Oh my God! What a lovely, soft, and deep voice she had. It used to go right through me, although I could never explain why. And that was even though she never had a lot to say!" She paused for a moment. "How many times I had to go and bring her back, or rather to bring back that heavenly voice. Actually I did bring her back once, twice, three times, but then she would stop coming of her own accord. I always agreed to have her back even though we had hired someone else in the meantime. She must have gone through agonies during her mental troubles, and then she left us and never came back."

So here is Muhammad now, with Gertrude right in front of him. He has left everything behind in order to join her in Paris.

He is seeing her now just as he saw her for the first time in Tangier, with a dreamy and soft-eyed expression, a modest, open, passionate smile on her face.

"I've never met a man who looks at me the way you do, Muhammad. Or let me rephrase it. I've never met anyone who used such different words as you did in Tangier."

Alice got up and said she was going upstairs with Hélène to get a room ready for Muhammad. She may well have been hoping that he would not be staying too long.

Muhammad managed to muster a response. "Gertrude," he said, "I fell in love with you as soon as I set eyes on you in Tangier."

"There's no time to waste," she commented immediately, "when you fall in love at the very first glance!"

She remembered the hotel Villa de France in Tangier, the nice Moroccan waiter in the bar, the local cheese sellers in front of hotel, others selling the round loaves of bread, the drunken tramp who used to stand under the hotel windows and yell out that he was a friend of Henri Matisse.

"Matisse painted me," he would yell, "from over there, up at that window!"

Now Muhammad was staring avidly into the face of a woman about whom it used to be said that "she was one of those Americans who were born along with the first skyscrapers in America." He listened as she talked to him in a tone of voice that sounded like a loudspeaker or a sound emerging from a recording studio.

"Do you remember that night in Tangier?" she asked. "Oh my! How I panicked, but how happy I felt as well! I swear to you, you magic Moroccan, that you purified me! What did you do to me to bring me down to earth from my distant sky? Oh my! You can't even imagine how I entered paradise and left it on one unrepeatable night…"

Alice came back downstairs and joined them both in the warmth of the salon, close by the fire and under the paintings by Cézanne, Renoir, and Matisse hanging on the wall next to Picasso's portrait of Gertrude.

"The room's ready," she told Muhammad. "You can go up whenever you wish."

Gertrude thanked her and continued her conversation with Muhammad as she adjusted the collar of her camel-hair jacket.

"Ever since I've come back to Paris," she said, "I've been asking myself what Muhammad would be doing there…in those empty spaces? True enough, Tangier is beautiful and surprising, but it does not suit the needs of a young man like you who still wants to live his life. Isn't that so, Muhammad?"

"I have to thank you, Gertrude," Muhammad replied. "Your letter was brief, but it gave me an incentive to look at the world a different way. The truth is that you are the one who has lifted me up to the skies!"

"By the way, how are things in Tangier and Morocco now that you've left? Have they constructed the port? What about the tramway project they were talking about?"

"The tramway is still a distant dream, but the port was recently completed. The city's not the way you found it and left it. Next time you won't need porters to carry you on their backs so the seawater doesn't get your clothes wet. My country, Morocco? Well, as you knew when it happened, the French and Spaniards have divided it up between them. The Sultan has been deposed, and his brother has been put on the throne in his place. Tangier has been turned into a completely international city, owing allegiance to no particular nationality, even though the Spaniards are doing their utmost to consolidate their control over it. Once in a while however, the Americans remind them that Tangier is not a Spanish appendix."

It was on the Tangier shore, and on an unforgettable starlit night, that they first met alone. The whole thing came about thanks to a recommendation that Gertrude received from a French friend: she should search out Muhammad on her visit to the city and get to know it well. His name was Monsieur

Marchand, the former French consul in Tangier. Muhammad was eager to volunteer, and served as a thoroughly trustworthy guide, yet he hesitated about becoming a friend and companion close to the heart in the days ahead. What I recall from Muhammad's comments about that encounter far in the past was that he did not sleep that night, even when the American woman fell into a deep sleep. Insomnia kept him wide awake. It is true that he was thrilled to have been singled out in this way, but, truth to tell, he was afraid he might fall asleep and start snoring loudly. Who knows what might happen when someone feels half dead at night? His intestines might explode with gas, and the entire scenario would be ruined!

I am delighted by the thought that Muhammad arrived in Paris in a delightful spring season. In fact, he never mentioned to me what the weather was like when he arrived at Gertrude's apartment, nor does he mention in any of the papers he left with me anything about the hot, extremely humid conditions that would occasionally affect Paris; nor for that matter does he mention temperate or cold weather conditions with heavy rains and mud...or the like. For that reason I have preferred to cover his arrival in Paris with a light drizzle, something that did not prevent people moving about, or an isolated moment when public spaces could be enjoyed, architecture especially, but people as well. I can envision him now, arriving by horse-drawn carriage at Rue de Fleurus, heaving his suitcase, briefcase, the carpet bound with poor Moroccan-style twine, and other rolled-up items either under his arms or on his shoulders. That is the way Moroccans always travel; they may initially plan to travel with one small suitcase, but that soon turns into two huge suitcases and often even more!

I can see him knocking on the door, on the pavilion side, not the atelier. I can see Hélène, the maidservant, opening the door and him going inside. There is the little white dog, Basket,

Alice extending a cold hand, and Gertrude putting out her cheek without bending down a little toward the Moroccan. I can see him too, stealing furtive glances at the women. So what had changed and what had stayed the same during all those long years when he had not seen her? I can see Gertrude as well, after their first stroll together, taking off her shoes, going on tiptoe to her bedroom, and coming back with her photo album to show Muhammad.

She said that it was just a childhood album, a beginning to her life story; she had other albums that he could look at in chronological order. She told Muhammad that, actually, she did not like looking at old photograph albums, especially pictures of herself, although once in a while she would take another look at photographs of her mother and father. But he should be grateful to her because she had decided that being a good hostess demanded that she let him know about what she described as "the source of her life's river." It had seemed necessary for her to put Muhammad right into its stream from the outset so that he could have all the data at his disposal and find out about her in considerable detail. She may also have wanted to confirm things he had heard from her during her ten days in Tangier.

At this point Gertrude noticed that Muhammad was still wrapped up in layers of clothing. One sweater was visible underneath a shirt buttoned at the front, and on top of these was another sweater, this one made of wool with a high, wide collar that covered his neck. She assured him that the apartment was warm, and he did not need to keep all those layers on. She helped him gently take off the outside sweater, and he immediately felt more relaxed in this atmosphere, which had a very different feel to it. He was sitting beside Gertrude, and wafts of her perfume intermingled with his own breathing. Opening the album, she invited Muhammad to look closely at the photographs: "Look at this one, now this one…"

Sitting in her normal chair, Alice looked uncomfortable, as though she were alarmed, aggravated, or suffering from a stomach ache or something else. It is the kind of state, with a high temperature, that will be familiar only to people with the same restless and excitable personality or those who feel the same level of searing jealousy. Even so, Gertrude and Muhammad simply carried on looking at the photographs in the album, exchanging remarks, explanations, and clarifications, totally oblivious of the high level of anger that was boiling to the surface right next to them; as though Alice were on another bank out of sight, one that could not be seen from where they were.

"Look at this one! That's me when I was four years old. I don't know what that white dress was made of; it was a very soft material. Just look at my hair, how thick it was, all the way down my back, and that ribbon. Good God! How pretty I was!"

"And who are those people?"

"My four brothers and sisters. That's Michael, who was nine years older than me. That's Simon, two years younger. My sister, Bertha, four years older. That's Leo, my wonderful brother, two years older than me; he was terrific! And that's me. I was the youngest. I told you that when we were in Tangier, didn't I?"

"Oh yes, that's right. You did."

"This is a photograph of my brother, Michael, and his wife, Sara."

"And that's obviously a picture of your parents!"

"Yes, there's my father, Daniel—Daniel Stein; he was an American of German origin, from Bavaria. That's my mother, Amelia Keyser; she was born in the United States, but she was of Bavarian origin too."

Gertrude looked up from the album.

"My father was a boy of eight when he came to America with his family. They settled in Oakland, a suburb of San Francisco. Later on, my father became the deputy director of the tramway company in that city. When he died, my mother outlived him for thirteen years, and, when she finally passed away, my eldest brother took on the financial affairs of the family.

"Look! Here's our sage Michael who, through good management and experience, has made it possible for us to live a refined life. We're still well off today. There's a picture of me with Sara, his wife, and their son, Allan, in San Francisco. You can see Sara and me wearing hats with feathers. Good heavens! I hadn't noticed before that Allan is wearing a miniature marine's uniform. Here's another picture of me, this time with Leo in London. I hated that trip; London shocked me with its fog and frigid people. Here's another picture with Leo, this time in Cambridge, Massachusetts. And here he is introducing me to Henri Matisse, the wonderful artist."

"Yes indeed, I know him!"

"Ah yes, you do know him. You made his acquaintance when he visited Tangier. Here's a picture to record our purchase of his wonderful painting 'The Woman with the Hat.'

"Here's a picture of me in front of this apartment. It's taken from the atelier door before we changed the rotten wood on the floor. It was when we had first rented the apartment. At that time Alice had not arrived in Paris; she came four years after this picture was taken. That was the year my first book was published, *Things As They Are*. In just a minute I can give you a copy of it."

"Thank you. I'd like you to sign it for me, of course!"

"OK, fine. Now here's Picasso, the Spanish artist, Pablo Picasso. You may at least have heard of him in Tangier." As she was talking, she kept looking at Muhammad, while he remained silent. "He's my friend," she went on. "He's the one who painted me in that wonderful portrait you can see over there."

From her sitting position she points over to the painting which is hanging on the wall over the fireplace whose dancing flames lend a warmth and a poetic mood to the occasion.

"This photograph of the two of us was taken in the studio of the art-seller Clovis Sagot." With that, Gertrude stood up. "Come on," she said. "Take a closer look at this fantastic painting."

"How did Picasso come to paint you like that? Did he imagine you from a distance?"

"No, I was in front of him all the time—almost ninety times, eighty-seven to be exact! I had to sit like a model. Do you know the meaning of the words 'artist's model'? I'll explain it later. We've lots of time to talk about details. What's important is that Picasso was ready and found me equally ready…so we embarked on it together. But let's postpone talk about this till another time, and look at some more photographs…

"Here's Leo again, in the studio, here in this apartment before we introduced some changes so that it looks the way it does now. Here's a picture of me between Michael and Leo, the family—the Stein Family Corporation, they call it!" She let out a laugh. "Aha, this is an important photograph. Look, it's Matisse between my brother Michael and Sara, and Heinz Burman is with them. It's in our old house…here in Paris: 58 Rue Madame. This is a photograph of Fernande Olivier when she was living with Picasso. There's a child with her, but I've no idea who it might be.

"Good heavens, how come I have this photograph? I've no idea… I put it in the childhood album, but it should go where it was in the original album. Do you see how I looked when I was young? What misery! I was the despair of my teachers! They did their level best to teach me, but I kept causing trouble and wearing them all out. Do you know Muha? What did a nasty teacher once tell my mother about me? 'She behaves like a child who refuses to be a child!' That sarcastic remark upset my mother a good deal, but as a child I was delighted. I still have that same instinct even today. That's why I like photography: in these photographs I can forever remain a child. Once we leave them, we age rapidly. Do you follow me?"

"Yes, indeed I do!"

Gertrude may have been laying the foundations for a personal relationship, but Muhammad was still in the ultimate moments of flight. It is true that human relationships, particularly those involving love, have to start with awe and surmise, or at the very least a moment of incredible mystique or some fleeting attraction. Even so, the essential linkage requires a montage of elements, a maturity of language that creates a mutual understanding between two people, a dialogue between two souls. Although Gertrude was a little over thirty years old, she still managed to convey the impression of being a woman of experience, like a mother. Muhammad on the other hand was arriving as a fugitive, like a bird with broken wings alighting on electric wires, without knowing how to cling to them or where to focus his penetrating yet still storm-tossed glances...

Within moments he realized that now he had to acquire new tastes and a different persona. It was no longer enough to play with a woman's bosom or clasp her buttocks in order to get some love. The walls pulsating with paintings and colors, the carvings, black African masks that filled the house, Gertrude's way of talking about those artworks and artists, the photograph album that she had shown him like a book to be read and not merely pictures to look at... All of it filled him with a new and different feeling, one that he would have to think about a great deal and at length. With regard to his personal tastes and this lack of esthetic experience, he did not find everything he had seen beautiful, or rather let us say that it did not convince him or speak to him. Thanks be to God that from his very first step inside the apartment, he had not expressed an opinion or been asked to state his viewpoint. He would continue simply to look and listen.

We can only imagine what Muhammad's feelings must have been as he looked at the pictures hanging on the walls, as he questioned himself in an attempt to understand something and asked why it was that he could not do so! Certainly there were pictures that sprang out at him, some that filled him with a strange joy whose source he could not explain, some others that made him smell a fresh human scent that he could not name, others that grabbed him powerfully as though they had been painted just for him, others that told him nothing—as though to confront him—others that gave him a big jolt, and still others where he could not understand why he was unable to tell where they started and finished. He liked some of the pictures for their brilliant or gold-inlaid patterning…

He stood there in silence looking at the paintings, stunned and surprised, like someone entering an art gallery for the very first time. He was scared about touching something that was not supposed to be touched or breaking something that might be breakable. I myself had the very same feeling when I attended the first exhibit in Tangier, the same silent panic before I gradually caught on and understood things. But Muhammad was lucky, since he was moving around under Gertrude's gaze, and she knew where he had come from and how to gauge the limits of his viewpoint. She was also a gifted instructor and was persuasive in her explanations. Muhammad was undoubtedly grateful for what Gertrude had to tell him about this visual art, something he had not encountered in his own country. In his particular situation and his winged condition he could see that Gertrude was giving him a special privilege in what she was telling him.

Could he see it all in just one day? Of course not! He found himself suddenly, and at one go, in an open museum of modern art, not in a mere house decorated with a few paintings and carvings. He was looking and touching at the same time, and all to the accompaniment of a knowledgeable commentary from a young woman in full control of what she was saying. Gertrude obviously possessed a remarkable skill for talking to other people and talking even when she actually preferred to be listening. Even though her French was far from idiomatic, she talked confidently to Muhammad. She told him on the side that Picasso was always saying that they both spoke a kind of French that no one else could speak! She went on to tell Muhammad that he would love Picasso when they met.

"You both have the same penetrating eyes!" she told Muhammad, then moved closer and whispered in his ear almost inaudibly, "I love being French!"

5. THE ROOM ON THE ROOF

There can be no forgetting the moment when Muhammad first entered the upper room on the roof. Hélène had prepared everything, something that always happened when Alice told her that a new guest would be staying there. Muhammad told me several times about his first night in Paris: to be precise, in that very room which he managed to fill for years. No sooner had he made his way up there than he took a deep breath and felt a special, strange feeling of exultation. At last, here he was, close to the woman who had inhabited his own life ever since she had touched him with her wing and then flown away.

Lying down and having a long, deep sleep was his one-overriding desire, and yet he just stood there in front of the wood-framed mirror hanging on the wall over the wash basin alongside the bed.

"Just imagine," he told himself, "what would have happened if you had not found her when you arrived and knocked on the door! Imagine too if you had found her, but she had rejected you, or if the invitation she had given you in Tangier had just been a pleasantry. If, once you had arrived, she had refused to greet you and had no valid excuses…. Wow! So Muhammad, what a relief it is to find someone you love and desire!"

He took off his clothes and doused himself in the hot water to get rid of the exhaustion and dust of the journey. In fact, there was not any real dust, either on the boat or the wide expanse of the Mediterranean between sea and sky, or in Marseille, or on the train to Paris. It is just a phrase invoked whenever anyone has arrived at his destination. Muhammad may in fact have been thinking about something else besides dust as he was washing himself.

Bearing in mind Muhammad's situation and the psychological halo that was in control of his mind, he would not have been bothering about water and cleansing himself of all his body odors—especially in his armpits and sensitive areas—if it were not for the fact that he was getting ready to experience his long-anticipated dream. He was totally convinced that Gertrude was thrilled that he had come. She had laughed, and so had he; she had made a few overtures, and so had he. She had not merely hinted, but had come straight out and said things. He had observed her body well when he moved close enough on her bench to actually make contact with her and they had been looking at her childhood album of photographs together. Up till that moment and maybe ever since they met, he had never been able to work out what made her so attractive. Was it her body, or simply her talk? He could not work out precisely what kind of magic that body possessed or how it was possible for a piece of flesh inside her mouth—with no bones to it—to offer so much passion.

As he threw himself down on the welcoming empty bed with its white sheets, the door to the room remained slightly ajar. He lay on his back, exhausted, like a broken shadow. The sloping wooden roof over his head looked greenish from traces of damp. He thought he might spend some time later on polishing it a bit and restoring it to its former sheen; he also decided to get some flower pots and different kinds of plants to change the look of the roof-room into a kind of small hanging garden. He looked all around him and noticed the modest furniture on the wooden floor, which creaked under his footsteps: the toilet just by the door, the wash basin, the wooden wardrobe, the table and chair, and the gas lamp next to it.

At first glance then, the room displayed its old, tarnished features and the cracked walls that needed replastering. He noticed a tiny window in the sloping roof and got out of bed to see what kind of view it gave. From up there, the field of vision afforded a general view of an elevated part of Paris; in the distance the Eiffel Tower, that legendary entity whose iron beams interlocked, inevitably caught your eye, giving the observer a remarkable sense of engineering ingenuity. Through another small window in the room you could glimpse a bridge over the River Seine and nearby avenues of dark green trees. Muhammad made a promise to himself that tomorrow he would take a stroll along the banks of the river about which he had heard so much.

He went back and lay down on the bed, doing his best to come to terms with this high room and the nonstop sound of barking dogs. A sudden idea alarmed him: he was not going to be living here in Paris the way he had in Tangier. Back there, he had been living in a ground-floor house surrounded by a garden, the greenery of which had flourished under his tender loving care. He was also worried by the notion that the big city he had come to kept its windows firmly shut in a cheerless fashion. In fact what he really had to do was fall asleep and get the rest he so dearly needed.

But Tangier kept following him to Paris. He had told himself he was running away to escape from it, and yet now Tangier was invoking all its images to impinge upon his mind, all kinds of places, every single face. He felt somewhat sad as he saw Bakhta, his cousin, waving a white handkerchief at him. How affectionate she was, and how she blended with his loneliness; perhaps she was loving him in silence! Other pictures too of his Bedouin cousins, fine, honest people living in the desert outside Tangier. A picture of the city divided into segments in his memory: the Petit Socco, the Café Hafa, Casa Barata, the Cave of Hercules, Lalla Jamila's Tomb, the neglected grave of Ibn Battuta, the virgin beaches, the port—ah, the port! Other images as well: Gertrude, Alice, suitcase, handbags, porters surrounding the two women after carrying them away from the boat, and the low, water-logged pavement. He can still remember how he had met and greeted them both, then put himself at their disposal, all in response to the request of their mutual French friend; how he had escorted them to the Villa de France hotel; and how he had talked to Gertrude about his early writings when she had questioned him to test his potential, something she had heard about from Monsieur Marchand. Then there was the lunch he had eaten with the American pair at the hotel restaurant, the agreement on the program of their visit; first exchanges of laughter; scandalous dirty jokes shared with Gertrude and Alice that had immediately annulled all the formality between them. Then the first stroll along the Atlantic beach in Tangier and the hill-climb to look out over the sea.

"From here," he told them, "I can plunge straight into the sea!"

"You're crazy," Gertrude responded with a laugh. "From up here? OK then, let's do it together, you and me!"

He did not say no.

"I agree, but only on condition that we embrace first and then throw ourselves in together."

They kept laughing at each other and making the motions of plunging down.

"Actually, Muhammad," Gertrude said, "I'm no good at playing mad. What I would really prefer is for us, you and me, to take the plunge somewhere else!"

Every sense in his body told him what she meant.

"In bed, for example?" he whispered.

It was a wonderful act of chance that they had a mutual French friend. He had got to know this person in Tangier, whereas Gertrude had met him on holiday in Majorca. It was the things that Matisse had told her that encouraged her to visit Tangier, and the urge intensified when the former French consul there, Monsieur

Marchand, told her about a nice young Moroccan whom he could get to escort her around, along with her friend. That way, she could get to know all about Tangier, the first spot of land that people encounter on the African continent: a beautiful place that tempts one to cross the short distance that separates Europe from Africa, and thus discover the real meaning of geography.

"It's all very easy," she told Muhammad on the first night in her separate room in the hotel. "I've never in my life imagined that this would happen."

"So let me thank this happy chance," he said.

But Gertrude replied that in essence it was not a matter of chance. One is led from one instinct to another, in the same way that bodily contact must be preceded by a communion of two souls. It is that gentle, acute contact created by the words we hear and others that we say.

"Not only that," Muhammad continued, "but the words we read as well."

Gertrude immediately explained that words that are read are actually spoken or heard words in any case, but the written form gives them a fresh context in which they can be said and heard again. We do not have to rely entirely on what we read, or, at the very least, on everything we read. Written words will often give the writer a sense of superiority over other people, in which case the carefree words that someone may have said or heard turn into mere banalities…

In this rooftop Parisian room with its sloping wooden roof inside and tiles outside, Muhammad kept trying to fall asleep, moving around awkwardly in the narrow space and bumping his head on the roof. He kept reconsidering his abrupt departure for these far-off skies; there had been no preliminaries whatsoever, as though he were running away from a gloomy land that could only instill a sense of dread in people's hearts. Even so, deep inside he did manage to find a rationale to convince himself, and, at any rate, he was not obliged to convince anyone else. For him, what mattered was that he had come to Paris to follow the tracks of someone he loved. Where love is concerned, no one should be blamed for following his heart, especially when it reaches the point at which he finds himself in a bitterly cold firmament and the feminine breeze hits him with its warmth—something that was now happening to Muhammad as he warmed himself with the memory!

The truth is that, after he returned to Morocco, Muhammad kept Gertrude's image stored deep in his heart, as though preserving it in a cloth purse, not just as part of his memory. He sent her letter after letter, but there was no reply, like a student writing out lines over and over again without being sure whether or not the teacher was happy. When a single, small, and tersely phrased letter did arrive, it managed to bolster anew Gertrude's presence in his inner self and make her flickering light that much brighter than it had been before. In Tangier he would picture the map, with Paris at the very top as far away as the fingers on his hand. He used to steep himself in memories of the distant body that had moved away. His dreams would help him recall the American woman, and he could find shade in her wide shadow. He could envisage himself climbing the ladder to the heavens of her bosom! From daydream to sleeping dream he would be able to transfer her image as though he never needed to wake up.

He woke up to hear someone knocking on the door. Hélène had come up to invite him down for dinner. The table had been set in his honor, and Gertrude was full of praise for Alice because of the menu she had chosen and the way everything had been cooked. He embellished the praise with words of his own and added to the compliments. As he ate and chatted, he took another look round to take in the details of this open salon. There was a small black-and-white iron sculpture right under Gertrude's portrait, another one in papier-mâché placed inside a small glass case which stood on top of a sideboard between two tall windows covered with curtains in muted colors. He started counting the paintings that Gertrude was pointing to and naming their artists: twenty paintings, drawings, and sculptures by Picasso alone, seven by Juan Gris, and two by Sir Francis Rose in a dark corner. Muhammad remarked that you could hardly see anything over there, to which Alice responded that that explained why they called any of their visitors who regularly sat in that corner "matchstick owners"! Gertrude continued with her detailed description of the oil and watercolor paintings of Paul Cézanne and Matisse's works—of which there were two whole rows—two works by Paul Gauguin, paintings by Manguin, and others by Monticelli. There was a picture of a naked woman by Vallotton and a single work by Toulouse-Lautrec. She also pointed out another portrait done by Vallotton, a portrait of Maurice Donnay, and two paintings by De Launay. There was also a small piece by Eugène Delacroix and some others as well that were difficult to look at while everyone was eating.

The walls were covered with paintings of all sizes, whether on the apartment side or the studio, which had been turned into a kind of exhibition hall. In addition, every wall in that latter space had a mirror, with brass pots as decoration. A table had been set up, and on it were all kinds of exotic objects: nails, tiny specimens of traditional weaponry, a variety of pens both useful and useless, writing quills, unused seals, keys, and a collection of pipes.... Once he had finished eating, Muhammad carried on looking at them all up close. Accompanied by Gertrude, he made his way in amazement through the glass cases, chairs, inlaid wooden sideboards, wonderfully patterned rugs, and Eastern miniatures. In the middle of them all was the wonderful Moroccan carpet that he had brought as a present that very day.

In responding to Muhammad's questions, Gertrude talked about herself, about writing and art. She also mentioned other things that kept her busy. She led him to understand that her daily life was not as empty as might be imagined. If she was not actually writing, she would be involved with other activities that took up a lot of time: dealing with the problems of Americans in Paris and even outside Paris at times. She used to visit people in hospital or offer assistance in finding a rest home. Both she and Alice had to search for these Americans, wherever they were, so they could fulfill their patriotic duties and do whatever was necessary to comply with the dictates of the American Humane Society Foundation. Muhammad seems to have sensed that Gertrude needed his services, because, even though she never asked him, he found himself telling her that he was at her disposal. She immediately welcomed the generous offer and beamed at Alice.

"Thanks for your generosity," she told him. "We're women with no protection. We need a real man with us!"

For his part, Muhammad continued looking at the weird art works without feeling that there was anything wrong or demeaning about his proposal. To the contrary, he seemed very happy about his new situation. He may have wondered whether it was a first step, with others to follow.

I made no attempt to hide from Lydia my anger at Gertrude's easy surrender to the dictates of the heart and nothing else, to a featureless love, but she scolded me with an arm gesture. We were sitting opposite each other in the Le Goéland Restaurant in Rabat; it was a candlelit dinner to celebrate New Year's Day. The owner of this exclusive restaurant kept moving from one table to another, offering his greetings and thanks to the customers. A short while earlier this wily Frenchman, who had become a Moroccan of sorts and whose restaurant was a regular resort of ministers and diplomats, had been standing by our table, telling a dirty joke in an old-fashioned Moroccan colloquial, so that Lydia could not enjoy it as much as we did.

When it came to what Lydia regarded as "my excessive enthusiasm" for analyzing an exceptional love story with its own particular circumstances, she took a totally different point of view. To a degree we were in agreement, needless to say, since I had no desire or intention to talk about Muhammad as though I were somehow more aware or intelligent than he was or could avoid the kind of mistakes he made if I were in his shoes. But was I supposed to be ashamed of him and myself, because it was understood that I was criticizing him in order to belittle him? Absolutely not! I am abundantly aware of the passage of time and fully understand that by now he has become a liability of the past and my own realization that, if I were in his place and living in his age, I might be behaving exactly the way he did at the time. What I am doing now is thinking things over; I am certainly not about to spit on the past. I am doing my best to understand without indulging in needless confrontations. There is no point in starting a fight with a past that is in fact long since over; I am doing my best to understand that and deal with it. What I cannot understand, however, is Gertrude's love for Muhammad in and of itself.

"So why do you think Gertrude fell in love with this poor Moroccan?"

"Maybe she was looking for some kind of exotic Oriental pleasure, meaning to experience the obscure and unknown..."

"If that's the case, she could have found any number of Orientals in Paris. Why go that far away to find someone?"

"Lydia, you know far better than I do that the people you meet when you're traveling are not like the people you meet where you live. For Gertrude, Muhammad wasn't simply a man; he was a bodily experience..."

"No, don't exaggerate!" she objected. "Such talk about machismo is simply ancient Arab bragging. Machismo exists everywhere, and so does sexual frigidity. If I've understood you right, she didn't attach herself to him as much as he did to her. Was your friend the type of man who's interested in the nine apertures of the female body? I suspect that may be why he bumped against the impossibility of love. We also have to take into consideration the other aspect of Gertrude's personality: she wasn't totally feminine. You know that. But, in spite of everything, we still need to keep searching. I don't know…. Love is full of secrets!"

At mile-marker 6/600 on the Z`ir Road on the east side of Rabat, and at one o'clock in the morning in the New Year, Lydia turned her KitKat car with diplomatic plates to the right toward her house. She was still talking to me about Muhammad, trying to divert my attention away from judgments about values.

"So let's suppose," she said, "that Muhammad did object to a situation that you consider demeaning. Let's suppose too that what happened to him had never actually happened. Was he ever thinking of writing a book about his life? Was he intending to ask you to write one? Would you have been asking about Gertrude Stein and Alice Toklas, and others as well…and about me too for that matter? Would you have entered my house so we could meet, make love—yes, us too—and exchange meaningful dialogue (at this point she touched my cheek with her finger) and nuances of language?"

Once we were inside her home, we went into the salon again. I tried to speak, but she put her finger on my lips.

"Don't say a word," she said, as she kissed me. "We can't make time go backwards and recreate people's lives. Whatever was going to happen happened. Nothing will ever happen if it can't happen. We're all part of this enormous process, my friend. So let's just think about it."

Lydia may have seemed as though she were embarking on her very first adventures in love, but in bed she behaved like a woman of experience, well aware of how to hug, clutch, and kiss, how to suck on her lover's lips and thrust her tongue in his mouth like a viper, so much so that she gave you the impression (and I am speaking about myself here) of having come to have me spend the entire night inside her mouth. She was an American woman, one of those who are more concerned about the sensual manifestation of love and want to be as neat in bed as they are with clothes, work, eating, and everything else in life. That is something that aggravates me. I don't like overpowering women. I have always much preferred the sound of a wolf howling in the desert to a woman who wants to sleep with you as neatly as if she were part of a television soap opera.

Beyond that I do not like any woman who wants to be in charge of my life, particularly by issuing homilies; one who knows or claims to know everything. It is true that I dislike ignorant or stupid women too, but I also hate women who have something to say about everything. Lydia, who claimed that, as a diplomat, she understood our reality, is incapable of being aware of her own psychological makeup. What kind of reality is it that she is supposed to know when she does not understand the people? Muhammad was never constrained to the extent of bartering his own self. He possessed a degree of intelligence, and he chose to get rid of it. He had to make a choice; he had options. He had to come to a decision, and he preferred a destiny that was not necessarily his own. When Lydia chooses to justify everything on the basis of its being a kind of understanding, I am not like her, nor do I wish to be so. I disagree with Thornton Wilder, a writer who had a big influence on her and whom she was always quoting in my hearing, who says that we can all fully understand Caesar's cook, who killed himself when he burned the food!

I simply told her that in his youth Muhammad had been very ambitious, but had not managed to break out of the stifling seashell in which he was trapped. The country itself had gone downhill, and, along with other people who had returned from abroad, he found himself compelled to bow down to the inexorable blast of traditionalist jurists who had neither profundity nor talent. They had memorized a set of ancient texts but never indulged in any kind of thought; all they did was yell and scream and occupy the entire public space. As a result, his enthusiasm dwindled along with everyone else's. A number of them chose to turn to religion and philology, but he made an effort to think for himself, even though it was purely external, and to write, albeit in a voice other than his own. Even so, he failed to cause a ripple or throw a stone, however tiny, into the fetid pond. When he began to worry that he was burying his spirit alive, he slunk away on a murky dawn and left the country.

In his room on the roof, every single location in Tangier, every face—everything, in fact—was still there, flashing in front of his drooping eyes. It would all come back and stay very close to him, attaching itself to his retina, as though he had only just spotted it. From time to time things might perhaps fade into the mist, and yet in Paris it would be converted into something closer, something that managed to keep everything remote and beyond his vision. He would look up and see the dark clouds forecasting imminent rain and not know whether they came from down there or were heading in that direction. He would then look down again and watch the first droplets as they trickled down the pane of his tiny window. No doubt he would recall that distant horizon in Morocco, or at least that is the way it seems to me on the basis of a short extract that I came across, something he must have written at this particular time. I cannot tell whether this sensation he had was the result of memory or research: "Over there," he wrote, "the world was not allowed to enter our heads. The air all around us may have been pure, and yet it neither entered our hearts nor reached our lungs."

From now on, Gertrude became his new habit; her time was his. When she came up to the room, his whole life blossomed anew, as though he was being born a second time in her embrace. His whole heart opened up to her, to such an extent that he felt the room was too small and did not allow his bliss to float on high. The bed was not big enough to encompass their twin bodies. On his second night in Paris Gertrude had stripped naked and removed her tight undergarments to reveal an ample body; she may have been eager and submissive, but there was no space left on the bed.

I can recall now the way Muhammad used to shudder as he described the scandalous sight. To be quite clear here, I will admit that, when I am talking about both him and her, it is his language that I am using. Wherever he put his hand, he was in contact with sweat-drenched soft skin steeped in a wonderful perfume that he could not identify. He touched her shoulder, her back, her waist, her breasts, everywhere on her body, and she writhed like a rhinoceros roaming wild in the bush. I still remember today the dirty language he used.

"The best thing about a body like that is the incredible pliability. As it plunges and heaves, you're overwhelmed. It's like a lake shrouded in smoke and decked in blue, with a light breeze rippling the water."

"But what about her, Abu Muhammad?" I asked. "Where was her hand?"

"Her hand? She left it dangling so she could touch a piece of flesh she knew all about. Do you get it?"

"Her hand was behind my waist. She used it first to explore every rib one by one, then all over my body. While I kept moving fingers, lips, and tongue without uttering a sound, she was totally incapable of making love without talking; it was almost as if she were addressing herself to my flesh—extremities, veins, and innards all at the same time. For her, any anticipation or exchange of talk was not a matter of give and take. No, speech was what gave everything its verve and warmth. Her passion was self-centered, rough, and crafty, and I loved her incredible energy. She was playful as well, like a heavily laden horse moving across hard, stony terrain covered in slippery rocks, trying to cling to everything. I found it all deeply satisfying, as though it were giving me a new burst of life." (This was a segment from Muhammad's account during the sessions in Tangier, although they too have now become distant memories.)

For a very long time he stands in the salon, staring at Gertrude's portrait. He has nothing to say about its artistic quality, since he has yet to acquire the necessary words used with such fluency by Gertrude to describe this picture or any other. Even so, he has his doubts, but he does not know how to put them into words. He will be learning more from the young woman; he will ask more questions and understand more, particularly once he has started welcoming for himself many visitors who come to the apartment every evening before five in the afternoon to see the art works which cover the walls—friends, many people who enter the apartment for the first time as though going to a public museum. He asks Gertrude if she intends to keep on tending this treasure trove of artworks for the rest of her life, hanging on the walls in the salon, on the side, in the studio, or else wrapped in paper or stowed in cardboard boxes in the storeroom. Will she still be looking at them morning and night, talking about them to visitors and all comers, and dusting them off every single day? She replies that without those paintings she would have no life.

"That's the way I'll be until I die," she said. "I'll read and write. These pictures will keep me company and I them. I may get tired of people and they of me, but these colorful pieces will never get tired of me or wear me out. I've embalmed my very soul in these paintings, and I'll remain alive just as long as they do!"

As time passed, Muhammad found himself tossed this way and that—open one minute and closed the next, hot and then cold. He became inured to mood swings, moments both amicable and inimical. He would dissimulate, and all around him places would coalesce and splinter. He would be a close and distant friend, companion and comrade, guard and driver. So often was he connected to Gertrude's body, up and down, back and forth, that he became like a shadow of her, as she did of him. The two shadows intermingled on the pathway till he turned into a kind of wraith, a type of Chinese shadow puppet behind the white screen. He did his utmost to preserve his own features, taking on the difficult task even though you might call the process sheer stubbornness. But if Gertrude was content, then so was he.

At this juncture we have to admit that it was thanks to her that he started writing on a daily basis. She taught him how to record everything he saw, heard, read, and said off the cuff. He used a pencil for this purpose, as did Gertrude herself; like her, he never did any trimming, revision, or editing. Like her too, he believed that everything written resulted from fresh human experience. It was as though they both—she from her viewpoint, he from his—were writing for the sheer purpose of writing, or else as being something they both could do. But at least she had started finding a way to get her writings published in magazines; in fact she even paid for it herself. And here we see Alice, whenever she was not otherwise engaged in urgent household business (like maidservants running away from the apartment for example), making her way to the office of Jean-Gabriel Daragnès, the publisher. Once there she used to squeeze past the slides of lead-printing letters and ingest the smell of printer's ink as she encouraged the workers at the press to produce excellent copy as quickly as possible. She was always particularly generous with the workers. That was Gertrude. Muhammad on the other hand used to make notes and write things down, but the pages and notebooks would simply pile up in drawers.

These days Muhammad seems to be keeping me company again, hardly ever leaving me. I wander around the streets of Rabat, and he is always with me. If I am in the market, he is there as well. I can almost touch the vegetable basket that he is carrying as he walks a few steps behind Alice in Paris. She would be making a selection from the tomatoes, potatoes, and onions, and sampling the fruit. The sunshine would feel close, and I could envision it shining diffidently on the tops of trees in the sixth arrondissement, in the Luxembourg Gardens, and along the Boulevard Saint-Germain. The sun used to peek through the cloud cover, a wan, yellowing glow would shine in your eyes, and you would feel a passing sense of gloom. I can visualize him passing by the shop of Luigi the barber, an amiable, warm-hearted Italian from a provincial area near Alexandria. Their greetings to each other reflected their mutual affection; Luigi would never accept payment.

"Don't bother," he used to say. "Your head is as my own, and so is your face!"

He would have to greet Monsieur Michot the butcher too, who would ask him about Gertrude's guests. Were there more of them this week? Red and white cuts of meat, with cutlets already prepared.

I can almost hear the noise of a Paris morning: carts passing by on the hard asphalt road; fiacre drivers, street cleaners, itinerant peddlers, young boys selling newspapers, all of them yelling their wares. He must have walked past the woman selling roses at the street corner not far from Saint-Sulpice, that Bretonne spinster with an acid tongue when occasion demanded. She would always tease the young Moroccan man, who did his best to overcome his bashfulness. Even though she had a scar that marred the line of her lips, she could still look pretty. I can see him too standing by the door of the bakery owned by his Algerian friend, Si Ibrahim al-Wannas, someone who was known for being sociable and teasing female servants. Muhammad himself had by now became a distinct daily feature all along the Rue de Fleurus and throughout the quarter. He would spend a good deal of time with these people whenever he had to go out for a short walk or to do the household chores.

"We hardly ever hear his voice," Gertrude tells Alice. "As you can tell, he never bothers us. He's just here, and that's it."

I can almost see him entering and leaving on tiptoe, just like Alice and the maids. Inside the big apartment Gertrude imposes her own silent regime; she cannot stand noise or din, plates clanging together, or glass breaking in the kitchen. In the corridors the maids have to walk barefoot so the sound of slippers and shoes will not bother her. She much prefers to have all the polishing, cleaning, and mending done when she is outside the house, walking the dog, visiting friends, or going to some appointment or other. She does not even like to listen to music.

Muhammad is residing in the apartment, but that's it. It is as though he has become part of the furniture. He has to dust the pictures, which is a tremendous honor for him because he realizes that he is actually touching great works of art! He also has to go to the bookstore of Mme. Sylvia Beach, a small English woman, on a side street near the Medical School, to take out books or return them. He will in fact continue to frequent this little bookstore even when it moves to the Place Odéon. He also has to look for the paper and pencils that Miss Gertrude uses all the time before she edits what she has written and writes it out in pen. She has gradually stopped using her typewriter. Ever since Alice has taken charge of the manuscripts, she has become especially adept at decoding the terrible handwriting that even Gertrude finds hard to read at times. Often he has to go back and forth to the studio of Monsieur Vollard carrying pictures; he may have heard the rumor that this crafty art dealer also sells vegetables in bulk! He also has to carry out a function for Monsieur Matarasso, a bookseller and trader in rare antiques who has a special passion for collecting Rimbaud documents. Rumor has it that he managed to get hold of a suitcase full of the papers of this mercurial poet, along with some of his clothes, pictures, and manuscripts. He collects anything connected with Rimbaud. Even if he came across some preserved shit of Rimbaud's, he would certainly bid for it at auction and make sure he got it! There are also some minor tasks that Gertrude wants done, involving the bookseller, Monsieur Marc Lolie, and his fat Belgian wife who loves singing opera. She cannot stand people, and they reciprocate the feeling, except for our Moroccan, who manages to make her happy by calling her "Carmen."

The thing that Muhammad really wants is to see Gertrude smile. That radiates a sense of safety and gives warmth to the entire apartment. But when she is angry or sad, everything looks gloomy and dank. How happy Muhammad feels when Gertrude invites him and Alice—and sometimes their housemates, the dreadful Henri-Pierre Roché and the much nicer Bernard Fay—to form a small audience to listen to her latest composition. There is always something that she can read in a pseudo-poetic tone from her most recent writings. He has to keep both eyes and ears peeled so he can look appropriately impressed and happy and be ready to express the necessary compliments.

Yesterday, he was making his way silently into the apartment, when he was astonished to hear voices while the two women were taking their afternoon nap.

"Oh Alice, I love the way your voice quavers. Oh Alice, Alice! Your eyes are like those of a cow in a green pasture, lifting its horns to see who is passing by. Oh my lovely cow. Oh, Alice!"

After a moment's pause, he hurried up the stairs.

"The sow!" he thought to himself. "She can't do anything without talking!"

There is one particular detail that I must not overlook. In the privacy of his own room, that afternoon and all evening,

Muhammad allowed himself to weep, the bitter tears of a man in the depths of despair. He covered his head with his bed pillow. When he stood in front of the wash basin and mirror to wash away the tears, he kept rubbing his face with water in an attempt to convince himself that the tears had come on suddenly because he was feeling nostalgic. If Alice had happened to see him throwing water on his face this way (since she was always with him), she would have told him something she had said on a previous occasion: "You wash your face too much; it's as if you're trying to rub it off! You rub your hands together a lot. Soon there won't be anything left!"

But water cannot wash everything away, especially the vestiges of hateful times, shrouded dust, the producers of nasty worms that burrow their way into places and souls and feed on corpses.

Setting other personal issues aside, the essential thing as far as Muhammad was concerned was that he had now become the man of the house. He was the close friend, the guardian of the women and the apartment, always intent on keeping the pictures, sculptures, and other possessions clear of evening dust. Gertrude gave him another task too, one that seemed reasonable and acceptable as part of his responsibilities as the man in the family. During the artistic and literary soirées that Gertrude regularly organized, Muhammad was asked to make sure that no one drank too much—Max Jacob and Artaud, for example, but anyone else who chose to behave in an inappropriate manner that might spoil the atmosphere of the gathering. Gertrude gave him explicit instructions, and he was expected to carry them out to the letter in order to preserve the propriety of the occasion. His stolid facial features, his Eastern appearance, and the very speed with which he adapted to his new role were clearly sufficient for things to remain under his general control. Max, for example, immediately understood that there was no need to pick Alice's pocket when she did not want to do something or offer something. That may explain too why Guillaume Apollinaire stopped coming to the salon and withdrew from the intimate circle before going off to war, drunk with sun and dust, only to be hit in the head by shrapnel and return shrouded in bandages. The rest of that particular story is well known. When it came to Antoine Artaud, he realized that the American woman's salon was no longer what it had been in the past, a place where truce could prevail with the more reckless partisans of art and writing, the kind of people for whom poetic sensitivity could rise to the level of schizophrenia. So he went away; all that was left was Anaïs Nin's salon, somewhere he could go and find an entirely different kind of woman. She too had her particular psychological traumas, true enough, but at least she knew how to deal respectfully with other people's traumas. Whenever Artaud walked along the Rue de Fleurus and saw Muhammad standing there, he would wave his hand in greeting (or maybe it was an expression of disgust), then continue on his way, whistling merrily!

Muhammad, our Moroccan, performed his functions exactly as if he were on a small farm that the heavens had given him. He turned into a malleable piece of dough, a blank sheet of paper. Even so, he did not feel hurt in spite of the august atmosphere that pervaded the place, thanks to his own efforts. That is precisely what he himself told me, exactly as I am saying it now. In fact, these accumulating daily chores made him think about himself in a way that aroused an ambiguously bitter sensation that he did not want to name.

"When I was there," he would say, "there were times when I felt proud of myself, but then there were others when I felt as though I were going down a staircase into an abyss from which there would be no escape!"

He longed for the spark, but felt it was always a long way away. He wanted body to rub against body, but once in a while the slightest rebuff, albeit suppressed, made him feel as though he were far away. Let us say that his feverish passion had no depth to it; that is the way to interpret the feeling that, while he was actually in Paris, he found himself adrift in featureless thickets.

No one who frequented Gertrude's apartment could possibly tell whether Muhammad the Moroccan was a friend, servant, driver, or keeper of the studio. In any case the image inside the apartment was not the one that presented itself to public view, nor indeed was there anyone who could infringe accepted boundaries to the extent of asking about everyone or everything. Even though Parisians as a rule are fanatical when it comes to collecting detailed information about the people they consort with, Muhammad remained—as far as I can tell—a person with no attributes worth mentioning. Even Parisian women, by which I mean specifically Miss Gertrude's nasty neighbors like Marie Le Branchu, Denise Ville, Claudine Hervé, Hélène Lazard, and Jacqueline Rossignol, failed to get all the data. They kept making inquiries, of course, but the baker, grocer, butcher, dentist, newspaper seller, milk seller, and bicycle repairman all turned out to know no more than they themselves did. As far as I can tell (and Muhammad did not talk to me about it), he preferred to play the game; he wanted to remain a mystery and his relationship with Gertrude to stay private.

There is one person with whom Muhammad was prepared to abjure a bit of his commitment to silence and share a few of his attributes, namely his French friend, Bernard Cacheux. He alone was someone with whom Muhammad could feel a sense of refuge and consolation. He had made Bernard's acquaintance in a small café on Rue Madame, and the two men had grown fond of each other. Bernard was one of those Frenchmen who can gain your affection very quickly for his basic simplicity, spontaneity, and open heart. He always wore a dark blue beret of the kind sported by sailors; the reason for covering his head like that may have been that he had previously worked for the French railways before he was forced to retire. As he explained to Muhammad, he now spent all his time taking care of his aged mother, who was sick and crippled. It was his misfortune that his only sister, who lived with him, was mentally handicapped.

Muhammad used to go to Bernard's home in his spare time, and he had a lot of it. This simple Frenchman fascinated him with tales of Paris and many other French cities, all of which he knew as well as the veins on his hand. They used to sit together on the stoop outside the house where Bernard lived, each one of them holding a glass of wine in one hand and a pipe in the other, sharing both time and memories. Sometimes Bernard would let his mind wander off, and his fingers would shift the beret to left and right. Muhammad knew how to hold a conversation, but he was equally adept when it came to respecting someone's need for silence. He would let Bernard have his moments of distraction, and then resume the conversation or broach a new topic.

Sometimes Alice used to pass by as they were having these chats. She would be wearing a hairnet to keep her hair tied back and huge earrings like a gypsy woman. She used to take a few steps with tiny feet like Spanish women so that Muhammad would get up and accompany her on a stroll or to market. In the same way Gertrude herself would often come up and take him with her while she was walking the dog. He used to get up and walk on her right-hand side, with the dog on her left. She used to move around like a bat, relishing life in Paris, especially when she was wearing her dark grey woolen sweater and the black hat with feathers. She used to wet her lips with her tongue and talk to him in the imperious tones of one issuing orders.

Because Bernard had learned almost everything there was to know about Muhammad, he was able to train him to endure his situation.

"You've chosen your lifestyle," he told Muhammad, "so now you have to live with your choice."

He was teaching Muhammad how to behave and control himself until some new horizon opened up for him. In response Muhammad told him that he had actually had another horizon, but he had closed it down, left it all behind him, and come to Paris. It was just like someone closing up a shop and completely changing professions.

"Muhammad," Bernard commented, "you've actually changed your entire direction."

The Frenchman was certainly sorry to observe the slight tinge of angst that would show itself once in a while in Muhammad's expression. Muhammad himself would sometimes question his motivations, as though thinking out loud. For example, how come he had not followed his own innate Bedouin instincts? The genuine Bedouin puts his ear to the ground and hears the clop of hooves passing by and moving on. It was as though he had lost his own spiritual compass; as Bernard put it, he was no longer rooted. The Frenchman, with all his life experience, did his best to reassure Muhammad that he was actually going through a transitional phase without realizing how wonderful it was. Without even questioning him, he went on to clarify that Muhammad might well be leaving behind the Bedouin stage that still lingered deep inside him—a close attachment to the earth—and was now moving into an itinerant gypsy mode, in motion and without roots.

"Do you understand what I'm saying, Muhammad? Of course you do. Of course. The gypsy, Muhammad, never listens to the earth because at heart he has none of his own. Instead he listens to the wind; that way he hears all the voices he needs in his life. Do you understand what I'm saying?"

Yes, yes indeed! And, while talking about gypsies, Bernard shocked Muhammad by announcing his intention to leave the quarter. He had decided to move to a Parisian suburb where he would be living among the gypsies, grave-diggers, and simple folk (as he put it). He could no longer reconcile himself to living on a paltry salary from the municipality, renting a place to live in central Paris, and dealing with the high cost of living. Out there a friend of his had managed to find a wooden house with no rent.

"Fairly soon," he said, "I'm going to leave you to your room on the roof where you can put out tidbits for the swarms of pigeons and expand your hanging garden. You can come and visit me out there whenever you want. I'll leave you the address, so you can get in touch."

Muhammad told Bernard that he would go with him until he was settled and got to know the new gypsy suburb. That was the very least he could do.

Gertrude announced that she would pass by Bernard's residence to say farewell and ask him if he needed any assistance from her. There was a Ford car, and that way nothing would be lost. "He's going to leave the quarter empty. He was always so nice and helpful."

She told Muhammad that she was seriously considering buying another small dog. In that case, the evening walk would involve two dogs when he was not with her. The wretched cat usually had its own ideas about the appropriate spot to deposit its mess. Muhammad asked her if the cat still needed more training, to which she replied that it did not; what it needed was to make up its mind!

When evening came, people gathered around the table to play cards—Gertrude, Alice, Roché, and Muhammad.

"For heaven's sake," Alice would say to Gertrude. "Play a bit more seriously. Why are you rushing so hard to lose? So you can go up to bed?"

Henri-Pierre Roché stated that he could not believe how early Gertrude went to sleep; he was afraid she might be playing the role of a crafty fox, ready to hunt her prey without their being aware of it. That made Gertrude burst out laughing, and everyone else joined in too. Even the newly hired Asian cook chuckled as he stood there waiting for final instructions from Gertrude, although more often than not she would tell him he could leave "till tomorrow."

The card game passed with rapid words—short, terse sentences not without their fair share of underhand allusions. Poor Muhammad had no idea where he was supposed to be amid all this verbiage and these terse utterances. But his hands were clever, and at heart he could understand why Gertrude was in such a hurry and Alice was not happy. That night it was Muhammad who was on Gertrude's mind.

6. THE GYPSY SUBURB

The drizzle that had been soaking Paris for days finally came to an end.

More than a month had passed since Bernard had left the quarter and moved to the new suburb. Muhammad had gone with him as far as his new tin-plate residence. He would have to repeat his visits several times as the two friends had agreed. As far as Muhammad was concerned, these visits were a pretext for spending some time away from the dull routine of Gertrude's house. Bernard was no longer able to leave his new home just for courtesy's sake, but he certainly managed to offer a refuge to the Moroccan, who never stopped venting his frustrations.

Gertrude announced that she was going to take him to the Italian hairdresser, Luigi Menardi. She herself had started going to his modest little salon, since she no longer preferred Madame Pichon's salon for women. The thing she liked about the Italian was that, when it came to cutting her hair, he was deft with his hands and fingers; in a word, he was not as creepy as that nosy, obnoxious French woman.

"From there," Gertrude told Muhammad, "I can take you in 'Aunt Tantine' to the gypsy suburb, if you like."

He told her he would rather not, preferring instead to take a hired horse-drawn cab.

"Next time we can go together," he teased her as he left. "There are enough empty spaces in that suburb for you to learn how to reverse the car easily! And that's assuming, of course, that your car can still move forwards!"

By this time Muhammad had become au fait not merely with the histories of the maidservants in Gertrude's apartments, but with those of her various cars. From "Aunt Pauline" to "Aunt Tantine," it had been a long trail of problems, breakdowns, scenes, and anxious situations. Just the previous week the two women had told him what had happened to them in the dreadful car right in front of the Luxembourg Palace. The car had totally refused to move, and the security police stationed in front of the palace entrance had found themselves dragooned into pushing it to one side so the head of the Senate could get into his office.

It was an aged and decrepit vehicle. There was no illuminated license plate, no clock, and no cigarette lighter or ashtray. You could not even rely on it for a short trip to Mildred Aldrich's residential garden or Picasso's house close by. The friendly mechanic at the garage where cars were carefully looked after and garaged for the night assured everyone that the car was no longer fit to drive and could not be relied on. A family friend, Georges Maratay, even suggested that this heap of scrap should be towed away to his family home outside of town. But Gertrude insisted on getting the car repaired and driving it, if only for a short while longer, all in anticipation of the arrival of a new Ford which she had been promised by the American Foundation for the Treatment of Wounded French Soldiers. However, even though the mechanic reluctantly agreed to bring the dead motor back to life, he still asked Gertrude to wait a while until his young assistant came back from his vacation. That vacation was already long; in fact, it had gone on much longer than usual, as now happened with members of the younger generation who much preferred a life of ease and sloth. That phrase that he used amazed Gertrude.

"Ah," the man said to her, "you know these young types, our lost generation!"

That expression was to stay with her later on.

In the Luxembourg Gardens the blossoming chestnut trees were an eye-catching sight. Nannies had brought the children in their care to run around the park and play and were now sitting on benches. There were some old and disabled men there too, with their canes handy beside them. Muhammad seemed delighted as he made his way across the gardens and exchanged greetings with everyone. A friend of his gestured to him with his ebony cane.

"What are you doing here, Monsieur Richard?" Muhammad asked him.

"Me?" he responded when asked the same question. "I'm not doing anything much, just taking a quick stroll while there's still time! As you can see, the sun's come back. It's a lovely day."

Muhammad was moving away when he heard Monsieur Richard point out that the sun normally comes and goes, and that's the way it is with all of us!

I can still remember details about that gypsy suburb that Si Muhammad never stopped telling me about, and I will remember them as long as I live. It was as though he was anxious that I should be able to have a direct view of it. I find myself going back to the papers he left behind in order to locate the things relevant to that particular period in his life. As I pick my way through the various bits of paper, I get the feeling that I'm also churning up the deepest recesses of my memory. I am worried in case I have forgotten events or descriptions and can no longer recall particular details. Even so, I have never completely forgotten the factors that tied him to that suburb and the things about its inhabitants that made him so happy.

Now I can write everything about it. But before I do, I have to recall that, when Si Muhammad talked to me about his memories of that time, there was a certain tension in his attitude. To be sure, he would still describe this gypsy area that served as a kind of refuge for him with a degree of serenity. But, in order for me to be able to give you a better idea of the connection that tied Muhammad to this location, I have to confess that I am now affected by a weird sensation. I feel as though I am almost losing myself, as though Muhammad is somehow taking me over, and his memory is taking the place of my own. I find myself poking around in this wide-open, dusty area shrouded in colors, smoke, smells, and those strange noises that he himself loved all his life.

I can see him now, getting off the bus and saying farewell to the driver. He walks slowly—as though I am actually the one doing the walking—along the outskirts of the district. Once again he is attracted by the sight of covered and uncovered wagons; clotheslines; wet, embroidered garments in multiple bright colors and shapes; families with multiple members, so many that you cannot distinguish the small children from the chickens, goats, dogs, and pigs tied up in front of the wooden and tin shacks and the carts. Violins and guitars are being played by numerous musicians, either standing or sitting by the doors; there are still more guitars and violins broken and discarded here and there on the garbage heaps or on the muddy ground.

Bernard was the first to speak. "I thought you wouldn't be coming back again!" he said. "That's why I've got some new friends, as you can see."

With that he introduced Muhammad to two people who were sitting and relaxing with him on the front step of his wooden house.

"This is Gonzalo, a friend from Peru," he went on. "I've no idea how fate managed to toss him into this vile city. By the way, he's a painter. He works at Jean-Gabriel Daragnès, where Miss Alice Toklas goes a lot. He knows her well, as she does him. And this is my friend, Moldovan, one of the damned gypsies from this suburb, from this particular gypsy tribe, if you like. They'll be your friends too. All through this rainy month when you've stayed away, I've been telling them about you." He paused for a moment, then went on. "If our Lord did not actually exist, you wouldn't have found us here. The rain and mud we've had recently almost wiped us out."

Muhammad kept looking round and seeing the effects of nature's declared war on human beings deprived of necessities.

"Moha," Bernard told Muhammad, "you know how fond of you I am. But I couldn't leave the old man and my innocent dumb-head on their own in this disaster zone. So don't forget me again. Keep coming, my friend, so we can see each other."

Sitting down together on occasions like this, in the open air and with a glass in hand, all of it having its own special ring, color, and taste, people can share their feelings without restraint; news and information are easily exchanged. Muhammad learned almost everything about his two new friends, by which I mean the basic stuff that anyone needs in order to befriend someone else. Moldovan has no idea where he came from; like the life stories of most gypsies, his is a long one. He was born on a horse-drawn wagon. He plays the violin with magic hands so he can earn a meager living as a busker. When he cannot find anything to eat, he is forced to steal. Muhammad cannot distinguish exactly the particular kind of shirt that gypsies wear: is it supposed to be male or female? Maybe that is the normal thing with gypsies; no one can tell their shirts apart. Gonzalo is harder to pin down: he is obviously very deep and has his secrets. He seems to know everything and everybody. Bernard hints that the Peruvian is a very close friend of an important woman writer; she likes paintings too and writes books. She too has a literary salon in Paris. Bernard turns to ask Gonzalo what her name is.

"Anaïs Nin," Gonzalo replies. "I've told you lots of times. What's your problem with forgetting names, my little railway-man?!"

Moldovan said that he meets her sometimes in the Closerie des Lilas Café which is always crowded with writers and artists. American writers go there too: Hemingway, Scott Fitzgerald, and Henry Miller. Even the one-armed Cendrars used to sit there every day.

"But the one thing I know," he went on, "is that Anaïs Nin always links her arm with that of the American writer, Miller!"

It seemed that this particular piece of gossip disturbed Bernard somewhat because he started fidgeting on his chair. Gonzalo meanwhile hurried to point out that gypsies never know about the secret relationships involving important people.

"You can pass by quickly with your violin," he went on to say, "but all you see is things happening as usual and hands putting a few measly francs in your hat." Then with a guffaw, "which has holes in it in any case, my dear friend!"

Gonzalo used to shift his glass from one quivering hand to another as he deluged the company with details. He explained that, when a man links arms with a woman, it doesn't mean anything particularly profound.

"But people say he's her husband…"

Gonzalo interrupted. "No, he's just there, with her. That's all. He can't do a thing. You don't realize that he only gets close to women so that he can write his stories about nude people. Enough! He's not her husband exactly. If he were, then he'd be the husband of every American, French, Greek, and Japanese woman with whom he has linked arms! As I understand things, he's turned cold. His thing is no longer good for anything but peeing!"

At this point Bernard entered the conversation as though to calm things down. "So, gypsy man," he said, "here you are seeing and hearing things. Pretty soon you're going to be seeing Anaïs in this quarter in person. She insists on coming to visit our tribe here. She wants to meet us, or so Gonzalo tells me. So don't rush.

Let's go back to the violin. Today we want to celebrate the arrival of my dear friend Moha…"

So this Parisian suburb became another haven for Muhammad; he would always be either going or coming back. It seemed as if he had stumbled on a tribe of his own, among those ostracized gypsies, people who had finished up in Paris from far distant locations without knowing why or what had led them to exchange one country for another. For some considerable time Muhammad did not sleep well, but gradually he reconciled himself to the situation. He inured himself to the sound of the bells at the Saint-Sulpice basilica, which was close to the apartment on Rue de Fleurus. Apart from those holy bells, no other loud noises could be heard inside the apartment, primarily so that Gertrude could be at ease, but also for fresh secrets to be kept. Even so, the entire neighborhood knew everything about the house. The maidservants were the principal volunteers when it came to spreading news about the two American women and the life of the Moroccan man— who had no clear idea, truth to tell, of exactly what his status in the apartment actually was. As Muhammad himself puts it in one of his papers, "That was in spite of the fact that everything pointed to my having an official function in the house, since I can say that by this time I had become a member of the family." However it was essentially a family of servants, male and female, who worked like ants, day and night, to serve the indolent and unemployed queen ant.

So Muhammad got used to all the habits, hints, and jokes that were part of the life inside the apartment. He did not hesitate for a moment before wiping the thin layer of dust off the paintings or adjusting their position in one direction or another. He did it all quite spontaneously, as a voluntary act or a kind of meddling, but, whenever Gertrude saw him doing that, she would make use of the situation to look over at Alice as though to convince her:

"Didn't I tell you that the house needed a man's touch?"

Visitors to the apartment on Rue de Fleurus would find Muhammad busy doing something; he never let his hands remain idle. You would see him in shorts and T-shirt washing the new Ford, "Aunt Godiva," as Gertrude christened it when she brought it home; either that, or repairing a table or a cracked wooden frame, or helping one of the servants move furniture upstairs or down, or putting out scraps for the pigeons, or watering the flowerpots on the roof.

He would be silent the entire time, reading or writing something once in a while. His life in Paris settled down like silent drizzle. Alice, who did not feel happy about him, used to needle him a lot.

"You're always so quiet! Talk, for heaven's sake. Say something!"

He explained to her that, if he had nothing to say, he preferred to remain silent. "That's the difference between us, Alice. You talk about everything, whereas I prefer to think about it!"

Alice may have provoked him all the time, but even so she enjoyed Muhammad's English, even though it was fairly weak, because his accent, voice, tone, and slight lisp sounded nice to her, along with the rise and fall of the voice that is so characteristic of people from Tangier. In spite of that, Gertrude preferred to have Muhammad talk to her in French in which he was extremely proficient (although his Spanish was even better).

From his papers I have now been able to track down some of the sources on his education and competence in languages. He received his basic education in Arabic in Tangier, where he was born, lived, and studied with its jurist educators and later with scholars in Fez where, as he informed me, he had attended some of al-Kattani's lectures. He learned his Spanish in Tangier and was able to improve his competence by joining the Spanish administration corps. He was taught his first French lessons by an Algerian named Kadudu al-Ghazuli who was a dragoman for al-Hajj al-Muqri, the Sultan's Grand Vizier, and was able to work some more on his competence during his educational trip to Marseille.

In Paris he spoke French both on the street and in Gertrude's home; she wanted him to talk French. She told him that he could practice his broken English with the friends of hers he met, especially Sherwood Anderson and Hemingway. He could use his Spanish on Picasso when she introduced him to Muhammad next time.

Picasso, Picasso! That name had come to mean a great deal to Muhammad. Ever since he had arrived at Gertrude's apartment, that name had been on everyone's lips.

"Take Picasso and hang him in that corner…. Lift that Picasso up a bit…. Picasso called this morning; Picasso called this evening…. This person came on Picasso's behalf."

And, of course, most of the walls in the apartment were covered in Picassos. The famous portrait of Gertrude was hanging over the fireplace; barely a day passed without her saying something about it. There it was, up high, like a mirror that she could look into and see her very soul as well as her face.

Muhammad stands there one more time, staring at the portrait which Gertrude has turned into the fulcrum of her daily existence, indeed her entire life. I can picture him now, standing there with his ample frame and puzzled gaze, looking round anxiously as he hears the sound of footsteps drawing close or moving away. There he is, standing there in front of the picture like some tacit version of Marlon Brando. Maybe he is pondering how he can learn how to speak or write better in various languages, since he had clearly not had the opportunity to learn the kind of language that would help him unlock the secrets of such paintings, and especially this particular one which he would stare at every single day but which for him remained a closed world. He may well have asked himself how one becomes a translator for other people when he cannot even perform the function for himself. Was it during this particular period or in this situation, I wonder, that he wrote a snippet that I really like:

"Sometimes language can carry us some distance…, far, far away. We dare to venture into the labyrinth, and yet we cannot get out of it the way we entered. Isn't it sad that we put such trust in a mirage simply because we are good at speaking its language?'

Did he write that at this particular time or facing Gertrude's portrait? I have no idea.

I have to confess that, now I have looked through Muhammad's private papers, I have discovered him anew: the way his abstract expressions sparkle, his spontaneous use of language, and the facility with which he can use dictionary items. I can almost say that he is imitating me (or maybe I am the one who is imitating him) in the construction of small ideas, in stumbling across isolated words that are the only ones to convey the sense, but without needing to be organized as sentences, phrases, or paragraphs. Truth to tell, circumstances were of no help to him, but he did nothing to help himself either. He could have been a very great writer!

"Muhammad!" he hears Gertrude calling him, and she comes toward him with a broad smile on her face. "Tomorrow you'll be going with me to meet Picasso," she says. "On the way we'll stop by an agency to look for a summer place we can rent. This year we'll spend the summer on the Côte d'Azur."

He told her jokingly that "Tante Godiva" probably would not hold all three of them.

"Just you and me!" she replied assertively. "That's all. Alice'll have things to do." She gave him a friendly shove. "Come on, I want you to take a look at the family album tonight. There are some pictures you haven't seen yet. But you must promise me to make complimentary remarks. I don't want you to be looking at the pictures and saying nothing. I'm interested in both the sound of your voice and your comments. I always enjoy listening to deep voices and thick accents."

He noticed that he liked the pictures of her more than the others, also that she was fond of the family pictures, the same kind of thing that you see the world over—the same arrangement of people, the same clustering around the two parents in the middle, the same joy in life, and the same sense of security to be seen on the smiling faces. Nothing in those pictures ever suggests obscure destinies, nothing in the expressions suggests that this snapped photograph will simply be a distant, fleeting memory.

This time Gertrude did not want to respond to all Muhammad's questions. She refused, for example, to talk about her brother, Leo, when he asked her about him.

"Let's not talk about that person," she told him. "The less said, the better."

No doubt he remembered at that point what Bernard had told him when he was talking about the Stein family: "Gertrude was very unkind to her brother Leo. He preferred to move far away. He settled in Florida. It was Leo himself who told me that it was difficult to be clever with Gertrude around!"

Even so, she was delighted at the same time to talk about other people who appeared in the pictures.

"That's my friend Valery Larbaud. He wanted to translate my book *Three Lives* into French. Ah, there's Tristan Tzara. Picabia brought him to my apartment; he's completely crazy. Alice liked him, so he's stuck to her and won't sit beside anyone else. She's a little devil! It's the weird combinations of language that she lets loose that fascinate him so much. However, he's never happy, like somebody's cousin who's just come in from the desert! Aha, that's Man Ray, who's dressed in women's clothing for this picture. He ruins other people's photographs, but when he's preparing his own, he's absolutely vicious, invoking all his photographic powers. That one? That's Georges Braque, my friend and Picasso's too. (Oh my, it's always Picasso, isn't it?!) But they no longer sympathize with each other the way they used to do. The day before yesterday, when I passed by Picasso's studio, Man Ray brought him some personal photographs. In one of the pictures Braque was standing with him. 'I think I know that man,' Picasso said. That's the way they always are now with each other, arguing and exchanging all sorts of emotions."

As she closed the first album, Gertrude turned toward Muhammad. "If you're tired, just tell me," she said. "We can make do with that for now…"

But he wanted to see some more, more pictures and more albums. Gertrude made use of the photographs as a pretext for talking a good deal about herself and other people as well. He was eager to learn more about her and to stay with her longer. Nothing made him as happy as being alone with Gertrude and sitting beside her.

As he looked at more pictures, the album was balanced on their knees. They were both sharing glances, laughs, winks, and comments. Muhammad was betting that, if they continued this way for a while longer, Alice would eventually get angry and stand up to go chicken-like to her coop. To have Gertrude so close to him, chatting and babbling on (as he was to describe her) bothered her—a very orally oriented woman who lacked the writerly spirit, hyperbole being her only talent. She would use three, four, or even five words in a context where one would certainly have been enough. But there was no way of objecting and refusing, even though things were intolerable or even hurtful. You had to go along with everything without even knowing why that was necessary.

Muhammad may actually have exaggerated his dislike for Alice, a woman who was there ahead of him. She had her place inside the house and in Gertrude's heart as well. He could not deny that she managed to fill every corner of the place with her very soul, her voice, and her interventions. In many of the photographs, there she was, a shadow of Gertrude herself; in many of the scenes and locations she was a kind of adjunct to her. It was clear that the two women not only shared locations and memories; the careful observer could not help noticing that they slept in the same bed. Muhammad was looking at a photograph of Alice and Gertrude embracing under the Eiffel Tower, and a courtesy question about it from Muhammad was enough for Alice to go over all the details of the occasion.

"You would get her worked up, wouldn't you?" Gertrude scoffed. "Old motor mouth when it comes to biographical details!"

With that, Gertrude stood up, announcing that she was going to read the new novel by Knut Hamsun. She could not stand listening for the thousandth time to the details concerning the celebration connected with Miss Toklas's arrival. For his part, Muhammad tried to listen politely to what Alice was saying, and he almost completely stopped looking at the photographs in the album....

"When I arrived in Paris," Alice told him, "I was lucky to find it looking splendid, colorful, and illuminated, living the impact of Christmas. The French were dancing in the streets and squares. Beneath the window in the Magellan Hotel not far from L'Etoile I could hear people singing wonderful French songs; the sheer sound was deeply affecting even though I could not understand what the words meant. I'm sure you know that kind of feeling, Mo, the one that makes you fall in love with a great song without knowing what it means: that electric charge, that flash of lightning, that raging storm that sneaks into you and plumbs the depths of your inner self until you begin to feel happy, amazed, and invigorated, or something else that I do not even know.

"We arrived—my friend Harriet Levy and I, that is—by train from Cherbourg where we had toured the lovely countryside of Normandy, fields full of daisies, anemones, and blue-green citron flowers stretching away beneath the blue, cloudless sky, as blue as a calm ocean that has ascended to become sky and horizon. Once we arrived, my first thought was that we should pay a visit to Monsieur Michael Stein and his wife, Sara, whom I had met in San Francisco. It was in that incredible house, which to me looked like an ancient temple turned into a family residence—its walls covered with artists' paintings, and most especially those of my French friend, Henri Matisse—that I first met Gertrude."

Alice swallowed hard, then continued. "In those days Gertrude looked as wonderful as she does now, with that crown of chestnut-colored hair, the same body that fills the vision and the horizon, and that childlike, circular face. I recall that at that particular time it was tanned by the Tuscan sun where she had been spending her summer vacation with the family. Her hands were tiny and delicate and yet full at the same time. She was wearing a dark, ribbed velvet dress and an eye-catching pearl necklace on her bosom. Whenever she spoke or laughed, I immediately assumed that the sound was coming out of that piece of jewelry. I was immediately captivated by the unique sound of her voice, deep and warm from one point of view and a light contralto from another."

"Mo, come over here when Alice has finished her story," Gertrude said. "I've something I want to say to you."

"Okay, Gertrude," he replied.

With that he went back to Alice's account of the way she had stayed in touch with Gertrude and visited her several times at the apartment on Rue de Fleurus. At that time, Alice explained to him, Gertrude was sharing it with her brother Leo. Immediately afterwards, Gertrude had asked Alice to come and live with her. She had spent three years living with the two siblings until Leo left for Italy. From the outset, Alice said, I found myself overwhelmed by Gertrude's busy life, with its friendship and many and varied relationships.

"Just imagine all of them coming here: artists, writers, poets, physicists, diplomats, soldiers—they all came here, and they still do. You've seen some of them and met others, and you'll be meeting still more. The strange thing is that you'll notice that everyone here is twenty-six-years old; even Gertrude, who is actually thirty-five now, cannot live or function without adopting the posture of a twenty-six year-old." At this point she laughs out loud. "And that's the way she'll stay, at that same age, however old she gets. You know of course—but then maybe you don't—that anyone who retains a child's spirit can never grow old. Even if he dies and the green grass starts to grow over his tomb, he still dies as a child. True or not?"

"Ah, yes indeed!"

Muhammad's memory must have taken him far and wide as he sat there listening to Alice, who was using her entire body as she shared her comments and hints.

"My friend Alice is a simple woman," Gertrude had written to him in a short letter she sent while he was in Tangier. All her letters to him (and I have found only five or six of them) were no longer than half a page, written on medium-size paper always torn out of an exercise book. "Alice is always asking me in her own spontaneous way whether you don't have a woman there in Tangier!"

Gertrude never used to reveal her own misgivings as a woman, nor do we have any response from Muhammad. (If he did reply to her, I have not found any copies of the letters up till now. Maybe I'll find some in the American archives.) However, I did find a fascinating sentence in the diary entries I managed to acquire, and it is one that seems to me to be relevant to this particular context. It may be able to explain things a little bit.

"When someone loves absence," it says, "he has no interest in presence."

There's actually a smudge of ink about an inch wide that covers a single word directly after "has no interest in"; I think it is either "never," "completely," or "absolutely"—in other words, he never has interest, or he has completely/absolutely no interest…. But, if that obscured word is "a lot," then the meaning is changed somewhat, although it does not alter the situation all that much. He does not have a lot of interest, or he is minimally interested! So why not?

To offer a little interpretation or a hurried impression on my part, I understand from this fleeting sentence that, if he had a relationship with a woman who was far away, then the intense proximity—if it involved a woman, by which I imply another woman—would not arouse his interest or attention a great deal. However, in spite of that, the frequency with which he talks about Spanish or Jewish Moroccan prostitutes was neither abstract nor purely mental. As I recall things now, it merely reveals to us a description of a personal situation or a decision to indulge in an experiment which he undoubtedly chose to regard as part of his own particular whims. And why not?

"A wonderful time!" That is how he once described to me the brothel phase in a man's life, one that he considered "glory days in the life of Tangier, but no more." To tell the truth, in all the many years that I kept him company I never witnessed any overt sexual inclinations in him. That might be because old age was creeping up on him, and I had made his acquaintance late in life, that time when men usually lay down their weapons. Or it might have been a certain bashfulness that demanded moderation.

Muhammad noticed that Alice was still reviving her first memories of Paris. For several moments he watched her tiny, slender, dark brown body without hearing a single thing she was saying. Then he abruptly came to and realized that she had a joyous tone to her voice that sidled its way into your heart. That may have been how she managed to control Gertrude, who would usually only be attracted by the voices of clever people. Alice knew how to be fresh, to play cute, and how to transform herself in a moment into a sweet kitten who would make an easy gift of herself and not tremble when she felt that she was being led into the "operation room."

Even now I can visualize the look in his eyes as he stared at Alice, sitting directly opposite her. When he looked at other people, his gaze was always firmly fixed, as though his eyes were seeing down to their very core. At least, that is the way it seemed to me whenever he looked at me or I found him staring at my facial expression.

I can also hazard a guess at the burning question that he was posing deep down as he sat there watching silently, the kind of question a man might ask about a woman living with another woman: Was this relationship merely a poor substitute for another natural relationship that was just as bad? How could a woman manage to liberate her body—her flesh and pleasure—from the natural dictates of a man? What was the significance of a bodily relationship that was merely a question of mutual touching, the rubbing of one body against another, no penetration or exchange provided by nature, so that life involving two opposites would have meaning, pleasure, and offspring. In brief, it would be sheer frustration!

He stood up to join Gertrude, who was still waiting for him.

"No, no," he was muttering as he walked, "it's desire. It really tears you apart...."

And because I know how he used to think and the sarcastic comments he had to make about ironies, I can almost hear him through the whispered words: "If the two women stayed this way, they'd produce a baby one day!"

Gradually, and through experience, he started to appreciate Miss Gertrude's situation.

A plenitude and sense of having achieved a kind of personal contentment, but then all of a sudden…a weird kind of trembling would come over her, making her seem like a woman whose emotions had dwindled. What she needed was a man who would use a magic thrust to insert day into night! A sense of deficiency, of incongruity, of body growing and swelling over an internal void. While that body would expand horizontally, its frame never rose, as though it were the Castilian farm woman peeling a potato in Goya's painting from his "black period." (And, by the way, I have no idea why people describe it as being "black," in spite of the fact that it is completely brown-colored, with a delicate, dark touch of shading that uses the brownish hues to create its graded textures.)

As Muhammad made his way to Gertrude's bedroom, Alice stared gloomily after him, realizing that the beautiful eyes of the plump Jewish woman would not be for her that night. She stayed in her seat, preparing some texts of new writing and letters by Gertrude for submission the next day to certain magazines and mostly to Karl von Feichten, who had recently been showing some sense of rapport with Miss Stein's cubist sentences. She would be corresponding with him rather than Gertrude.

"I hope," she writes, "that you'll put this text on an appropriate page!"

She will use the same level of enthusiasm when she writes to Alfred Stieglitz and his magazine *Camera Work* and to Hemingway and his *Transatlantic Review*.

She never abandons her duties and obligations inside the house, and yet she still cannot appreciate why her companion should agree to put her body in the hands of this Moroccan man to play with, just as though it were on a table for dissection. He's a shabby, indolent Moroccan; he hardly does anything useful other than read and edit Gertrude's manuscripts occasionally and play the part of a writer who is incapable of finishing what he is writing. He does not even know what to call the stuff he is writing!

Like a black widow spider, there is a kind of cryptic circle that has to be broken.

How can the family's latest cat stay castrated like this? All it does is eat whatever food the kitchen provides and yawn as it watches the mice in the bedroom enjoying the food on offer and the way flesh comes together! But then, what is a cat supposed to do when its mistress orders it to do something? Does it not have to respond, immediately and eagerly? Even when she moves her magnetic eyes, it rushes toward her, swishing its tail in greeting.

Didn't Gertrude invite him quite openly, in her own voice? True enough, Gertrude has a body that lacks many of the special qualities of femininity, but this is something entirely different: an Oriental from the villages who is still a frothing camel deep down. What he needs is pictures of women as fully rounded as horses, walking heavily across the desert sands or even along the Tangier shoreline.

It may have been at that particular moment or some other similar occasion when he was alone with Gertrude that Muhammad wrote a blatant text that I stumbled across among his papers. In it he piles up descriptions and goes into great detail about bodily features; it is almost as though he is preparing arguments for a postulated trial. Right up till now, every time I read or reread this particular note, I find myself paying more attention to his sentences. They are more advanced that the ones he was normally writing and publishing at the time. I also contemplate the shape of the visual trace of things, particularly when he shows such obvious relish in his descriptions of a body that for a period in his life belonged to him, thus making him abundantly aware of the painful burden of loss when it was denied him.

"A large body." The description begins with size, as though he is clutching the body he is describing. "A white body, with candle-smooth skin, moistened with a sweet gleam that others never see; a whiteness tinged with freckles that are profusely and obviously scattered over her body. At the top of her back, just under her right shoulder, there is a soft mole. When I kiss it, Gertrude squirms, then lets out a chuckle and shudders. There is a nice conformity between her round, stolid German face and the fullness of her body. Her tensed thighs give the impression of being twin exclamation points, and the dots are the points where the upper half of her body meets the lower half. Her blue-green veins which to the eye look like gently flowing brooks seem almost to cascade across her pores. Her taut breasts with their nipples display their brownish illumination, as though they are to lead you into the dark and take you back to your suckling days and the first smell of milk long, long ago!'

Lest I forget and the associations elude me, Muhammad is now in Gertrude's bedroom. For sure, the two bodies become naked, moment by moment, article by article. Needless to say, Gertrude would take her time removing her clothes while Muhammad was still involved in Alice's nonstop account. He would find her already in her diaphanous nightgown, and the Hamsun novel would have fallen over the edge of the bed. It would be obvious to Muhammad quite how overweight Gertrude was from the way she had to change her position from lying on her side to lying on her back or her stomach. By now he was used to a practical method whereby her copious black hair was allowed to decorate the moment without obstructing. He would certainly be well aware of the weighty responsibility he had and would know how to dodge the waves of this night in their ebb and flow....

There is another small detail that keeps nagging at me; I think that this is the appropriate context for it. On one occasion I had stopped him while we were walking along a Tangier street in the evening after leaving the Café Paris. I asked him about her, about the identity of this American friend who filled his memories and daily round of stories.

"Oh, that was an old body!" he said.

At the time the unexpected response staggered me, and I wondered if he really wanted to bury her name beneath some unseen layer of sand. "Let's walk a bit further," I said. "Tell me some more about her."

I watched as he gestured angrily with his right hand like someone eager to clear his vision of something. We completed our stroll in silence, but that single phrase, "an old body," kept repeating itself inside my head as though it were coming through a loudspeaker. It is only now that I realize that, when we parted at the crossroads, we were directly opposite the hospital, the very same hospital where neither he nor I realized at the time he would be spending his final moments in just a few months.

It seems only yesterday that we were sharing conversation and silence till we went our own ways by the hospital gate, as though all he did was to cross the road from one sidewalk to another so he could go inside and die, leaving behind this vague phrase "that was an old body!"

So here I am in Rabat, with night falling. I am on my way to meet Lydia at her home. Rapid fleeting images and pictures keep crowding inside my head: the things Si Muhammad had said, the things I had read in his papers, what Lydia had said, what I had read in books and imagined by dint of experience or questioning.

The storm began to subside and, as happens every evening, it turned gloomy and foreboding. Too much administrative stuff during the day, too little to do in the evening: maybe that was to blame, or perhaps because it all composed an ambiguous kind of beauty that no one knew what to call or how to enjoy, a kind of grayish beauty that might have been shown in some incomplete pencil drawing. In spite of it all, I can still see the trees on my way and ask myself what their greenery is supposed to say to a sky with no blue. Why is that seagull flying on its own, far from the sea, soaring high over the River Abu Riqraq as though it were going back to its birthplace?

"This is no way to grow old!"

Gertrude's voice comes back to me like a distant echo. In the midst of her excursion with the Moroccan, she is obviously happy. She hears the sound of a glass breaking.

"Alice, Alice!" she yells in annoyance. "You're going to break everything in the house if you keep on trembling all the time!"

She goes back and kisses Muhammad again. By now he has moistened his lips and surrendered to her embrace. He too is thinking about the way Alice's hands keep trembling and breaking glasses.

"That old kite, she wants to be in complete control of everything! She has this weird, selfish possessive instinct and wants all the flesh for herself and no one else!"

Gertrude preferred to fall from her huge bed floating on the carpet, whereas Muhammad let himself blend in with the soft, smooth sheets.

"You wanted flesh, Muhammad, so here it is!"

His face gleamed like a child's on her chest. That perfumed piece of dough made his entire body taut and ready to do anything. Now here I am toying with my own brown woman, Lydia.

"As you see, women won't leave us in peace!"

She pulls me toward her and leans over to kiss me. She comes even closer, as though we were about to start dancing. We slowly dissolve onto the firm woolen carpet.

"I adore your hair like that!" Muhammad says, loving his fingers as he relishes the moment.

"I know what you like," Gertrude replies. "Every time I take two steps in your direction, I can feel your glances ranging over my back!"

"Shave your beard," Lydia tells me, "and get your hair cut."

"Have I grown a bit old?" I ask her.

Gertrude asks him, "Mo, do you like Apollinaire's new poem? What a damned debauchee he is! He's rhapsodizing about every aperture in the body!"

"It's the first time," Muhammad replies, "that I've ever read anyone talking about the ninth bodily aperture: the one between two pearly mountains!"

"Damn you!" Gertrude tells him. "You're even more of a disgrace than he is!"

"Gertrude sounds like a woman of experience," Lydia tells me, "at least on the basis of what I've read."

"True enough," I reply. "It's almost as if everyone who entered the house entered her bedroom as well."

"No, not that far," Lydia replies. "She was different, that's all. You know that…."

"I don't know," I say. "I don't know anything."

But I do know, by which I mean that I've started to know. Now everything is in the books.

7. AGAINST A YELLOW BACKGROUND

Muhammad woke up early and got out of bed. Gertrude still had her eyes closed and was sound asleep. She was not bothered by the clock chiming on the wall or the dog snoring by the foot of the bed.

On his way to the washroom he noticed that Lucienne had rolled up her sleeves and was kneading dough. The Bretonne maidservant was preparing rye bread today. As he went back to sit at the low, glass breakfast table, he noticed that Alice did not seem to have woken up yet. The maid told him that she had already gone out with Trac, the Cambodian cook; they had gone to the market. So she had done without him today, then; either that or she was going along with Gertrude's plan to go with him to meet Picasso.

As he ate his breakfast, he looked up at the portrait of Gertrude, which always managed to transport him far away. The young Gertrude had failed in her medical studies. She had been thwarted in her desire to fall in love with her professor, a psycho-analyst. Once he had realized how impetuous she was and noticed how she could not control her passionate feelings, he had known how to handle her. Afterwards she had come to Paris with her brother Leo. It was Henri-Pierre Roché who had accompanied Leo to Picasso's house so the two men could get to know each other, and it was Leo who had introduced Gertrude to Picasso at the atelier of Clovis Sagot, the art dealer. Picasso had suggested to her the idea of the portrait. He was well acquainted with women's bodily makeup and had noticed how plump she was. He knew how to cajole her into being a model for a while and was anxious to paint things as they really were!

Muhammad poured himself another café au lait and put some butter and jam on a piece of toast. He was thinking about the night he had just spent enfolded in her arms and all the other nights so close to her breathing. He could remember the honey-colored gleam in her eyes that made him lower his gaze in embarrassment or shame. All her secret power issued from that particular gleam. He recalled the way it was on his very first night with her in Paris, as she told him the things that excited her about men when she needed a man to stimulate her. Most of the time, she said, she did not like a man to be polite and gentle.

"For things like that," she told him, "I can use a woman if that's what I want!"

He heard what she said, but at the time he did not pay sufficient attention to what it meant.

Trac came back loaded with vegetables, fruit, and other provisions. Muhammad went over at once and asked him if he needed anything else, with due apologies for not going with him. Muhammad asked him about Alice.

"I left her talking to some neighbors at the top of the street," Trac replied. "She didn't seem in a good mood today, sir."

Muhammad had a lot of sympathy for the cook; he was also deeply fond of this Cambodian. Trac told him that, ever since he had come back from his vacation, he had been thinking about opening a small restaurant. He told Muhammad that he had come back with his share of the family's inheritance. From Hanoi he had managed to bring a number of colored birds, a monkey, and some lengths of silk cloth. He had found a suitable spot for his minor project on Boulevard du Montparnasse. At this point Lucienne intervened to tell Muhammad that she had decided to leave Miss Gertrude's employment and help Trac in his restaurant. That made Muhammad tease her.

"So, this isn't just a restaurant project. It's a marriage project as well. Ha, ha, ha!" Muhammad went on in a serious tone. "What matters is that you must let Miss Gertrude know that you're leaving."

They told him that she already knew everything. A new Cambodian servant would be coming. Trac had been in touch with him and convinced him to work for the Stein family.

With that, they heard a noise coming from the bedroom, and the corridor meeting broke up into three segments. The little dog, Basket, came ahead to prepare the way. The late riser was finally getting out of bed....

Muhammad had gone to get the Ford from the garage on Rue de Vaugirard. He saw Gertrude waiting for him on the corner of Rue de Fleurus. She asked him if he liked "Tante Godiva," and he told her that it was smooth and comfortable to drive.

"On that basis, Mo," she went on, "we'll be spending our vacation in the South of France. I only hope we can find somewhere nice to stay in either Cannes or Antibes. If not, I'll go back to the Hotel Pernollet, with my kind friend Madame Pierlot. By the way, Picasso spends his summer vacation in Antibes. He has his own house there. He was thinking of buying a place in Biarritz, but Ben discovered this place for him."

Sunny sky in Paris. He was sitting beside Gertrude, who had taken over the driving, feeling proud of herself and happy. He noticed that this time she had put on bright-colored clothes: a white transparent shirt and a gold necklace that dangled as far as the dividing line of her breasts.

"This aunt of ours is really relaxing and enjoyable...," she said as she clutched the steering wheel.

She grabbed his shoulder, then his thigh, and started humming her favorite song: "The Trail of the Lonesome Pine." No sooner had they arrived in front of the tourist rental agency than she got out of the car, wrapped her woolen coat around her waist, and let the rest of it hang down around the lower half of her body.

Muhammad's expression broadened into a smile as he heard Monsieur Ben Darras advising her to change her plans. "There's nowhere suitable for you on the Côte d'Azur any longer, in Cannes or anywhere else. Think of other places instead. I've some magical locations, genuine pieces of paradise on earth!"

It was obvious that this Jewish Frenchman, born in Algeria, knew how to sell his wares, but he was still relying on his long-standing friendship with Gertrude to persuade her. He had been advising her of the importance of changing locations so that she could discover different types of lifestyle and people.

"Anyone who really loves you, Mademoiselle," he told her, "is going to join you no matter where you are!"

She stared at him in disbelief, obviously not agreeing with him.

"If I have to go somewhere other than the Côte d'Azur," she said, "then I'll go back to the Rhone Valley, which I've always loved ever since I discovered it by chance, thanks to you. You can do that with other people, Ben, but this time find me a quick solution with that soldier, if you can. I must have that magical little manor house. I won't be bothering you again when it's about summer places on the Côte d'Azur!"

She watched as he nodded his agreement.

"Don't worry," he said. "But just give me a bit of time to think about things."

On the way to meet Picasso, she was still talking about the owner of the summer rental agency, who had never had a writer or artist whom he could not tempt with a summer or winter stay somewhere or other. He was very good at following up on things and knew exactly how to link the very last place that he had available with the interests of the customer who happened to be in search of the very first retreat offered to him as a place of escape, somewhere he could write or draw.

"I know him well," she went on. "He's clever and tricky. He's placed Jean Cocteau in Menton, Stefan Zweig in Nice, Blaise Cendrars in Aix-en-Provence, Picasso in Antibes, Paul Valéry in Sète, and Jacques Prévert in Toulon. If his office had been here before, I have no doubt that he would have placed Mallarmé in Avignon and sent Artur Rimbaud to Aden and Abyssinia!"

Picasso was standing on one leg with the other propped against the door to his studio. There were traces of paint on his shirt and hands.

"Here's the Moroccan I've told you about," Gertrude told him. "He knows how to say a lot of things! Mo, my friend."

"Picasso looked me over from top to bottom, staring out of his dwarfish frame."

That is the way Muhammad described this meeting to me, one that seemed to have left a mild impression on him. It may have been a cold glance, or simply conservative, but Muhammad insisted on mulling it over all the time we were in Tangier.

"Its intentions were not clear," he said. "It wasn't totally ambiguous, but it wasn't clear either. In other words, I managed to gather what it meant with no trouble!"

Muhammad talked about Picasso a great deal. His meeting with Picasso was his one and only revenue source. He was clearly a fulsome presence. He told Muhammad, for instance, that, when he came to France from Spain, he spent his first days in Paris at the Hotel du Maroc; Morocco was obviously holding onto him now that Spain had been destroyed!

Picasso was not happy when Muhammad asked him why he had painted only half of Gertrude, confining it to the face and part of the arms. Picasso glared at him, and Muhammad noticed how red his eyes looked from the long hours Picasso kept or from too much drinking.

"I couldn't paint her entire body," he said, a cigarette dangling from his lips. "I was scared that the red-hot lower half would burn me!"

He gave a laugh (which was also intended as a scoff, no doubt) while he smoothed his shiny hair with a quivering right hand. But he soon lightened the atmosphere by inviting Muhammad and Gertrude to have a drink with him; they could choose to have something at his studio or else join him at a neighborhood bar. Gertrude preferred for them to get away from the choking smell of oil paint. Pablo too said that he needed to get out and go somewhere with noise. In the bar, he tested the wine and looked annoyed. They changed the bottle, and he looked even angrier. Finally he settled on one with a nod of his head.

"Everything's acid in this city," he said.

The drinks made the rounds, and Gertrude seemed to be toying with Picasso.

"You really long for the wines from your Spain, don't you?" she said.

He shook his head. "I don't believe in anything called longing," he said. "My longing is in front of me."

He noticed that Muhammad was not drinking a lot. Gertrude told him that this young man did not usually drink wine; he had only just started. In his country drinking wine was forbidden, but in spite of that Muhammad had never avoided the company of people who drank. Some people over there pressed grapes and produced wonderful wine.

Once they were back home, Gertrude told Alice that Picasso had been asking about her all the time they were at the bar. He had been very affectionate with Mo; in fact, he had been in a very good mood, something that rarely happened with strangers.

"Just imagine, Alice my dear," Gertrude said, "Picasso told me that Muhammad looked like the Moroccan in Matisse's painting. That's an incredible thing for a genius like him to say.

In fact, I've recorded it in my personal notebook."

Muhammad entered the conversation to suggest that that might explain why his first glance had seemed so cold; he was actually looking at him through a Matisse filter.

"Oh, be quiet, Mo, for heaven's sake," Alice sighed. "Basically, Picasso doesn't like Matisse. They're two friends in spite of each other. They exchange hugs and paintings, but in fact they never stop making scathing and sarcastic comments about each other!"

Gertrude was sitting there, going through the letters and packages that had arrived in the mail. Alice was sitting beside her, having performed her usual function of emptying the mailbox. Gertrude let out a whoop of joy when she opened the latest issue of the magazine *Atlantic Review*. They had published part of her new book, *The Making of Americans*.

"Oh thanks, Hem," she shouted. "Thank you, my dear Hem!"

It was clear that Hemingway had in fact been a loyal friend. Ever since he had read the manuscript during one of his visits to Paris—actually at the Rue de Fleurus apartment—and revised certain chapters, he had been keen on publishing parts of it before trying to find a publisher for it in book form.

Here is what Muhammad writes about this particular moment (or maybe some other moment): "Gertrude looked proud and self-assured. She was laughing like a child, and her laughter rang out in the apartment. Even though she was short and plump, she looked really beautiful and refined. While I was looking at her, she fixed her clever eyes on mine and gave me a long, profound look, almost spiritual. It may have been that purity that I loved, the feminine delicacy that is always spoiled by a crude silence and the sound of the male voice."

Trac and Lucienne came in and went over to the place where Gertrude was sitting. They both stood there like brass shadows of brown and yellow. They apologized for leaving.

"Tomorrow," said Trac, "my friend Nguyen, the one I've told you about, is going to come to the apartment. You'll be able to rely on him completely."

But Gertrude asked them both to continue working for her at least until the Saturday salon was over. Then they could leave and start their little project. Because the lovable Cambodian was expecting some monetary support from Gertrude, he did not object and immediately agreed to stay, as did Lucienne.

On an evening walk with Gertrude, Muhammad kept repeating what Picasso had said about his nostalgia. "I've abandoned my nostalgia as well," he said, "especially since I've no family to regret my absence or me theirs."

Gertrude turned to look at him as she dragged Basket along. "Ah, and by the way," she said, "I never saw your father when I was in Tangier, nor even your mother."

He explained to her that his father had died during an incursion by the Sultan's army into South Morocco. She then noticed that he hesitated to talk about his mother.

"I'm sorry," she said. "You don't have to talk about your mother if there's a reason not to do so!"

For a few moments he said nothing, but then he started talking about his mother. After spending month after month alone while her husband was away fighting in the Sultan's army, she had died while giving birth to her son. Muhammad had grown up without ever seeing his mother's face. His father was still away when he was born, so his cousins had taken charge of him. Even when he was older, he could still not recall his father's face; he had been a child when news had arrived of his father's death in a campaign.

Muhammad's feelings were obscure, as I well realized. However, when he found someone who was good at listening, and especially someone like Gertrude who knew how to stitch him up like a felt sheet with stories, memories, and personal secrets, he would turn into an expert storyteller who could come up with the right words that would make his feelings that much clearer.

Miss Gertrude inundated Muhammad with questions and expressions of amazement and curiosity. (Wow, Oh my, etc.) She also made a point of spicing the conversation with some of her own feelings. She used to make her voice that much softer, as though she were trying to sound like a playful child.

"To tell the truth," Gertrude said, "I don't know about my own longings, either. I have no idea how to open my heart up to other people!" She went on, "Picasso's an exceptional person. There's no one like him, nor is he like anyone else. He has his Spanish side and a Russian one as well!"

She laughed out loud as she said that. Muhammad asked her about this Russian dimension in Picasso: was she implying that he had Bolshevik tendencies? As it was, she had her own unique perspective on things, somewhat peculiar. She said that there was a bit of Russian in Spaniards; of all people, they are the least receptive to love, and their marriages always end up deeply unhappy. They are also the least concerned about time; for them night is day and day night. They are closed off to emotions and never listen. They do not hear what you are telling them. But when they really want something, they make use of precisely what it is they have not heard!!

"I used to think Picasso was a gypsy," Gertrude explained. "A gypsy perhaps, but he doesn't look like you!"

Muhammad told her that, like him, Picasso had the demeanor of a Mediterranean person, Mediterranean feelings, and, like him, a gypsy spirit. This was Muhammad's chance to tell Gertrude about gypsies. How he loved them! They have a basic instinct that is not rooted in the earth. Whenever they leave a land behind them, they abandon any notion of nostalgia along with the dust traversed by their caravans. (That may be why gypsies will tell you that they are nobody or are from nowhere.) For gypsies, any and every place is place, and not all at the same time. As Muhammad and Gertrude were chatting, he may have been asking himself about the meaning of anyone being somebody or in the end being in a particular place.

Gertrude drew him out a little further. "That's all relative," she said, "and less significant than most people believe or imagine. What's important is to be who you are and to live where you freely choose, or where you agree to live, albeit reluctantly, but still of your own free will! One could even be deprived of that place which seemed to be his own," she added, "but at heart one had first to exist, and then that existence had to be given some meaning. One can live in honor in both his own space and that of other people, and equally can be the object of contempt in both."

At this point she stopped, and so did he; it was as though they were both thinking out loud.

"You yourself, Mo," she said, "have just told me about someone who was born and whose first space was a loaded wagon. You can imagine how many places, boundaries, and maps that wagon has traversed. What all that means is that both he himself and anyone like him, born in the open without a name, in a ditch, in a ruin, in a train carriage crossing borders, can establish his identity through his guitar, his violin, his voice, his language, or even his shoes! What's really crucial is that he is elevated by his very existence. Do you understand me?"

At that moment the echo of a quiet French chanson made itself heard.

"Ah," Gertrude said, "we're near that café where Guillaume usually hangs out. Come on, come and meet another gypsy you're going to love, even from afar...."

"Who's this then?" Apollinaire asked when he saw her entering the café followed by Muhammad.

"My guardian angel!" she replied in the French that she used for thinking.

Muhammad relished the compliment. Such fleeting remarks were enough for him to live on at that time. "Ah, my guardian angel," she would say quietly in a tone that brooked no detail.

For the most part Muhammad stayed in the background as he looked at Apollinaire's head, with its signs of reconstruction. How could someone so incredibly big be a poet? He might be a platoon commander in the army or even a black trainer in a circus. Those would be more appropriate, but a poet? Poets are supposed to be thin, as though the words they use feed off their bodies; their bodies shrink a few centimeters every day under the effects of all the images and ideas that fall on their heads. When Gertrude invited Guillaume to her Saturday salon, he told her that her Moroccan friend did not have much to say. The profound poet may well have realized that behind Muhammad's slight hesitancy there lay a concealed boldness; he had things to say.

"There'll be time enough to please you. At least he admires you. At this point he's still admiring you from afar and is learning some of your poetry by heart."

"What is it that you like about my poetry?" he asks Muhammad.

"I've liked everything I've read so far," Muhammad replies, "but I particularly admire *Poèmes à Lou*, and from that collection, 'En allant chercher des obus' ['Going to look for shells'], especially your celebration of the body's nine orifices!"

Apollinaire laughed. "I know you! Now I know you! You're like me." He turned toward Gertrude. "He's crafty, like me! I think I'll like him…"

On the way back to the apartment, Gertrude questioned him.

"Ahem…. You didn't say a word! What's your impression of him? You always sit there and listen when we're with other people. You've trained yourself to be silent…too well!"

In fact, Guillaume Apollinaire had impressed him; that was clear enough.

"I noticed he complained a lot about the sound of church bells in Paris!"

Gertrude told him that Guillaume was a fine poet who liked quiet, but could never find any, either in the city or within himself.

"I won't hide from you, Gertrude," Muhammad went on, "that I got the impression he was like a gypsy that time had passed by."

"How can you know that?"

"Just a feeling I had, but he gave me the impression that he loves things a lot, he loves quickly and easily. With him one may even have the sense that he's a missionary for love, someone who practices love standing up, like peeing!"

"No, that's just the way he is…. He lives his poetry before he even writes it down. That's why I used to write down some of his fleeting remarks, as you noticed. He writes poetry and speaks it! We'll talk some more about Apollinaire later," she told him as they reached the apartment door.

Alice was waiting for them in the courtyard as though all she had been doing was awaiting their return.

"Gertrude," she said, "Picasso called. He can't come to the salon. He told me jokingly that he's afraid of mingling with other people these days. The Spanish flu has caught the flu itself. I think he's joking as usual, but he suggested that he might introduce you to a Spanish artist named Salvador Dali. Do you know him?"

"Yes, I know him; he's a surrealist. But I don't like surrealist painters. Not only that, but I prefer another Spaniard whom I've been introduced to, Joan Miró. I'm told he's modest and shy. In any case, I'll get in touch with Pablo tomorrow morning."

Alice turned to Muhammad. "Mo," she told him, "our friend Gonzalo has been in touch with me. He was talking to me about printing, and asked me to tell you that the gang's expecting you! Ah, Gerty," she went on, "I forgot to mention that, while I was chatting to Picasso, he told me that the three works by Picabia are 'the worst pieces Gertrude has.' When I asked him why, he replied that the man doesn't know how to draw, the poor, stupid genius!"

I have to mention here that in the rooftop room nighttime passes slowly and heavily. Muhammad is well aware of that, of course, even before he goes upstairs. He only has to glance to see how Gertrude has sat opposite Alice. Stretching out her hand, she grabs Alice's and starts massaging her fingers, stroking her cheeks. One shudder follows another….

"Ohhhh, my sweet little Jewess!"

Muhammad gets up to leave. Once outside, he quickens his pace so he will get to the suburb before sunset. Getting out of the fiacre, he gives the driver a wave of thanks.

In a panoramic sweep he can take in the entire chaos of the gypsy site: smoke, glaring colors, girls with bosoms exposed, men with long hair, harsh voices, animal pens—goats, dogs, chickens, pigs, all where they have been left. Everyone here is totally unconcerned about time or place. Who knows? Maybe tomorrow they will not even be here! It felt as though they were in the rearguard, oblivious to everything.

"These are the gypsies," Bernard told him. "Don't bother about them too much; they don't like sympathy. Don't look on them your usual way, my friend Mo; they're different from you and me…!"

"But they're human beings, just like us!"

Bernard now told him that they were indeed different. They had come from obscure places and had no idea of their own history. Even so, Muhammad kept insisting that they were human beings, and people had to think about their horizons, willy nilly.

By this time Gonzalo had joined the conversation. "Listen a bit, Mo!" he said. "Gypsies don't need to think about their horizons. They don't even have such a word in their lexicon!"

Moldovan arrived next, bringing two friends with him who were soon introduced to Muhammad.

"This is Emilian who can play every single wind instrument. And this is Helena. All she can do is bang on drums."

Moldovan was wearing jeans (actually, it may always have been the same pair) along with a red shirt with black squares and a brown leather vest with dirty patches of grease on it. He wore a cowherd's hat on his head and had let his hair grow very long.

"So this is our music troupe, Mo," he said. "All Paris knows us!"

"And my friend," Gonzalo added, "you're going to see how the violin can keen and the wind can speak through the reeds. And when this devilish woman taps with her fingers, it's as though she's touching our very skin, not the drum's goat-skin!"

The young girl wanted to return the compliment. "Just forget what Gonzalo's telling you," she said. "We just sing; that's all. It's better for you to listen with your own senses; try to listen to us tonight with whatever's inside your head, not other people's. We ourselves sing what's inside our heads!"

As they started to perform, Emilian tried to finish what his companion had just been saying. "We sing what's in our very blood; that's where our music comes from!"

It is difficult for a writer to write about music or singing; they are like breathing. In fact, it is difficult in fact to write about anything that cannot be said or told. One listens to it at the very moment of creation, and it transmits electric pulses to the body and reaches the soul. Unexpected things start to happen: shudders, sobs, screams, tears, rapture. Yes indeed, down with books! You people who only read books, curses on you! All you see and hear are books. You folk who pile books on shelves and do not put them inside your head as well, curses on you too! Yes indeed, come on and tell me where this magic gypsy asp can find such a voice! (It's her blood, that's where it comes from!) Oh yes, here's to women, women from whom blood itself emerges, women whose blood comes in vocal form. Oh, my God!

Bernard's garden next to his house had been demolished by a significant crowd of gypsies. Muhammad heard him raising his voice without knowing what he was saying. At some point late at night he still had a question to pose: "Who are these people, Bernard?"

It may have been Gonzalo or someone else who responded. "We can't stop people playing their music."

He could no longer remember what time it was when he went to sleep, nor where or how.

When he woke up next morning, it was to discover that he had been resting his shoes on the bodily frame of a piglet. Other people had made use of pillows or else unused bicycle tires, cardboard boxes, or threadbare rugs and blankets.

"I slept like a log," Muhammad said, "with no nightmares. I needed that. But I slept like a dog with no family! It's all thanks to your being such a generous host, my dear Bernard."

Bernard returned the compliment. "We're your people," he said once again. "You, Muhammad, are the gypsy who's come back to his people. Yesterday, Mo, you were superb! Where did all that poetry come from, all that singing? Did you really like Helena? She seemed very attached to you...."

Muhammad shuddered; he looked really scared. "Oh no, my friend," he said. "I might have drunk too much. You know me. I don't play around with such things; I'm a restrained type. I can't put honor and its opposite into one and the same basket!"

"You need to rethink your identity," Bernard muttered as they said farewell. "You only have one life, my friend, and you can't live it twice!"

When Muhammad got back to the apartment, it was in pre-campaign mode, all in anticipation of the Saturday salon.

The new Cambodian servant had arrived, and Alice Toklas was supervising the staff in an uncharacteristically gentle tone; she seemed polite, affectionate, and formal. She even apologized. She then told Muhammad that Gertrude was expecting him in the studio; she wanted him to go with her to Monsieur Vollard's studio, and then, if there was enough time, to Sylvia Beach's bookstore as well.

When he entered the studio, he found Gertrude sitting underneath Picasso's two works, "Girl with Basket of Flowers" and "Nude Woman Standing." She held out her hand to him as she clasped the chair on which she was sitting and reading. She did not offer him her cheek as usual, and he surmised that she had chosen this particular morning to surround herself with the spirit of the "ugly Spaniard." It felt as though she had shut herself off so that no other spirits could get through to her. That of course did not suit Muhammad in his current gypsy phase, with his friends, who, he said, were still closest to nature, and their fiery music, which never seemed to emerge from simple musical instruments but to descend from heaven along with the angels!

"Be careful, Mo, I beg you!" she told him. "They're dirty. That disgusting music you keep talking about can never rise to the level I expect you to reach."

Gertrude was determined. She stood up and headed for the door. Muhammad followed her, uncomfortably aware that he may well have lost a battle in his cold war with Alice.

Ambroise Vollard's salon was on Rue Laffitte. In its first four years of existence it had been a small place, but then it grew larger and transferred to its new larger location. Vollard himself was a clever salesman. Rumor had it that he would talk to his customers half asleep and half awake; that way, every time a customer was interested in a painting but assumed that the owner of the studio was half asleep because he was not satisfied with the price, it could then be said that the price of the painting in question had doubled.

Muhammad knew Vollard well, even though he had never met him before. He had heard a great deal about him at the apartment, especially at the Saturday salons, and almost everywhere else. He knew that he had been born on the island of La Réunion and came to Paris at an early age to pursue legal studies. He had given that up and changed course. Muhammad was also well aware of his incredible instincts and his unbelievable memory; he could recall every painting he had ever sold, the ones he had acquired and resold. He could also remember their names, their artists, their dimensions, their supports and frames, even their lines, colors, shadings, and light patterns.

Now here stands Vollard in front of him, with his bald pate, shining eyes, and small, trimmed goatee covering his chin.

"So, Mo," Gertrude tells him, "here's another Parisian devil you must get to know. Just imagine anyone else being able in a single year to exhibit Gauguin, Van Gogh, and Cézanne—the first in March, the second in May, and the third, if I remember correctly, in November. The following year he purchases the rights to Mallarmé's collection of poetry, *Un coup de dés* [A throw of the dice], put on an exhibit of Les Nabis, shows Picasso's work for the first time in Paris, buys all Cézanne's work, and signs a contract to take on everything Gauguin has painted while he's in Tahiti!"

Vollard was obviously a real devil, accepting the American woman's verbal assaults with a generous spirit and probably with all the cunning of a thoroughly experienced salesman as well.

"Even so," she told Muhammad, "he acts the fool with me, assuming he's being smart" (which may have been her way of using harsh expressions with regard to him).

"Oh, Gertrude," Muhammad said, trying to be nice.

But Vollard calmed him with a hand gesture. "Don't worry, sir!" he told Muhammad. "I know her very well. I am well aware of how to behave with Americans, men and women!"

It was as if Gertrude had not even heard what he said, because she was so involved in choosing the paintings she wanted and imposing her own price. "You want payment on the spot, you old fox?!" she told him as she wagged her finger in his face.

Vollard winked at Muhammad through his spectacles while she was still talking to him.

"So listen!" she said. "I'm going to give you back Bonnard's 'Siesta' and take a Renoir instead, either this one or that one. This Gauguin, 'Three Tahitian Women Against a Yellow Background,' I'll take with me, and 'Sunflowers on an Armchair' as well. My next Saturday salon will be decorated with works by this painter who wanders around the jungle! Aha, and this one too by Toulouse-Lautrec, 'At the Café,' I'll take it too. Fine, so make out your bill as you wish, but listen to what I'm saying: this time I'll be setting the price, no matter what you say!"

They went straight back to the apartment without passing by Sylvia's bookstore; it would have been impossible to park the open car with such a load of paintings. While Muhammad drove, Gertrude looked behind at the back seat where this collection of fascinating paintings was placed.

"If we stop for just a moment to go into the bookstore, gypsy thieves will snatch them. Who knows, the police might even stumble on them in the hovel of that female singer friend of yours…. What's her name again? You told me once?"

"Helena, Helena…Helena something or other," he told her after a moment's pause to suppress his anger. "I already told you."

He found himself having to endure a sudden burning sensation of shame at being the friend of a female gypsy singer! On the way back he kept trawling his memory to see if he had told her anything about Helena or the musical night with the gypsies that might make Gertrude this jealous or conservative. Then he thought of Gonzalo and wondered if he had told Alice anything (meaning in his absence) relating to what had happened during their evening's session the day before. No, that is not the way he behaves. So what kind of game is Gertrude playing with me, he wondered. He noticed (but kept to himself, of course) that every time he broached a new threshold with Gertrude, she always managed to touch a sensitive nerve, and that made him so angry that, like everyone else, he had no idea how to react.

Lucienne told Gertrude that Olga, Picasso's wife, had telephoned to say that she could not come to the salon on Saturday.

"She wants you to know, Miss Gertrude, that Monsieur Apollinaire has been admitted to hospital on an urgent basis; he is suffering from the Spanish flu. He is very ill indeed."

The servant was clutching the wooden table as she finished her message. Gertrude was shocked by the news. "Poor man!" she said. "Where did he catch it, I wonder? He was a soldier, so why didn't he take the necessary precautions? After all, he knows about injections. Oh dear, good God, we were expecting him to come to the salon!"

Alice now volunteered some information about exactly what Guillaume meant for Gertrude. Muhammad was listening to her with particular interest as Gertrude herself came in, maybe to get changed.

"I just can't imagine him being ill," Gertrude said, as though she did not believe the news. "But then, he's careless. He could catch flu anywhere and anytime. Even if there's no such thing as a Spanish flu epidemic, he could make one up all on his own so that he could catch it. He's such a nice, wonderful, and lovable person. If only he didn't drink so much and ruin his temperament! Sometimes he turns into a completely different person, violent and intolerable."

Alice stood up and raised her right hand to dramatize the scene. "I can see him this tall," she said. "The only other visitors like him are Georges Braque and Durand. Along with Max Jacob, he makes a much-loved duo, but they're always scrapping about everything: poetry, drink, love, and relationships. Because Max is so neat, poor Apollinaire has to borrow his brother's clothes. But Guillaume is more culturally adept than Max. As Gertrude keeps telling me, he knows at least something about everything! And when he doesn't know anything about something, he's very good at listening at first, and then he'll set his imagination to work and at times even his madness.

"Gerty used to love him deeply," Alice continued, "and so did I. Right up to today we have no idea why he made his sudden, strange decision to go to war. There was absolutely no reason for him to do so. His mother is Polish and his father is Italian" (and here she lowered her voice to a minimum) "if in fact he had a real father! He lived his life to the full, then suddenly decided to join the army. In the last war he was right at the front and returned the way you see him now, with his skull partially missing and bandages as a permanent turban!"

Muhammad would have liked to hear some more details, but Alice turned her attention to preparing the meals and organizing the necessary spices. Gertrude came back in and asked Muhammad to help her put the new paintings in appropriate places. "These are our new guests!" she said.

By now Muhammad had realized through experience inside the apartment what he would have to do whenever "new guests" like these arrived at the Rue de Fleurus apartment. He would gradually liaise with the paintings, both the older residents and the new arrivals, and stand in front of them for long periods familiarizing himself with them. He knew them all, the ones he liked and the ones he did not, those he understood and those he did not. He continued his personal policy of not revealing to any artist which paintings he liked and which he did not appreciate, nor would he tell any artist what another artist thought of his work. He became well acquainted with the secrets of art and the minor wars among artists. Invoking the language of dyeing, we might say that Muhammad had not discovered his green period when his spirit was filled with his excessive love of a hanging nature scene, nor had he discovered his blue phase whenever his heart overflowed with admiration for the blue of a sea in one of the water pictures.

Gertrude pulled up a chair and sat there watching as Muhammad set up a ladder and climbed up, with a hammer in his hand. He then climbed down again to take one of the paintings and attach it to the spot that Gertrude had indicated. Nguyen, the new Cambodian servant, arrived with a tray of drinks.

"Cheers, Mo," Gertrude said. "In celebration of Gauguin and Renoir!"

"And cheers for beautiful art," he replied, raising his glass, "beautiful love and beautiful life!"

The two of them chatted about these particular paintings and their creators. She may have alluded to the extent to which Muhammad had become so enthusiastic and knowledgeable about the craft. By now his eye had changed, having been acculturated by an accumulation of a lengthy period spent looking, a good deal of listening, the experience of silence, and concentrated reading. Allow me to say—as someone who knew him very well as a friend, and to the extent possible, of course—that Miss Gertrude reeducated him. I am not exaggerating when I claim that she created him anew!

I can almost hear her now, looking up at him from where she was sitting on her chair to where he was perched on the ladder. "I think you've started getting over the gypsies!" she said.

8. GERTRUDE'S SALON

Saturday, after a normal, event-free Friday.

The day before and even the day before that had gone by without his doing anything worthwhile. Usually, if Muhammad had nothing to do inside the house and no requirements for Gertrude, he would go out and find something to do far removed from the routine in his rooftop room. True enough, once in a while he would prefer to put up with Alice's chatter about cooking or women's stuff, while she would listen to him talking about his country, about Tangier, his childhood, his family, his revelations about life and people, his readings, his first attempts at art, and other things....

Muhammad would enjoy spending time wandering the streets of Paris and its empty back alleys. He used to meander slowly from one quarter to another, looking at the buildings, the bridges over the Seine, and the rush of people. He could feel the heavy burden of the present and the dust of history on the walls, some of which stood lofty and strong while others were chipped away at the edges or in the sculpted façade. Everything drew him in—clotheslines full of washing, colored shirts, shops and stalls in rows under the arches of tall buildings, vegetable markets, fishmongers, sellers of roasted pork, and vendors of novelties. The things that most attracted him about Paris were the fiacres and the gypsy suburb. He was unable to conceal his silent desire for a leather vest like Moldovan's, a violin like Alalto's, a plaintive flute like Emilian's, or a soft-toned drum like Helena's. Why did he not own a leaden horse with heavy hooves pounding on the asphalt and a cart with rubber wheels? Why was he not a gypsy cabdriver who would spend his days on the Paris streets and return home in the evening to the gypsy suburb?

All the time Muhammad spent in Paris, the gypsy suburb was, as far as he was concerned, the very heart of Paris! The entire universe of tin, wood, verdant arbors; those grave robbers, barbers, trainers, clowns, troubadour singers, beggars, servants, thieves, fortune-tellers, exchangeable escorts—all of them found within his heart a haven for love and interaction. It was only there, either on his own or in other people's company, that he actually discovered his own self.

Within the scope of that mire, made up of dust kneaded together with rainwater and the sweat of people's brows, he was able to contemplate another kind of humanity, one that lived in life's suburbs, not acknowledging time or anything else—as though, in shifting from Gertrude's apartment to a totally different scenario, he were leaving the twentieth century and returning to another, earlier one. Families with lots of children; semi-naked women, breasts exposed; men unconcerned about sinister looks, with scruffy hair, bushy moustaches, and sharp-eyed expressions. Their clothes looked soiled, covered in the dust of roads and frequent travel; smoke drifted from many fires; and children were charging around in clumps like multicolored pieces of cloth. This man from Tangier was no longer shocked to see bodies in contact with others or even to spot naked lovemaking in the shade of trees or in tall grass…, and all to the accompaniment of grasshoppers chirping or frogs croaking in the marshes close by.

Saturday: a minor festival in Miss Stein's apartment.

The guests were arriving, all highly perfumed; there were so many different brands of scent that some of the guests had prolonged sneezing fits. In a neat, intimate space like Gertrude's apartment, everyone was afraid of sweat, so every conceivable aid was invoked, and such things provoked allergies that made people cough and wheeze. But such attacks were soon over, and everyone could inure themselves to everyone else's scent. As at previous salons, the same scenario was taking place: embraces, kisses, handshakes with new acquaintances or as a confirmation of existing friendships. Gertrude always had a gift of introducing men to men and women to women, and sometimes women to men and vice versa. We can only guess what kind of bodily electric charges were afforded by the atmosphere!

Once inside the salon, everyone noticed Gertrude's gleaming visage as she offered her cheek to be kissed, with Alice standing right behind her with her hand extended as though she had brought Gertrude down from upstairs before taking her back up again. Then there were the ambiguous smiles exchanged by people who did not know the others. Who is that man? Who is that woman? Where have I seen that face before? In surveying one scenario after another, Muhammad seemed to know almost everyone, whether because he had met them at previous salons, because they were frequent visitors to the apartment, or because Gertrude had gone to visit them. Even so, he could not resist sneaking glances at people's faces, their features, their clothes, ties, handkerchiefs, sweaters, fans, shoes, hair-clips, and coiffure styles, not to mention winks and gestures, as they broke up into groups and circles.

Muhammad felt as though he were standing in line for something and was worried about missing his turn, so he moved slowly through the crowd, one step at a time, listening carefully to what was going on around him. That way he could find out things about the men and women whom he did not know, people dressed up like this, drinking as much as they were, and indulging in a veritable spread of wonderful food for which Alice was the only one who knew the recipes. How much she relished the compliments on it all!

"Looking back now to this throng of people in the salon and also in the studio, it seems that Gertrude's apartment—and this particular moment—manages to encapsulate all the luminaries of Paris.... All else is darkness. I may be exaggerating, a lot or a little, but everyone who matters was there; everyone who produces light in Paris, and not only light but also beauty, creativity, and ideas, they're all there. The entire scene, the moment, delights me, as does my own self, in that I too am present. I have to show myself some respect because I'm here and I deserve to be. Why not?" (That is what Muhammad writes in one of his fragments.)

I can well remember the way Muhammad used to tell me about that salon, stressing and underlining what he was saying like someone using his shoes to stamp on a cigarette butt as a way of making a decision or rounding off a particularly meaningful phrase.

"Everyone was there!"

Now I know what that phrase means, and the sense of pride that he alone had and none of us could share with him—quite simply, because of a contemptuous look he would give us or through our sheer ignorance.

In fact, everyone *was* there.

Leaving aside Picasso, who stayed away for fear of catching the Spanish flu, and even his wife, Olga, who was much more adventurous than he and had gone to get Apollinaire, who was now out of danger, everyone else was there. Matisse and Imelda Matisse, Juan Gris, André Green, E.E. Cummings, Robert Delaunay, Maria Laurencin, Jean Cocteau, Pierre Reverdy, Max Jacob, Sherwood Anderson, Francis Scott Fitzgerald (who this time came on his own after his wife, Zelda, had left him for a young airman whom she had met in a plane bringing them to Paris), Sylvia Beach (with her soft black hair, her long nose, sculpted face, and haute culture), Ford Madox Ford, Henri-Pierre Roché, André Salmon, Romaine Brooks, John Dos Passos, Cecil Beaton, Marcel Duchamp, Mina Loy, Valery Larbaud, Man Ray (like a wolf in the wild, carrying his Leica snaps), Djuna Barnes, Erik Satie, Natalie Clifford Barney, Jules Supervielle, René Laloux, Mabel Dodge, the poet and astronomer Conrad Moricand (a friend of Picasso and Max Jacob), Eugene Paul Ullman (an American painter living in Paris) and his wife Alice Wood (herself a writer and journalist), Henri Kahnweiler, and Clovis Sagot.

Now Virgil Thompson arrived as well, he being someone we had known through his music criticism for the *New York Herald Tribune*, and the *Times* correspondent, Carl van Vechten. For the first time, Serge Yasterbzov came to the salon (the one whom they used to call "Serge Férat," the owner of the magazine *Les soirées de Paris*), and his cousin, the baroness. On this occasion the Catalan artist Ramon Pichot came too, along with his wife, Germaine; he preferred his friends to call her Madame Pichot, as did she. She brought her sister with her, Madame Fornerod—Antoinette Fornerod—who was also the wife of an artist, Rodolphe Fornerod. Gonzalo, Muhammad's friend, came too, although in his capacity as Alice's friend, and, needless to say, Vollard arrive late as usual. There were others as well.

Gertrude was wearing a neat grey outfit, thoroughly enjoying her friends and making sure to look after each one of them. She spoke to one and joked with another, but left it to Alice, who was dressed in a neat, multicolored dress with pink decoration, to entertain the women and give them all the necessary attention. As usual, Gertrude was issuing instructions to the servants while clasping someone's shoulder or welcoming someone by stroking his back.

The largest group clustered around Henri Matisse. Picasso had not come to this salon to share the evening's limelight with him. Matisse had serene features and was stockily built. He sported a neatly trimmed, reddish-colored beard, and kept fiddling with his spectacles as he talked about some of his pictures that the Stein family had acquired. He had all the self-assurance of a Buddhist, calm and in control, only talking when someone asked a question, which gave certain people the impression that he was dull, even though he actually could be very amusing, particularly in his own environment or among people whom he trusted and knew well. He used to come to Gertrude's salon out of politeness, but it was quite clear that he came reluctantly; in fact, he loved Michael and Leo Stein much more. He did not like Picasso's infantile behavior with the young American woman, whom he regarded as somewhat frivolous. Actually, Matisse never had a genuine friendship with Picasso. Muhammad used to tell us—when we were in Tangier—about the ironic relationship between the two artists; in fact, he used to talk about the minor cold war that prevailed between the two creative artists, something that almost burst out into the open to become a kind of cosmic human phenomenon, albeit never tied solely to a specific geography or a particular culture!

When Muhammad went to visit Matisse at his home, he found him playing the violin. Matisse once told him that he does that every evening. Memories of Tangier are always what they talk about. For Matisse, the north Moroccan city is like a spiritual retreat for a great artist, a place where he can find his lost equilibrium. Muhammad had asked him about the painting "The Moroccan Amido" that he had done in Tangier.

"Oh my," he said. "You still remember that one! The Russian Sergei Ivanovich Shchukin bought it from me."

Muhammad told him that he could remember it well, and in fact he remembered Amido himself as well. "Do you remember him, Monsieur Matisse?"

"Oh yes, of course I do," Matisse replied. "How can I ever forget him?"

"It's the same for me," Muhammad said, "although the picture doesn't look like him..."

"I didn't do the painting to resemble him," Matisse interrupted. "It's supposed to look like me!"

Muhammad decided to explain what he meant. "If you'll permit me, Monsieur Matisse," he said, "what I implied by my remark is that in your painting Amido looks like a deluded Moroccan, someone who's had his picture taken without even being aware of it. The poor devil in your painting, someone who's inured to serving other people and bending low, cannot raise his eyes even a little to look toward the person he's looking at. In the picture he seems in a hurry, as though he's anxious to get away and continue his work as a servant who's reconciled to his fate. Isn't that so?"

"I realize," Matisse commented, "that you've developed your own way of interpreting my works. That's the main thing. But you always need to bear in mind that, when we paint, we're not presenting actual reality, only artistic reality. Of course it's not actually Amido; it's a work of art...."

Muhammad never forgot that lesson.

"You need to adjust your eyes a bit," Matisse told him as he bade him a gentle farewell by the door. "The human eye is not merely an organ that reflects what it sees or even what it knows (the way you know Amido, for example). It's a shaping tool."

Once the door had closed, Muhammad stood there for a moment to write down some of Matisse's phrases, then went on his way. Once he was back at the apartment, he told Gertrude what had happened.

"Matisse is a great teacher," she told him. "He knows what he's talking about. He's right, Mo. The vision we have is neither normal nor biased. Actually, it involves our minds coming out into the open. Do you understand?"

Needless to say, at that point Muhammad was not in a position to understand anything she said. He simply made do with showing his agreement by nodding his head.

"It's only with your imaginative eye that you can understand what Henri was saying," she went on. "For example, I can appreciate what Rodin meant when he said, 'A woman combing her hair is imitating the movement of the stars.' Do you follow me?"

She asks him that a second time, and he nods his head again.

He probably had to take a good deal of time before he understood the obscure space between what is real and what is imagined, between a Matisse or a Cézanne painting hanging on one of the walls in the Rue de Fleurus apartment and the reality as envisaged by this or that painter.

"The Amido in Tangier…is not the one in the painting?"

How was he supposed to understand these hieroglyphics? What was the difference? Who was going to help him realize that the eye that saw Amido and painted him was motivated by a different kind of imagination, one that was able to transform real things and run with them far into the distance?

For sure, Gertrude always saw the minor confusion that Muhammad felt as a result of his surprise and lack of esthetic experience as a golden opportunity to take him just a few short steps to the portrait where she appears as Picasso saw and perceived her. There is obviously a lesson that Muhammad needs to grasp, one in which she will repeat things he has heard many times before. She will examine her face in the painting as though it were a light on a water surface, with her looking at it from above as though hovering on wings. He will listen in silence, moving his head a lot, like someone who has stumbled on a fate that offers no other choice—or, let us say, like a person who humbles himself so that the sheer profusion of meaning will not overwhelm him.

Muhammad is very aware that, no matter what the occasion, whenever he stands in front of her glimmering image, he must choose his words with care and intelligence and behave the proper way; in other words to be as direct as someone needs to be to express himself clearly, as though he were opening the white handkerchief in the middle of the shirt in the painting or exposing her ample bosom. He knows full well how the words he chooses at such a sensual moment can arouse this soft, plump American woman so immersed in a riot of colors and give her such feelings of delight!

So, with the salon at its acme, here she is taking some of her guests to the same spot; there they listen as she tells them for the very first time the things that he himself knows and has remembered almost by heart. He is standing a bit further away and watches as she stretches out her arm and hand to explain something—as if she is about to take off. He is almost certain that he knows exactly what words are now emerging from her lips. Some nice remark will, no doubt, be made by one of her guests, and that will make her happy; such comments are like a sudden shower of rain that arrives with a dance on a sunny day. He has certainly learned a lot from the associations that always emerge from her talk about herself and her personal portrait. By now Muhammad is content with his eyes and the liberal way they see things, even though his solitary spirit may still feel a prisoner!

In a corner Max Jacob is sharing his experience and fondness for astrology with his friend the poet and astronomer Conrad Moricand. A group of salon women who like having their horoscopes read and their zodiacal signs analyzed has gathered around the two of them. Henri-Pierre Roché is sharing with Muhammad some memories of Leo Stein in the Rue de Fleurus apartment. He can never forget escorting him to the atelier of Clovis Sagot, the former circus clown who has now become a successful art dealer. He had bought a painting by Picasso from him and still remembered the title, "Family of Acrobats with Monkey." It was that picture that had made him want to get to know Picasso. He had asked Sagot to introduce him, and he had done so.

Roché never stayed in one corner of the salon because he wanted to get to know everyone and to make sure everyone met everyone else. Whenever Muhammad looked around, he could see Roché standing there looking tall, with eyes that kept ceaselessly searching, then settling (actually never settling) beneath a probing brow.

"A successful busybody will always succeed in finding out everything about everything!"

That was Alice's comment as she followed the old family friend. Gertrude always enjoyed Roché's trove of stories, news, and details about Paris, particularly when he would respond to her desire for gossip about artists, their women, and the people who loved their paintings. He would usually make a point of digressing to talk, with a fair amount of exaggeration, about what he termed the major painters' "debauched desires."

"My dear Gerty," he would say, "have you ever even thought about this totally phony interest in Vollard's baldness? Cézanne has done a painting called 'Vollard dreaming,' Bonnard has done 'Vollard at home with his cat,' and Renoir has 'Vollard as toreador.' Even Picasso—unbelievable!—has discovered 'Vollard as cubist'! Is this art? Is this really art history?"

Miss Gertrude did not remain silent, of course, but interrupted to put an end to Roché's objections. "Don't exaggerate," she said. "We can't produce any history of art as long as your voice is choked with so much anger...."

"Maybe not," he interrupted, "but not so long as this awful, gigantic ape is the subject of every artist's work!"

They are almost all here on this particular night, famous people and famous people's wives, artists, poets, publicists, publishers, diplomats, financiers, and businessmen, soldiers and civilians, old and young, interlopers and phonies. It is very difficult to get a conversation going or finish a discussion. Circles form quickly and dissolve just as quickly. Every time Muhammad moves, he hears languages, whispers, and phrases falling apart, while others come together or illuminate each other. Allusions, winks. It may have been an opening he heard, as though he enjoyed the sheer sound of people's voices while he watched everything so closely:

"He said he's come to see the paintings…"

"Her legs look crooked…"

"They say he isn't just a servant in the house…"

"A circular or maybe square woman…"

"There are many faces here that I've seen before at Anaïs Nin's salon…"

"Just look at the scars on his face…"

"What a barrel. He's only come tonight to drink all the wine…"

"Oh, the poor dear! She doesn't even know what's going on all around her…"

"No, I'm talking about 'Young Woman Carrying a Water Pitcher' by Vermeer…"

"You're strangely quiet tonight…"

"Make a note: she's only drinking tonight…"

"I've never come here with him before. I thought it was just an exhibition hall…"

"…Especially Cézanne and Monet, they've both moved beyond the movement whose birth they both proclaimed."

That last was Matisse's explanation as he took Muhammad off to one side of the salon.

"What exactly is it that we artists do?" he asked. "We open up the desire for life and teach others how to immerse themselves in it. There may be a bit of ego involved, but it's not good enough to become a kind of watchtower! You keep on asking me about Gertrude's portrait, and I'm sure you notice that I'm avoiding any response. I don't like getting involved with any painting that I can't look at as a child. Sometimes I can understand an ancient Greek statue that is partially broken—no head, no legs, even no hands—and still not understand portraits these days, even when the body is fully there, head, trunk, and hands. My friend, I don't like turning things into cubes, and I don't admire superficial embellishments!"

Muhammad accompanied Henri Matisse outside. Henri had put his beret on, buttoned up his wool coat, carefully wrapped the scarf around his neck, and waved goodbye to everyone with his left hand while clutching his ebony cane in his right.

"Be careful, Moroccan," he said giving Muhammad a sideways glance. "I see that you're going a bit too far in your convictions about things and people. I know the Stein family very well; they've moved ahead in front of my very eyes. This young woman is very moody. She can love and hate at the same time. My boy, the fruit on her tree is forbidden!"

Muhammad must have swallowed hard and moved his tongue as though to say something. People in love will usually be struck by a special kind of blindness, almost as though they have had it from birth. But Matisse went on.

"I beg you not to engross yourself in a wild fancy. I know the meaning of intense emotion and mutual affection…it's not everything. The American woman may get rid of you at any moment as though she were finishing a job!"

Matisse's image gradually disappeared as he walked along the low wall of the Luxembourg Gardens, while at night the leafless trees were saturated with a light drizzle and reflected the lights on their branches. Once the image had finally disappeared around a corner, Muhammad walked back, his tread heavy as he walked along the rain-washed sidewalk.

"What Henri said doesn't matter," he told himself. "No, it's what I take away from it that matters!"

His breathing may have quickened. Every time he tried to get close to Gertrude, the sheer fullness of the advice he had received but not asked for drove him away. He kept hoping that he would feel better inside, and yet inside he was beset by a flaming inferno.

The two doors were still open, but the apartment had now emptied of its crowd of guests. With no one still there, the three servants were collecting plates and rearranging the furniture; the whole place looked like a long gallery in a huge museum. The radiator was still on, dispensing a heat that warmed both body and soul. Muhammad improvised a few complimentary phrases to thank Alice and the servants for the delicious food.

"Everything was wonderful: food, desserts, and wine. Even our guests' eyes were sparkling at such a colorful display."

The female servant noticed Gertrude approaching. "Thanks are due mostly to the generosity of Miss Gertrude, sir," she said. "It's all due to her!"

"I feel like walking for a bit," Gertrude told him, urging him to come out with her and Roché whom he spotted coming out of the toilet. "You're still here?!" she said to Roché. "You seem to have drunk a lot!"

"He's just like a barrel," she explained to Muhammad. "Fortunately, he never gets drunk."

Muhammad stopped her going out. "Gerty," he told her, "it's cold and wet outside. The car's in the garage, and in any case it's closed now, as you know."

"What am I supposed to do then?" she asked. "I can't just sit or stand around here when I don't feel like going to sleep. I could stretch my legs for just a bit."

At this point Roché intervened to suggest that they sit at the table and continue the soirée by playing cards along with a glass of light wine. When everyone else approved of the idea, Gertrude gave way, and the four of them sat around the table facing each other, the two women, and Muhammad and Roché.

When the emotional situation is so fraught, Muhammad will completely refrain from all conversation, as though he is withdrawing within himself. Just then, there appeared before him the image of Bakhta, his cousin, running toward him in a white dress, a joyful bride opening her arms in a field of grain while he too was opening his arms and running toward her! But, of course, none of that was actually happening. He soon came to his senses and looked at his hands moving the cards on the table in Gertrude's apartment in Paris.

"No fantasy will ever be achieved through an excess of desire or passion," he told himself.

His skill at cards was clearly dwindling. On that nasty, cold night, his hands betrayed him; Roché beat him time after time. Along with Alice, he was the opposing team in the game. For her part, Gertrude seemed distracted and uninvolved.

"We're both no good tonight!" he told her, and got up suddenly to leave the room.

As he slowly climbed the stone staircase, he was cursing Roché, Alice, and Gertrude—and all the other drunken sots as well. Up under the roof he paused before entering his room and looked out at the pigeon scraps before going to sleep; it was as if he were talking to the pigeons, even though they were obviously not there and would not return until morning.

"When you're playing cards," he continued his drunken rant, "there are good nights and bad ones. What's to do? The important thing is for me to get some sleep now. That pervert Roché, Monsieur Roché Kick Shoes that is, can go and pee in the pissoir at the Lido Macho, the Jardin des Lilacs, or somewhere else I don't even know. But what about me?"

Inside the room he looked in the mirror.

"Roché feels sorry for me," he told himself. "This lousy dog, Roché, feels sorry for me! Doesn't he realize, the son of a bitch, that sympathy…is a kind of insult! Oui, oui! Sympathy piles insult on pain. Oui! C'est comme ça! What's he going to say about me today or tomorrow? He's won, and I've lost…. Ha, ha, ha. Shit. For what? With whom? With me? Well, Monsieur Roché, we'll see, you women's dog!"

Now Bakhta appeared again in her bridal gown, looming through the mist of his vision on the mirror's surface; he just stood there staring. He stretched out his arms to dance with her, and she let out a ringing, childish laugh as she did the same. Her voice echoed across a green expanse as though they were in a field full of greenery, and, from then on, the dance seemed to be atop the high asphalt roofs of Tangier, which filled the entire background. He got his hand to turn the gramophone and started dancing with Bakhta while singing a song that may have been one of his favorites:

Your hand on my chest is my own hand,
When you close your eyes, I too fall asleep.

Bakhta was putting her hand on his chest and stroking him; as he closed his eyes, she was placing her two white wings on either side of him. Together they flew high in the sky, and he started watching as everything below disappeared into the distance—cities, forests, mountains, hillocks, rises, seas, rivers, and people…, until it faded and everything disappeared.

"I can see that I'm too concerned about matters of the body," I admitted to myself. Lydia was still lying beside me, naked. At first she had taken a quick nap, but in moments that had turned into a deep sleep. I looked at her wrinkled body, the light brown skin, the protruding veins, the light foam on her mouth, the folds, bends, and curves…everything. It was as though an African totem was lying next to me. I had tested that bronzed body, and she had me. Lydia had managed to bring out the wild animal in me and imposed on me the modest rhythm of her silence while she was asleep. I had tested her, like a picture that condensed the dark shadows, and then she had gone to sleep. It felt as though we had spent our time together in a cave. Every time it got cold, I would move the coal to bring out the burning embers underneath. I cannot hide the pleasure I feel whenever I manage to bring out each obscure ember from beneath the layer of ash. I flee toward such obscurity in order to escape a clarity that has completely drained both me and itself, to such an extent that there is nothing left that is worth investigation or discovery.

Here my body is recovering alongside a woman who appears to me in a dark mirror, a woman who has no need to confirm that the origins of the bronze body are from clay.

"That virgin kiss," she told me just yesterday as she sat barefoot beside me, "how can I forget it?" As she said that, she lowered the lights in the room and stretched a foot toward me. I grabbed it and moved my fingers over her soft, moist skin. This tickled her, and she let out a sigh. That is how we started playing a hand-and-foot game—in silence. We were listening to the stream of Greek music from a disk she had surprised me with, obviously one of her favorites, which she kept underneath the shiny black playback system.

When she woke up this morning, she looked up at the window.

"I don't like days with no sun like this one!" she said.

I told her that there would be a frigid sun outside the room, which was enclosed by dark blue curtains, but it would be a sun with its neck cut off!

When Lydia wakes up late, her face is usually frowning, as though she were feeling angry about something; either that, or else she cannot control an insomnia that lasts into the morning, at which point she has to go to work. Perhaps it is because her brown complexion leads her to reject an ashen sky. Truth to tell, anyone who sets eyes on her finds it hard to believe at first that she is an American diplomat. She hails from the regions of the southern sun in Africa. In my very first impressions of her, I could envision her as a painter from Senegal, a Camerounian singer, or a poet from Mozambique! Her copious braids so carefully arranged still manage to attract my attention, interest, and desire, as though I am climbing up to some sunny heights without even blinking when I am with her, or in her warm embrace, if you want to be more precise.

Lydia said that she was not feeling well that morning and had decided not to go to her office at the embassy.

"It's better for me to come up with a health reason," she said, "and avoid going in looking all puffy-eyed and disheveled—a real mess and all tired!"

A phone call was all that was needed to communicate her unwell condition to the other party. She put down the phone and looked at me, silent and somewhat uneasy, as though she were not very happy with herself. I looked up, and for a few moments we kept looking at each other. Moving over to the breakfast table, we continued our conversation of yesterday. She pulled up a chair and sat down. I brought my lips close to her shoulder.

"Like you," I said, "I can never forget our first kiss. I can almost smell the way it felt, just as one can recall the scent of the first lime one pees!"

She was still sleepy, so she kept stretching and yawning, and I caught the smell of her breath, something to which I had grown accustomed by now.

I chose to devote myself to her for another hour before I left. I was well aware of the fact that I needed to offer her some help by sticking around, since she could not stand to stay at home while her male and female colleagues were at work. At the same time she was scared of being seen in a guise that she had not chosen for herself. Above all, she did not want any rumors to start circulating about her, not least because some of her male and female colleagues at work had been cautioning her about getting too intimate with a young Moroccan journalist who seemed to be thinking about something more than some purported writing project. By now they were expressing their doubts and disapproval on a regular basis.

We were still trying to get our best out of the morning when she suddenly asked me why I had not chosen another girlfriend besides her. It was hard from me to tell her frankly that she was the one who had chosen me.

"Our twin horizons summoned each other," I told her. "I came to you, and you to me!"

It sounded just like an American kind of question, exactly the same kind that Gertrude posed to Muhammad: why had he not thought of another girlfriend than her?

"I had one," he had replied, "and I still do," referring, of course, to Bakhta his cousin who, for him, simply represented the distant features of a would-be girlfriend.

It is not hard to imagine the reason that made Lydia ask me that question, but with Gertrude it was different: she had misgivings and wanted to know why a young man would leave his homeland and people, and maybe even his position in life, all in order to join up with a woman whom he had met almost by chance during her trip abroad.... The thing she did not ask was why a woman would bring a young man whom she had met by chance on that very trip into her own home, her life, and subsequently her body as well. But these are the kinds of things that happen just as much in real life as they do in novels and films. People do a lot of things while losing control over themselves.

It is entirely possible for people to involve themselves in a love that is more than love: something more than heart and body can stand, a love with features more akin to madness than to discretion. I am talking here about that condition where the head is smaller than its own ideas. We all know what it means when one is beset by madness; there is a sudden onrush of boldness that was previously missing, one that leads a man to throw himself into the abyss, risk his very existence, or discover his genius. I can recall broaching this topic with Muhammad; I had let him talk about it, and I have to rely on my memory now to recall what it was he said.

"I never thought about my decision when I took it. I was following my heart and let it guide my steps. As you know, the heart has its own particular logic, one that's different from the mind's; there's no relationship between the two…, even though there are those people who believe that, when the mind is not functioning, the heart is effectively not functioning, either. But I'm not sure about that!"

Lydia said she thought there was a firm connection between heart and mind, but it was a certain state of backwardness—whether due to culture or civilization—that was responsible for the divide between decisions of heart and mind. I did not like the idea at all, which seemed to me more American than necessary. I told her that the concept of absolute backwardness she envisaged simply did not exist. True enough, from a management or economic perspective there might appear to be a kind of backwardness, but culture and thought are an entirely different matter. You're portraying culture or civilization, I told her, in exactly the same way as we do. On that level, you may be ahead in one area, and we may be in another. For things to continue and achieve fruition, what is needed is an exchange of peace, my little Condi (and here I stroked her cheek playfully), the same way that you and I are sharing love." She put her face on the palm of my hand.

"*Ah, mon fourbe!* [Oh, my little rascal]," she said in a soft-spoken French with more than a hint of passion in it.

It looked as though the hour I had dedicated to myself with her was drawing to a close. Lydia was talking nonstop. Deep down she obviously did not want me to leave her morning self, preferring to see me link this day to the night before. She kept on talking about everything, in her desire, as she explained to me, to "reeducate" me now that she had failed to "recreate" me. She was talking about the bedroom, the paint color, the curtain materials, the sitting room, the kitchen and food dishes, the value of having a man use his hands somehow, even if it was only to peel carrots or onions.

"At least," she said, "you can hunt down a few images or similes!"

She noticed how disturbed I was by the number of appointments I was missing, and that led her to talk about the symbolic and material value of time.

"For American businessmen and financiers, every minute is a matter of money," she said.

She turned next to my current projects, but discovered that I did not have any. I almost told her that I did not really have a life either; a few passing thoughts or minor fantasies perhaps, the kind of thing that comes and goes at random. Grasping my hands, she sat me down on one of the kitchen chairs and bent over slightly so that her eyes were looking directly into mine. When I tried to put my arms out to hug her, she pushed them away.

"No," she said. "Not now and not here. Let's talk about the fundamentals." Pulling up a chair, she sat directly opposite me. "You don't realize the meaning of future. I see that you've too much self-confidence. What you lack is an instinct for planning, even for adventure maybe!"

I told her that the time was long past, relatively speaking. If I was supposed to do something for myself, I should have done it earlier. But she insisted once again. "If I'd been with you twenty years ago," she said, "I would have forced you to put forty years of your future life on the table and consider carefully the possibility of dividing the period into major and minor projects, the steps to take, the decisions to be made—not only that, but contracts with banks and insurance companies. That's the way life creates individuals in our country...."

Her anxious expression almost implanted itself in mine.

"You're weird, my friend!" she said as she pulled back a lock of her hair in a spontaneous gesture. She then broached quite openly the possibility of our having a relationship, indeed of binding ourselves to each other seriously and getting married. The abruptness of the suggestion shocked me, or—let me be frank about it—it scared me. She noticed my hesitation, and it was obvious that I had no idea what to say. "Has the idea shocked or frightened you?" she asked me.

For a few moments I said nothing. "The whole idea obviously needs a lot of thought," I replied, trying to make the best of things.

She shocked me again by not being in any particular hurry. "Think as long as you like," she said. "But you need to take some bold steps in your life. You need to take a few risks..."

"Lydia," I interrupted, "I can't separate my heart from my mind."

She did not stay silent: "You're crushing my heart."

I stood up, put on my wool jacket, and finished tying my shoelaces in the garden. As I left, I was replaying the entire tape in my memory, page by page, image by image—her face right in front of me with its full cheeks, her sunny body that I could only envisage spread out beneath a translucent muslin sheet, her soft-toned voice which I hear direct and in echo wherever I am, as though it does not actually emerge through her lips but somehow descends from the painted plaster ceiling. Those luscious, full lips that need no silicone! That red-hot body!

I am on my way to the newspaper office, walking in Rabat beneath a glowering sky with scant daylight and high humidity. The atmosphere is choked with the gases emitted on the other side of the valley toward Oulja.

I felt soaked; I must have been sweating all over. The ancient rock had to be weighing my chest down, but, truth to tell, I had no idea how to lift it off, neither where to put it down or when. My situation at the moment is really strange! I close my eyes for a moment and breathe hard. I am tottering along, waiting for a taxi to appear. Ever since I have given up my teaching job, I have had to make do without my old car. Actually I have had to shed a lot of things—except my conscience, that is!

I've turned into something like a statue in motion, not able to look back.

9. THE PORTRAIT

"It's a different Paris. Paris without Guillaume is missing something!"

That is what Gertrude said with a deep sigh on the morning in France that was to be the saddest since she had decided to leave America with its dreadful vacuity and live in Paris.

Muhammad was keeping track in silence of this heightened level of emotion. He may have had some detached thoughts about the connection between Gertrude and Apollinaire; where he was concerned, everything about such scenarios was plausible, but this was not the moment. He was simply observing as a kind of cloud passed over the heads of the two women whose tears seemed to be genuine; their facial expressions looked really sad, almost pained in fact. Expressions had changed, features had blurred, and now the sound of weeping had a different tone to it. Paris without Apollinaire. The city has lost one of its poets, so its lively round is now different; words weigh heavier on its tongue; certain gentle words of love flee from lovers' mouths. A poet who has lived his entire life in fragmentary form—in name, identity, place, language, body, and love—all that has come together in bodily form…and now it has gone!

Olga—Olga Picasso, that is—said that he died in her arms.

"How come you risked your own life by exposing yourself to that awful Spanish flu?" Gertrude asked Olga during a phone conversation.

"I don't think it was the fever you're referring to that killed Guillaume," Olga replied immediately. "I spent the night by his side, and he was clearly dying. His temperature was no higher than usual in Paris."

She paused for a moment. "Just imagine," she went on. "He just happens to die on the night of the peace treaty to end the war. The poor man gets to hear voices crowding in the street below, shouting 'Down with Guillaume!' Of course, that's the other Guillaume they're talking about, Guillaume of the war, not him. At the very end he thought the street was disavowing him, and that caused him great pain."

Gertrude listened to Olga crying on the phone. "That mistaken feeling," Olga stumbled on," that…that…was his final agony!"

"Poor man," Gertrude said softly. "He never had the chance to put that agony into words!"

Like someone waking up with a jolt, Muhammad looked at this different version of Gertrude, her hands shaking and not knowing what to do. As though talking to herself, she started going over her memories involving Apollinaire.

"What a lot we did together!" she said audibly, expressing a palpable grief as though the things they had done together were somehow causes for regret.

But she kept on talking about her associations involving the departed poet: "He was completely magical and masculine—absolutely fantastic, giving much of himself to other people. He seemed to come from another planet, and now he's gone back. I can't believe that Guillaume has left us so simply. He was always standing there, looking like a Greek statue, commanding your attention. How can that statue have fallen? He was overflowing with emotions that were extremely personal to him, not like any others…"

"Not now, my Gerty!" Alice said, trying to get Gertrude to stop weeping.

Gertrude let out a sigh as she wiped away her tears. She went over to her portrait on the wall and stood in front of it. "Here's where he stood," she said, "to talk to me about myself and the picture." She sighed again as she recalled the first thing she had heard him say about the portrait.

"How serene your face looks!" he had said.

She remembered too that he had told her that Picasso had devoted everything he had and indeed things he did not have to this portrait. "The painter had been motivated by something even bigger than himself; as he painted you, he was observing you from the future."

When Picasso had painted the portrait, Muhammad was not in Paris; he was still in Tangier. Indeed he had not even met Gertrude yet. For that reason there is nothing he can tell us about that particular period; all we have is a set of surmises from later on when he was directly connected to the portrait, its owner, and the apartment on Rue de Fleurus where it was on display.

He was well aware that those surmises of his were not worth talking about, particularly since it was so long ago and contexts had changed. Even so, he used to think out loud about such things, in terms of both present and future; not only that, but he was sufficiently curious to make surmises about the past as well! He was like someone planning to get married, someone who has made up his mind and entrusted matters to his Maker, but who then starts asking all sorts of questions left and right about the woman of his dreams. Even though Gertrude was no more successful than when talking about herself or talking about other people as a means of talking about herself, Muhammad was not satisfied or even convinced. He kept asking questions.

Gertrude never said a single word about the initial idea for the portrait, nor indeed did Picasso himself have anything to say to Muhammad or anyone else. The two of them maintained that they did not remember when or how the idea had come up. She can remember very well the first time Picasso noticed her, the first time he came to dinner at the apartment on Rue de Fleurus. So how come she cannot recall when they both thought (or one of them thought) about pursuing the idea? Personally Muhammad wants to believe his hunch about it, being well aware of the effect a full-bodied female would have on the young Spaniard, someone who had nothing about him to attract a woman and at a time when he had none of the fame that was to come later.

It was Muhammad's guess that a woman with so much savvy and aristocratic spirit would not submit easily to the idea of ninety sittings as a model in a closed room. The principal factor had to be a red-hot electrical charge binding two desires or two bodies to each other, with the one in need of the other. In Muhammad's opinion, critics and art historians had gone too far in their interest in the portrait, the technique, the colors, the light and shade, the technical aspect of it, the veiled aspect of the eyes, and things like that. What they had missed was what was going on while the work was being done. His reasoning was the Picasso was moving from one phase to another, and at the same time from one woman to another; he was, at one and the same time, changing phases and women. His other pretext was the one that would be talked about, or talked about when he was present, concerning stories relating to artists and their female models: Rembrandt, for example. He would rather that the woman spoke—the model in front of him.

"What am I supposed to say?'

"You can say whatever you like!"

The woman would talk, and the magic of speech (the magic of voice, in fact) would be added to that of colors, the magic of the moment. Body would move toward body, and they would fuse together.

Modigliani used to stand for a long time in front of the model before him, as though he were sucking her body.

"Why have you left my eyes like that?" his model, Jeanne, asked him once when he had stopped depicting her eyes and left them blank.

"When I have learned about your soul," he replied, "then I'll paint your eyes!"

Faced with such a response, Muhammad must inevitably have asked a question with his usual crafty spontaneity:

"How can Modigliani get to the spirit without traversing the body first? That's especially true if every spirit is allowed to flutter as much as it wishes, but then has to alight on the body, like a pretty, multicolored bird landing on an electric wire."

The whole thing is obvious enough. There's no need of more guesswork or pretext. Muhammad gave himself plenty of time to consider Picasso's paintings where he was working with female models. It is obvious enough that Pablo was fond of fully rounded bodies as in his painting "Les baigneuses" ("The Bathers," 1918) or "Les baigneuses regardent un avion" ("Bathers watch an airplane," 1920) and of large pendulous breasts as in "Deux femmes courent sur la plage" ("Two women running on the beach," 1922). There are a number of other works of his that show this attachment to one particular type of woman and special bodily characteristics. Gertrude was no exception.

"Picasso may have started the portrait from the head downwards," Muhammad commented in his usual fashion, "but actually he had started work on the model from another part!"

My Tangier friend was talking to me about that particular moment as he assumed things to have been, as though he were actually looking at them naked in the studio.

"Lucky for me that I wasn't in Paris at that time," he said. "If I had been, I would have had to drive Gertrude in 'Aunt Pauline' to Montmartre and stay standing by the door while Gertrude carried her fruit up to the ugly Spaniard!"

Muhammad remembered Montmartre all his life. He told me that it was not simply a district, but essential Paris when it invites you to pause; the place where you remain standing, waiting there but with nothing in particular to wait for. That's Montmartre—you just stand there, simply in order to linger.

It was in Montmartre, in Rue Ravignan to be precise, that the Spaniard lived and worked in a strange wooden building. In his blue outfit he looked at first like an electrician or municipal worker. His place was always bustling with his friends' rowdiness as they sat there drinking, exchanging jokes, rude gossip, and laughter. Picasso's own brand of jokes was both harsh and cruel, of a kind that purveyors of the normal dirty joke found difficult to take. But he was also generous; any fresh visitor who came knocking on his door could come in and take a look at the riot of different works and colors. Visual artists, poets, clowns, jugglers, performers at the nearby circus, interlopers, everyone used to meet at Picasso's place....

When a woman arrived to offer her body as a model, Pablo would lock the studio door to be alone for a while. It may be that Picasso's divorce from Fernande Olivier (his first wife) may have been caused by his prolonged periods spent alone with the American woman. Who knows? Every time Fernande herself met Muhammad, she would keep on talking about the obsessive admiration Picasso showed for Gertrude's body, going all the way back to the first time he had ever seen her with her brother Leo at Clovis Sagot's atelier.

"He used to draw me sitting right in front of him," Gertrude told the timid Moroccan. "We used the occasion to talk on and on…"

"There were a lot of problems about our modes of communication," Picasso said.

"They had trouble communicating about details," Alice commented.

Muhammad kept asking himself what a young Spaniard could possibly have to say to an American woman who was no good at Spanish or, for that matter, what the same American woman could say to a Spaniard who did not understand English. His focus was basically on what the two of them were not saying, but rather doing.

In accordance with Picasso's wishes, Gertrude used to go to his studio every day and sit close to the canvas that had been carefully and firmly fixed in its frame—medium-size, about thirty-two centimeters by thirty-two and three eighths. He would then start work. He actually started with her head, but it did not work; he kept stopping, breaking off, and interrupting work on it. Once in a while he would turn the easel toward the wall and toss the palette and brush on the studio floor.

"Ouuuuuuuf!" he would say. "Every time I look at you, I stop seeing you!"

All his initial attempts at starting the portrait without the head failed. He was so frustrated that there were times when he was afraid that he would not be able to finish the painting. He was not convinced about Gertrude's face, and in that he was absolutely right. At that particular time his moods were hard and rough, and Fernande, his wife, had her doubts about this model and the numerous lengthy sittings that were not producing any noticeable result. All that spoiled his mood. In addition, the generally chaotic atmosphere in the place certainly contributed to his inability to concentrate. The furniture was not well arranged, the dishes were never washed, the ashtray was full of cigarette butts, pieces of dry bread were left on the table, and the bench Gertrude was sitting on was broken and leaned to one side. Alongside her was the couch on which Picasso used to lie down; it was covered in dust, and the leather edging was coming apart.

All that may explain why progress was so slow, but another reason may be that the artist's mind kept wandering away from the square canvas in front of him to another context beyond that frame.

At the age of thirty-one Gertrude Stein was in the initial phase of her contact with Picasso's world, his moods, his cunning, and his cruel gaze.

"I have no idea what feelings Picasso kept having deep down when he was doing that painting!"

As Muhammad heard Gertrude say that, he was thinking to himself that many works of art are not necessarily motivated by feelings, but dictated by the senses.

If the Spaniard had simply followed his esthetic feelings, he would not have achieved what he did. It was his senses that served as his compass. At the very least, in doing this portrait he was following what inspired him; he had no need for information about anything! That is why he used to turn the incomplete portrait toward the wall and pretend to be angry again, tossing down his painting tools. That way, one sitting would have to lead to another, and so on.

Did Miss Gertrude realize what he was wanting? Did she want the same thing as well?

Needless to say, she would ask him in broken French what was going on. He would respond that the important thing was not simply to portray her, but to show her in a different guise, to use her to create a new way of looking.

Later on he may have become aware of the insistent way that the Moroccan was asking questions. "I like your questions," he told Muhammad, "although they also make me laugh. Are you aware that at some point I no longer needed Gertrude? I was no longer bothered—if you prefer—about having her with me every day. At that point I started looking for her other face, the ideal face perhaps. When I finally located that face, Gertrude was not even there!"

Which only served to amplify the Moroccan's doubts.

When the portrait was finished, everyone at the time said that it did not look like Gertrude. The only people who were happy with it were the artist and the model.

"It doesn't look like her now," was Picasso's comment in response to these objections, "but the time will come when they do look alike."

And with that he let out one of his ringing sarcastic laughs, a guttural noise that Gertrude described as being "very Spanish."

When Muhammad first came to the Rue de Fleurus apartment, he too was not convinced that the portrait looked like its model. He also had his own criteria and found it hard to get rid of them: thus he was either surmising or else making up his own mind—even if it meant not paying a great deal of attention to what his friend Alberto Gonzalo was saying, namely that he should pause for a while before letting his own opinions on the portrait be known. He would have to develop his intuitions one step at a time and not allow a disastrous misstep to dominate his feelings. He never stopped reminding himself that he had his own sensitivities, and on one occasion they had let him down!

As far as Muhammad was concerned, Picasso had only succeeded in expressing the outpouring of productivity that was Gertrude's hallmark. That is what had so excited the ugly Spaniard, and that is where his painting stopped! Anyone who knew Gerty from close up would see her in the picture as some other woman. The halo of hair on the top of her head was not enough on its own to make the portrait look like her. That may be why Picasso had also made use of the large, round coral brooch which he felt compelled to put on a white scarf around her neck so that the picture would look more like her. No one ever set eyes on Gertrude without seeing her wearing that brooch. Even Alice herself, who was so inured to seeing the image of that brooch, kept saying that, whenever Gertrude said anything, be it short or long, or whenever she laughed, she would give the impression that her voice was emerging from that brooch.

"And as a result, Picasso never really painted Gertrude."

"So what exactly did he paint, Mo?"

"What he actually did was to paint a mask of a woman with large eyes that do not match, nor are their feminine qualities evident."

"It's good that you saw a mask in those eyes of hers," said his friend, Bernard, whose opinions he trusted more than his own. "It means that Picasso had discovered her mask. As human beings, all of us have masks, and we find it hard to get rid of them! Every day we watch as people put on masks, and they in turn see us doing the same thing to our own faces. But all we get to see is the visual aspect that is presented to view; we never see the masks, even though they're there, attached to people's faces. It needs a really perspicacious individual to see people's masks, and I think that Picasso has that talent, at least as I understand things. He has painted Gertrude's mask in the process of portraying her face!"

The portrait gradually became the focus of Muhammad's interest, just as it had with Gertrude. For her it may actually have become the focus of her entire existence. Muhammad never met any artist, critic, or journalist among all the friends who came to the apartment on Rue de Fleurus who did not have a conversation with him about the portrait. He was never convinced by anyone's arguments; all the explanations and interpretations seemed to him to be wrong. His own hunch was the only proof he had. It could be that he was not prepared to allow for the possibility of enhancing his opinion with the ideas and suppositions of other people.

Muhammad's sensitivity was too anxiety-driven. He had laughed when André Salmon had told him that Picasso had produced the portrait at a time when spirit was guiding his vision.

Pablo, he said, was using the picture to locate some kind of balance. But soon after his return to Tangier, Muhammad simply refused to believe in every aspect of what he had started calling the entire tainted brothel. He even refused to acknowledge what Salmon told him about the horizon involved.

"Don't you see," he told Muhammad, "that Picasso has pointed her eye-shape toward the void that is typical of African masks? What does that mean exactly? It means that the first masks that Picasso came to admire—from Polynesia and Dahomey—provided him with an opportunity to change his esthetic approach. He started painting our friend Gertrude's portrait during a transitional phase in his artistic life. Picasso had decided to choose primitive artists as his guide when he decided to do Gertrude's portrait. By imitating African masks he set his Spanish side free, and his fortunes started to rise…"

As far as I can tell, Muhammad did not possess the necessary intellectual equipment to contest other people's premises. He had his own hunches and doubts, and observed and decoded things from that perspective. Where he was concerned, other people's views were alien, emerging from books, not from tangible reality.

Lydia and I were eating dinner at the L'éperon Restaurant on Algeria Street in Rabat.

"Your friend Muhammad's viewpoint was very impetuous," she said. "His sun was hot!"

What she found so peculiar was that so much intensity could exist in a person in love. It was fair enough for him to want to take good care of the body he loved, starting from the time when he had started to love it. But that his jealousy could extend so far as to completely sequester the past—that was something no woman could tolerate.

"You're right, Lydia," I told her.

"Once in a while," she went on, still perplexed, "someone can embark on a splendid adventure and have some success. But no sooner does he get back on the straight and narrow than something inside makes him meddle and destroy everything."

"You're right," I agreed once again.

It could be that at that particular time Muhammad did not fully appreciate what it meant for Picasso to spend a long time—close to ninety separate sittings—just to paint a portrait. The notion of cubism had begun to percolate in his mind, and he had started running away from unidimensional portrayals of objects. As he painted her, he was really afraid that he would manage to capture only the surface layer of her face.

Picasso was not sure of himself or of anything for that matter. He was searching, so on several occasions he focused on the crux of the painting, turning it toward the wall, so that he could forget that first layer whose outlines he had drawn and strive to capture the fleeting image inside his own imagination. At the time Muhammad did not understand what we two could appreciate now—meaning Lydia Altman and myself—as we exchanged opinions inside that quiet Rabat restaurant. The Spanish genius kept aspiring to capture the unattainable aspect of a woman to whom he felt attached or whose body he craved. And what is the problem if an artist has decided to paint a full-bodied woman with a large backside, someone whose image is setting his senses ablaze?

Muhammad obviously failed to understand the import of the passing remark that he once heard Gertrude make to him and some other visitors: "That's me in this picture," she said, "but at the same time it's not me!"

He was lacking the particular quality that would enable him to rise to the level of appreciation where he could understand the uniqueness of the work and the way in which the portrait shaped a very particular existence that was almost divorced from the person represented in it.

I started seeing Muhammad's face all over again.

There can be nothing worse for a man than to have profound doubts about a woman he loves. And what a woman! Gertrude was like the women described in poetry; in fact, when he was talking to me about her, he used to say that he still envisaged her emerging from one of Baudelaire's poems:

A woman passing by, with pampered hand,
Raising and swishing the folds of her skirt…,
Lashes of bewildering sweetness,
All such pleasure that kills.

As we sat there in the Café Paris, he used to stand up and recite the poem using his voice and entire body, focusing in particular on the those lines which reminded him of Gertrude:

Une femme passa, d'une main fastueuse,
Soulevant, balançant le festoon et l'ourlet…,
La douceur qui fascine et le plaisir qui tue.
[Baudelaire, *Les fleurs du mal*, "A une passante."]

Poor man! When he had first set eyes on her in Tangier, he felt as though it actually was not the first time; she had always been lurking somewhere in his existence. He was amazed to see that she was so easily impressed; everything delighted her; everything she set eyes on filled her with joy. He came to see it as a kind of magnanimity and drew him closer to her. Maybe he immediately told himself that this woman was his, rushing ahead like all Moroccans who see a stork in the distance and tell themselves that it is a woman! When Gertrude asked him to dance on that first night in the Hotel Villa de France, he knew that he was no good at dancing, but nevertheless took hold of himself and got up to do something new.

He kept talking about that first contact with her; how she had encouraged him to hold her close, and how she seemed like a woman scared of her own body.

"I'm no good at dancing," he told her.

"Nor am I!" she replied somewhat sadly, since, even though she had really wanted to learn how to dance well, she had never managed, mostly because she was too plump.

When Muhammad told her she had a beautiful body and it should not stand in the way, she laughed. He went on to tell her that the main thing was to have a musical ear. He had no idea where he had come up with this thought, but it was one that managed to light up her face

"When you have a musical ear, something that comes with practice," he went on, feeling a strange sensation of conquest, "then the body responds and discovers its own rhythms!"

When the two of them left the dance floor and went back to their seats beside Alice, Muhammad noticed that Gertrude took her notebook out so she could write down the things he had said to her a short while ago. That was the first time he realized that she was always on the lookout for pleasant and unusual words and phrases.

"I love it when words and ideas strike a chord with me!" she said.

He still recalled the fact that he had merited such a mutual display of approbation, although he could not remember whether the unforgettable kiss was him thanking her or vice versa.

As the two of them drew closer together, it seems that Alice was not paying any attention—as though with so much customer din, she was not really sitting with them both. Either she was distracted and uninvolved, or else something was making her feel unhappy.

I stretched my arm out to touch Lydia's hands lying there on the dining table. I hesitated a little because I was about to broach the topic of marriage, something that she herself had suggested but that seemed to me to be utterly impossible.

"I have to tell you," I said, "that Muhammad himself took the wrong road in his own adventure. He could have behaved otherwise, but he didn't. I may have told you my thoughts on that before."

With that, I told her again about Muhammad's career in Tangier as I still remembered it, with certain particular details still riveted in my mind.

Gertrude had been glowing with life; her dewy eyes had an eager silvery gleam to them. She said that a strange nameless sensation had come over her while she was crossing from Europe to the African continent on her way to Tangier (and, as she said that, she put her hand into her handbag and brought out a bottle of perfume that she proceeded to dab on her neck and chest). She went on to say that she was now fully aware of the reasons that had brought Matisse to Tangier, while other European artists had gone to Tunis, Algiers, or Tahiti. It was this light that had brought Delacroix, not to mention the shapes and colors (and, as she spoke, she was unbuttoning her carefully ironed coat). They were all escaping from the thick layer of clouds in the North.

In a fleeting moment Muhammad got the impression that by any yardstick this was an exceptional woman. She possessed both an unrivaled strength and a special kind of attraction. His instincts told him that she was a woman with a strong desire for intimacy. She had a yearning for other people and offered her body like sweets stuffed with fresh meat. At that point the young Tangerine had started to lay open his words a bit and launched a gradual assault.

"You don't need to remind the hen who's the cock!" she told him in a determined tone.

Realizing the intent, Muhammad swallowed hard and resumed his more modest guise through bits of silence and a certain give and take in conversation. "I do hope that you both like the place," he said.

"I'm the one who chose it," Gertrude interrupted. "Let's see tomorrow what places you can recommend for us to see!"

When Muhammad went out to urinate, Gertrude put her hand on Alice's shoulder.

"Alice," she said, "I beg you to understand what it is this Moroccan can give me. Don't get too jealous. You know how much I love you. Trust me, please. Let me test myself a bit. The routine of similar bodies is going to kill me!"

"I can see," Lydia commented in her usual joking fashion, "that your research has taken you a long way with this American hermaphrodite!"

We both laughed out loud, and that disturbed the customers eating at the table next to ours. They were right, of course, because the restaurant was small and neat and was not large enough for boisterous laugher. I watched as she gazed silently into my eyes. She advised me to reserve my respect for Gertrude for the book I would be writing; she was afraid that I might be so concerned about my friend Muhammad that I would prejudice my opinion of other people's reputations.

"Actually she was telling the truth," she said, coming to Gertrude's support once again. "Nature had not opened the gates of her female body merely to serve as apertures for Alice to look at or caress with her hand.

"At some point," Lydia went on, "Gertrude must have realized that touching the buttons on the accordion or working its leather pouches (as she did with Alice) was not enough to make the melody complete. She needed something more than merely putting her fingers on the body's tufts of hair."

She invited me to say something else, but, pouring some more wine in her glass and mine, I told her that I was listening to what she was saying. "You don't have much to say tonight," she said. "I see that you're in league against me with this enemy wine. You know me well enough; I like to talk a lot."

I explained to her patiently that in her country soothsayers do not improvise other people's confessions.

"Okay then," she interrupted me, "let's allow the soothsayer to confess first…"

We talked a lot. She liked hearing me talk about Muhammad and Gertrude, their first night in Tangier, how Alice had felt drowsy and gone into the next room in the hotel suite, leaving Muhammad to continue with his first night in the arms of the infatuated American woman.

Lydia smiled, while I used my hand to brush my face, the kind of gesture to swish a fly off your nose. It may have been the same thought I had had a few moments before but had not found the strength to tell her frankly. She was no fly, of course! At that point Tangier loomed before me once again, just as it was supposed to be on that night long ago. It felt as if I were watching a black-and-white film: Tangier, the shore, the Hotel Villa de France, the dance floor in the night club, the cold drizzle-soaked entryway, the two women on their own, traveling from continent to continent to continent.

"There are species of turtle," Lydia told me, clasping her glass in both hands, "that can cover thousands of kilometers, traversing seas and oceans in order to reach a strange shore, isolated and empty, in order to lay their eggs there!"

I brushed my face again.

Gertrude seemed almost to be questioning herself when she suddenly asked Muhammad a really weird question, something he had certainly not been expecting: "Have you ever taken a virgin before? [*As-tu déjà pris une vierge?*]" she asked in a low voice and in halting French. "Yes, I have," he replied quietly, almost without having to lie. "It happened once. It was in the desert with a reckless shepherd girl, a member of my family. I was just as reckless as she was…"

She sat back a bit in a studied gesture as though to take another look at his face. Still staring at him, she moved closer again. "Oh, that disgusts me!" she said.

Her reaction as she moved away again really shocked him, and he immediately realized how scared she was feeling. But he knew how to handle the situation, realizing that she would like him to tell her about the virgin girl, the simple Bedouin who had lost her virginity for fear that she would get older and never enjoy life's pleasures. In the desert she had tried masturbation, but, in an impetuous decision, she had preferred to be rid of her virginity. From the initial question and the eagerness with which Gertrude was listening to him, Muhammad may have guessed what Gertrude was going through in spite of her attempts to hide it. Leaning forward, he kissed her on her cheek and neck.

"Don't think you can have me," she said, acting all coy and flirting like a little girl. "That's not going to happen, not with you or anyone else, even if I do love him!"

Muhammad did not want to make her any more anxious. "So what does making love mean, then?" he asked her quietly.

She surrendered herself to Muhammad's passionate kisses and long and fervent embrace, quivering as she did so. He hugged her, and they went over to the bed. She listened intently as he continued telling her about his cousin, Bakhta, and the way she had so brazenly stripped naked, something that had shocked him; the girl was looking for an escape in the desert prowled by wolves, hyenas, and foxes.

On nights such as that one there are rituals that need to be respected.

Kisses play a major role in cutting down distances. Muhammad will first kiss the two lips to set the scene, followed by the two eyes. With his tongue he will turn to her ears before kissing the famous straight nose. The mouth, of course, possesses its own powerful electric pull; in fact it is the body's fulcrum, the crossroads from which kisses are launched across cheeks and various other creases and folds of the body.

So now, Lydia, just imagine the significance of that moment when Gertrude lies on her back.

"The garden wall is low," she tells Muhammad, "so jump a bit and come on in!"

He will lower his lips from her neck to her chest. The kiss sets her breasts on fire, and the dark brown nipples rise up and fill out as though they were about to nurse a child. Reaching her navel he pauses for a moment to indulge in more foreplay, maybe to listen to her sighs. After that he can fumble his way down to the dark thicket.

I do not imagine that Muhammad is the type to forget his hands in the frenzy of the moment; no doubt, he thinks of his fingers and embeds them in the thick black hair that crowns her head.

He will gently continue his probing of the fresh virgin surface with awe and warmth. Lower and lower and lower. He will come to understand the profound meaning of the double image of the world's desert in the Bedouin mind, one in which the curves of the sand dune and those of the female body are evenly distributed, the scene in which the desert stretches off into the distance mingled with the image of a woman spread out like a warm sand dune!

"Maybe my body was too heavy for you?"

This was the very first moment of elevation in his entire life, he thought to himself. "No, quite the contrary," he replied.

"When the spirit floats, the body does as well."

She responded immediately, holding him in an engulfing hug. "That's a wonderful response."

10. THREE LIVES

Gertrude preferred to leave Paris early on an open holiday. The problem about the much-to-be-desired stay in Bilignin had finally been resolved, thanks to the suggestions of her friend, Ben Darras, and the experience of Monsieur Saint-Pierre, the notary. That made her really happy. It was pure chance that had led her to this possibility whereby she had got hold of the place she really wanted, one that had seemed like a gift that it had become impossible to dispense with easily.

The black car moved steadily along the almost empty road. Muhammad was in the driver's seat, tapping on the steering wheel as though singing a song to himself. Alice was snoozing in the back seat, having dozed off after noon. Gertrude meanwhile was staring off into the blue horizon that hovered above the ground all around them and looking ahead at the grey road surface. She said nothing, preferring not to talk on the journey and not wanting anyone to talk to her, either; it seemed that these extended trips were intended for random thoughts, or else she was engaged in internal dialogues with characters in her stories. Like most writers who are thinking about their next project, they try to write it inside their body. At every single empty bend in the road or with reduced ambient noise, they will return to their ongoing writing process—composing, recomposing, adding, adjusting, editing, correcting—as though staring at some invisible manuscript. Needless to say, this is not the only way to write well, but it certainly is the prevalent mode.

Once in a while Muhammad looked over at Gertrude; she seemed far away and deep in thought. In the back seat Alice was still asleep, or at least that is the way it looked in the rearview mirror. She was breathing softly, and her prominent nose looked like a kite fixed high in the sky. Muhammad always did his best to avoid that wan, narrow face and the nose in particular because, whenever he came into contact with it, there was always an air of supercilious disapproval.

We can say that this was by no means the first time that Muhammad was thinking about Alice, the way she normally spoke to him, and the lackadaisical attitude she sometimes showed. Whenever she looked at him, her hand would lightly brush against his in a gesture that made her brassiere jiggle. That glare of hers may have been somewhat scary in itself, but his larger worry was the extent to which his doubts about her managed to blunt all his senses. When it came to talking, Alice's glibness may simply have been either a shield for a troubled person or a confirmation of a particular kind of posture, but it certainly did not merit the aggravation that it aroused inside him. He told himself that one should not dismiss someone simply because that person treats one roughly or ignores one due to an excessive attachment to someone else. In spite of that, Muhammad knew nothing about the details of what went on between the two women when they were alone together. He used to hear the occasional comment or hint, "Ah, my little cow!" for instance. As though the two women were in some kind of permanent kitchen, he would hear words and actions that seemed like preludes to passion: "Let me eat…let me sip…let me swallow…oh my, this apple…oh my, these dates!" He surmised that Gertrude ate more than she should, which explained why she kept on gaining weight and her clothes were too tight!

Muhammad was aware of the way that the remote village housing had been made available to Gertrude. He had been following the saga in every detail. In fact, the estate agent, Ben Darras, had been behind the whole thing. He had found for Gertrude a place in the Rhone Valley not far from Aix-en-Provence at a time when he had not been able to locate anything on the Cote d'Azur itself. Gertrude had quickly fallen in love with this summer abode, one that she had found only by pure chance. It may have been the absolute quiet of the location, coupled to which was the kindness and generosity of the owner, Madame Pierlot, when she first became acquainted with the region, that encouraged her to look for a permanent residence in the area.

From the start Muhammad was aware that Gertrude was growing to like the place more and more. He encouraged her to extend the stay for several additional nights. When Madame Pierlot learned that they had decided to extend their stay, she surprised them all by moving them out of the small room into much larger ones that looked out on the gardens and green hills on the opposite bank of the Rhone that stretched away into the distance.

From her balcony Gertrude could look out and see a superb house. It seemed to be calling out to her, something she kept on repeating and that Muhammad recounted to me as part of his many detailed recollections when we were in Tangier.

The idea of building, purchasing, or renting a place in the countryside near Belley had been developing in Gertrude's mind. We kept reminding ourselves of how much we would be missing if we started making the rounds every single day in our search for a place, checking out farms, residences, and mansions. Madame Pierlot was enthusiastic about the idea as well. By now she had started treating us like friends rather than transient guests. We in turn had grown very fond of her. She was a charming French woman who loved her job and devoted herself to it wholeheartedly. Her husband was out of work but did nothing to help her. He spent all his time reading Lamartine; once in a while he would pick up something by Paul Claudel, who was a family friend and frequently visited the village inn deep in the French countryside.

All of them fell in love with residences that were not for sale or rent, so much so that Gertrude almost gave up hope. On every possible occasion she used to go out on to the balcony and stare at the distant mansion, nestling on top the green hills on the Rhone's far bank.

"Why don't we go over there, my dear?" Alice suggested. "Let's see if we could buy it…"

Gertrude did not hesitate. Putting on her best black suit and a fetching hat with a red bow tie, she set off. It took only a short while in the car for them to be knocking on the door and making inquiries. They learned about the place in detail and were introduced to its family. They were particularly taken by the location, the way the house was laid out in its green surroundings, and the attractive vistas that nature offered all around it.

In this particular expansive region that had engendered Cézanne, Impressionism could not simply be a name for a new kind of painting, but rather a whole collection of sensations and fresh ways of envisioning things. It involves that impression, the one that knows how to encapsulate the fleeting and eternal moment, that different vision of vistas, objects, beings; the world bathed in light and the purest blue sky; that quiver in the eye; that sensory truth that affords one the possibility of appreciating the real meaning of residing on earth.

The need to wait must have made things that much more difficult. At the time, the house was occupied; in fact, it was being rented by a French army captain who was temporarily in charge of a small military garrison made up mostly of Moroccan soldiers (known as "*les indigènes*"). They had been brought over to France during the last war and had been kept there, perhaps with some future war in mind.

"I have to have this place," Gertrude told the owner of the property, "no matter what the conditions or how much the rent."

"I've never seen such crazy people," the kindly French

owner commented. "How can I get rid of the soldiers?" he asked Gertrude. "I'd like to do it, but how can I? Find me a way of doing it, and I'll stamp the agreement with every one of my fingers, not just my signature! The man's a captain, Madame…!"

It was a piece of good luck that Gertrude saw this house from the balcony of their hotel—across the valley, in other words, from where you could glimpse the white mountain behind it as well. Gertrude dreamed of having this house, which led into the small estate. She could put down roots there and fill her eyes with greenery that stretched away into the distance. Even the walls were covered all over with ivy, which led Madame Pierlot to comment that it was not a house so much as a tree!

It required only a short telephone call to her friend Ben Darras for Gertrude to have a suggestion as to what to do. The crafty agent had just stumbled on the most convenient way to get hold of this house with a minimum of difficulty.

"Since this captain is only here on a temporary basis," Darras told her, "why don't you use your network of acquaintances and your influence to get him transferred somewhere else? They all owe you a lot; France owes you a lot. If you make an effort to get the captain promoted, he won't be able to stay in that house. Believe me. He'll be transferred, and they'll appoint a new commander down here. A single garrison can only put up with one captain!"

By the entrance to the Army High Command building in Paris, Muhammad parked the car so that the two women, both dressed in their very best clothes, could get out and head for the main entrance. Muhammad stayed behind the wheel, skimming the pages of an old French newspaper. The amiable military official listened to Gertrude, whose presence seemed to occupy the entire space, and then suggested that the only possible solution was to appoint this particular captain to the French mobile forces in Morocco.

"You've told me, Gertrude," he went on, "that he's a captain in the south of France in charge of our Moroccan soldiers in that particular post. Isn't that so? Well then, here's the logical solution. A decent proposal such as this one will surely please him a lot since he'll be earning double salary over there. That's much better than promoting him, and in any case it's very difficult to promote a military officer outside the usual bounds and parameters. No French officer would ever accept such a thing. Do you understand what I mean? The captain will give the house back to its owners and yourself and then go on to something more significant for him and, needless to say, for us as well. Just wait and see, he won't refuse this heaven-sent salary raise."

"It was a very clever solution," Gertrude commented in the car on the way back. "But it's all due to that crafty devil Ben Darras. How can I thank him?"

Darras had to pursue the matter for over a month. Her admiration for him was only enhanced when the owner of the original property sent her a telegram informing her that the captain had been delighted by the decision. It had come as a complete surprise, although, of course, he had no idea of what had prompted it; he assumed that it was his competence that had been responsible. He may well have surmised that the chief factor in his raise in salary had been the cruel way he treated his Moroccan soldiers, but he was also aware that this was not the promotion for which he had been waiting for some time.

"Willing to offer the house to Miss Gertrude," the telegram said, "for a period of two years only, and on condition that she pay him a deposit for the furniture that he would be leaving in place until his return."

It was Muhammad's opinion that this particular headache needed to be dealt with from the outset, or else it would turn into a chronic illness later on. On this topic he had his own particular mountain Bedouin hunch. The file needed to be consigned to the attorney, Monsieur Saint-Pierre, the scion of an illustrious family of French attorneys stretching all the way back to the eleventh century. There was little doubt that he alone had the qualifications to deal with a question such as this; he knew the principles of his profession, and in particular he knew how to come up with alternatives, find solutions, and give his customers some hope.

In those days Muhammad seems to have been really happy living with Gertrude and enjoying one of the brightest periods in his life, one that was filled with pride, happiness, and joy. "It's important," he said, "for one to dream of what he wants and then to go out and find the will needed to fulfill that dream."

"It's a fantastic piece of luck," Gertrude added, "that Ben managed to find us a hotel in this region. He thought he would be getting rid of me and my nagging by housing us with Madame Pierlot, but the so-and-so was actually right when he was wrong! We owe some thanks to Madame Pierlot as well; she was the one who gave us a larger room instead of the small one, and the one she gave us overlooked the Rhone and that endless green space. It was also quite by chance that she gave me the opportunity to look out at that house on the opposite bank of the river, so that I can now reside at long last in a house that resembles those splendid mansions you read about in early English novels. My God, how beautiful this house is, and how right Madame Pierlot was when she said it looked like a tree sprouting out of the ground!"

Days and nights went serenely by, almost in silence except for the lowing of cattle in the meadows and nearby residences. You could hear the noise of bells on the sheep and goats as they made their way toward the white mountain slopes, urged on by the barks of sheepdogs. Madame Pierlot started coming to the house regularly, and her laughter, something she insisted on stretching out as long as possible, lent their evenings a particular rhythm of their own. She actually preferred coming in order to while away some time with Alice, and she always brought cheeses, baskets of eggs, and various vegetables from her own garden.

"Is all that food in the basket for us?" Gertrude would tease her as a compliment. "There's only three of us!"

"What about your servant," the kindly Frenchwoman would ask, "not to mention various friends passing through? And don't I eat meals at your place all the time."

"But what about Monsieur Pierlot?"

Muhammad now started reading a lot and acquainting himself with French literature. Madame Pierlot brought him books that her husband suggested and that he had in the hotel library. The Moroccan read Balzac, Victor Hugo, Zola, de Maupassant, and others. He was particular taken by *Madame Bovary*, although he could not explain why he was so fascinated by the story of a woman who deceives her husband with a number of lovers or by the superb style of a writer who knew how to lift human frailty to the level of a genuine literary masterpiece. Muhammad was relishing his new life with the person he loved, without being entirely sure of anything. From the outset he had never really known how to talk about the details of his relationship; he kept insisting that, as far as both he and Gertrude were concerned— and maybe other people as well—the entire situation was not necessarily auspicious. He was there, and that was all there was to it. Why ask? One can be in love without needing to ask questions. Questions about what exactly? People who drink do not need to ask why they do so, and it is the same with eating and breathing air. It is there, and that is it!

Muhammad would be totally absorbed in his reading, but once in a while he would look up from the book and stare at the distant heavens, the clusters of grey clouds, that one separate white cumulus perched right over his head, and the thread of white moving steadily downwards in his direction. He would take in the pine tree to his left and the various fruit trees and bushes—apples, cherries, and raspberries—that stretched upwards in order to grow larger. He would then turn to enjoy the serried rows of grapes anchored to the soil, loaded down with white, red, and black fruit, just like a carefully organized rack of colored wine bottles on the earth's invisible table.

Gertrude is there in front of him, pulling herself away early today from Madame Pierlot's chatter. She goes back inside the house, trailed by the little dog that is her permanent shadow. She comes back again with a book and her notepad. She is currently devouring Dashiell Hammett; nothing keeps her so involved as detective and crime novels. Muhammad glances at her and notices that, like him, she is crouched on the lawn looking away from the solitary cloud and the horizontal streak of light. Nothing escapes his notice: not her determined pace, the moves of her ample body, or the folds of her skirts.

That is the way he was, always probing, curious, in the belief that anyone in love with a woman needed to fill his eyes with her, walking, stopping, sitting, and standing up; to console himself with her talk and her silence; to feast his eyes on her, whether clothed or naked; in fact, to make use of every one of his senses, including a sixth sense if one were available—one that flowed out of the spirit and equipped a man to see his woman whenever she was not actually present, to hear her voice even when she was not speaking, to realize what she was thinking, and to anticipate her wishes even before she asked or requested.

He goes back to reading the novel and is surprised by Monsieur Bovary's naiveté and his inability to comprehend his wife's dreams. "This stupid Frenchman, Monsieur Bovary," Muhammad thinks to himself. "It's almost as though he didn't have his head straight on his shoulders! He watches as his wife falls into the abyss, but doesn't know how to behave or what he needs to do apart from finding all kinds of excuses for his fallen woman!"

But then he thinks a bit more about it and tells himself that he really needs to appreciate the poor man's situation and to understand what it means for a woman to live in a domestic situation of such emptiness, especially in a closed environment in which life is the same boring routine every single day, the same square, the same faces, the same chatter, the same roles, the same actions, the same gestures, the same words, the same language…

"What spacious dreams she had…," Muhammad thought to himself in silence. "But they were all dreams with no will!"

Muhammad made a habit of sprawling on the lawn where he could smell the moist earth as it steamed in the gentle sunlight. For him the moments on the grass glistened when Gertrude came out with her reading book and lay down beside him. Whenever she grew tired of the book or something in it annoyed her, she would remember that Muhammad was right beside her and move toward him to ask about something or other. He would respond with something or other as well. She spoke, he spoke, and then her usual flirting would start. By now he had come to the conclusion (as I myself know) that full-bodied women are never more lustful than when they discard their bed-loungings and grab hold instead of that elemental power that comes with a sudden, uncontrollable, tumultuous roll in the grass. How often did Muhammad find himself consumed by such rabid moments, such amazement!

During the nighttime gathering in the open air under the pear trees, Gertrude asked Muhammad to look after the garden. "I've asked the owner," she told him, "for permission to take down the plum tree, which is too old, and to plant some new trees." She decided to get rid of the long grass which had turned into breeding grounds for annoying hornets and kept talking about the bats and frogs that lived all around the house. She also mentioned the fact that some neighbors had been talking about a fox's den that they had stumbled across not far from the rows of grapes.

When a cat let out a loud meow, Gertrude leapt up in panic. "Ay," she said, "my heart almost stopped!" and put her hand on her chest.

"Oh Gerty, it might be just a feral cat," Muhammad said.

Gertrude's response was intended to show how much she admired the way cats mingled. "You can never tell," she said, "if it's a male or female cat. But it's fine for cats to consort and make love without others knowing about it. No one pays any attention to them as they live their lives to the full in the wild!"

On their way back to the house, Gertrude was telling him how happy she was with this place.

"Picasso can come here and paint whatever he likes. He's not far away; as I told you earlier, he's in Antibes. We can welcome more friends here too; there are plenty of rooms, and more often than not most of the vegetables rot because they aren't picked enough."

Gertrude had some more ideas. "We need to get some more seeds to plant," she told him. "How about going to Marseille to get some different kinds of flowers, especially acacia, daisies, magnolia, and lilies that we can plant around the house? We'll have to do the gardening ourselves."

She gave him permission, if he wished, to use the garden shed, which looked like a Red Indian hut or a small Buddhist temple; all this in spite of the fact that he could perfectly well make use of the other room whenever he wished.

He looked over at Gertrude to try to glean the significance of this offer: was she being really generous or was this a presage of something bad? A few wrinkles had started to appear on her face and in the corners of her eyes, and others as well that could be seen only in light and shadow or in a closeup inspection of her face around her cheeks and lower chin. Her neck, however, was still intact, inviting the admirer to rest his gaze on it and relax, a welcoming neck that could never leave the observer feeling neutral.

Along with her soft skin, Gertrude had a mellowness to her that gave her clothes a number of wrinkles that were both fascinating and exciting. Upstairs inside the house, where the lights were on in Gertrude's room, she invited Muhammad to help her take off her white gown. He reached for the zipper at the top of her back and slid it down to the bottom; he felt wonderfully happy at that special moment when lovers usually swing to and fro between the stars in an infinite lift that makes them survey life from above and discover it all over again.

A sunny morning in the L'Ain region. Gertrude has been looking out of her bedroom window, which is tall and wide, like a locked door on high stone wall covered in ivy. She is wearing a diaphanous white nightgown and has just climbed out of bed after another warm night spent with the Moroccan; the scene looks like a flash of white paint flashing out of an area of green in an eye-catching abstract picture.

Muhammad had woken up earlier and slunk out from under the sheets like a well- trained wolf. He found Alice with her normal dubious look and the servant with breakfast already prepared in the wonderful, abstemious French style: black coffee, butter, goat cheese, toasted bread, croissants, strawberry jam, cheery jam, raspberry jam, fig jam—each in its tiny pot. The servant was waiting for Gertrude to come down, that being a daily ritual to initiate the rhythm of the days as they sped by.

From the upstairs window, with its brown wooden shutters, Gertrude was able to embrace the entire landscape as far as the eye could see, the hills and valleys that afforded the earth verdant feminine curves: trees, vines, and fields of grain spread out in terraces, ranging in color from dark to light. There was no noise, there were no crowds, no fumes, no dust; only a space woven in silence and modesty, a green expanse, and a gentle, indulgent sun.

This time it was fine for the Moroccan to be here, but there was one person who could not stand the sight of him, as he filled his lungs with the pure, invigorating air and lived his life.

At long last Gertrude came downstairs; it was as if life could begin only when she arrived at the breakfast table. She seemed to be in a good mood, and Muhammad watched as she extended her hand to the cheek of Alice who was standing behind the flowering oleander tree; as she toyed with the thin, flowering branches, she seemed to be doing her best to hide her sorrows. He watched as they exchanged a kiss, then Gertrude clasped Alice's shoulder and took her over to the table. They had to eat breakfast quickly, Gertrude said, because Madame Pierlot and her husband would be coming; they were all going out for a trip along the banks of the Rhone.

The water was flowing gently by; once in a while its edges rippled with small waves that broke on the bank. To Muhammad they looked like sea waves in a convalescent phase. A few seagulls were flying overhead, but he had no idea where they had come from. There was a whole crowd of women carrying umbrellas and waving handkerchiefs and fans as they chatted to each other or their husbands. On the far bank a few fishermen were patiently watching their lines cast into the water. A solitary man was crossing the river in his boat, looking like someone in a watercolor. Muhammad conveyed his instant impression to Gertrude who smiled back at him.

"You seem to see things that I don't," she said.

"I only see through your eyes," he replied, and that loving response impressed her deeply. She took out her notepad and noted it down.

He thought about doing the same thing when he had returned to his own room in the evening. "When it comes to writing," he told himself, "I must try to avoid copying other people."

What he was implying, of course, was that a writer should not reveal to other people those fresh impressions and minor ideas that he captures through his own senses and particular point of view. What he needs to do is to keep them to himself or allow them to filter through his body and memory until such time as they can mature and coalesce. At that point they will take embryonic shape as sentences, phrases, and compact paragraphs. Eventually that will lead to labor pains, followed by birth.

But, as Muhammad has recently explained to me, he used to be delighted whenever Gertrude expressed her pleasure at the things he said. "I'm not going to lie," he said. "When she was happy, so was I. Her delight was mine too."

Actually, at the time Muhammad was not bothered about the chemistry of writing; he was still at the initial stage in the process. Unlike genuine authors, he was not yet feeling jealously protective of his ideas and individual acts of creativity. He was different from most of us today, since writing for him was not such a personal and individual issue, one that could not tolerate being splintered between two bodies, a special chemistry that was absolutely opposed to any kind of subdivision.

He went over to a copse that had attracted his attention and lay down on the grass, contemplating the clear water, which was coming from some unknown source and flowing toward some outlet where it could finally put itself to bed. Gertrude caught up with him; using her fingers and gestures in the air, she had volunteered to provide him with detailed explanations of the region's geography. "Here's where the Rhone's source is, and here's where it passes through on its way to the Mediterranean."

Alice and their maidservant now caught up with the two of them, then along came Madame Pierlot and her husband. This was followed by a replication of the scene in Manet's painting, "The Luncheon on the Grass," which Muhammad proceeded to describe in a voice that drew everyone's attention. Madame Pierlot now went over to the servant and discussed certain cooking details, while Monsieur Pierlot went back to his book. Gertrude lay down between Muhammad and Alice and had a little nap.

But suddenly, she leapt to her feet, looking delighted. "It's only now," she mumbled, as though talking only to herself, "that I've had a brilliant idea!"

"A new writing project?" Muhammad asked.

"No," she clarified. "A new love!"

The riverbanks were there for men and women to stroll along, and Gertrude went for a walk in the afternoon sun. She started running. When Alice declined, she invited Muhammad to run with her. She seemed just like the four-year-old girl in the photograph album, running over the rain-soaked grass, jumping over rocks and bricks, and adjusting her stride to the way the wind kept playing with her hair. When after a while she eventually stopped to catch her breath, she looked at Muhammad with a laugh. He in turn gazed back at her.

"There's a gleam in your eye," he said, and that made her very happy. "No, actually there's something gleaming in your heart!"

She paused for a moment. "Let me write that down."

He asked her if she had liked the expression he had used.

"No," she replied, "this time it was the expression's reflection that I liked."

No words can possibly describe precisely that amazing feeling of intoxication that comes over an Oriental male like Muhammad as he is lying with a woman and resting on top of a proud female body. Muhammad's problem, as he explained to me during our Tangier days, was that he could not say "no," especially to Gertrude. The American woman realized that Muhammad could be easily led on by simply giving him a wink or ruffling his hair as though she were his mother or elder sister!

Gertrude was totally steadfast about her life; she could not love anything she did not control. Muhammad had this particular prerequisite, since his love was that of one who would willingly accept servitude. I know him well, and he could never be certain as to why Gertrude struck him as comely (he never described her as being beautiful), but he would readily confess to me that it was never her face that excited him, but rather her body: that fact that she was buxom and had a full, rounded body.

"She was a woman," he used to say, "who made use of the lower part of her body to move."

Ever since her brother Leo had left for Italy and finally settled in Settignano in Tuscany, she had started to feel a greater degree of freedom, not least because she had started making use of her wealth, in her house and with her body, without considering anyone else's opinion or owing anything to others.

Deep down, the Moroccan had no idea what it was he was looking for in his peculiar love for a strange woman. At first he may have been acting like a wolf waiting in ambush before pouncing on a lamb and making off with it, but he soon found himself being swept far out to sea with the current against him. In the long run it was acceptance that gave his life some meaning. He may have tried to wrap himself in the wolf's primitive innocence, but any number of bad things have started from such an instinct. That explains why he was no good at playing a reticent role when Gertrude invited him to her "joint-bed game," the idea that flashed in her mind while the three of them were calmly lying on the green grass beside the Rhone on that day trip.

The two women were sitting on the bed in their nightclothes when Gertrude invited him to snuggle in between them. She noticed that he was hesitant, so she encouraged him to overcome an inhibition which was meaningless. "Once in a while," she told him, "it's a man's right not to feel innocent…"

Now Alice joined in. "What are you afraid of?" she asked. "No one else is here. No one can see us."

He remembered the children's tale that teachers in grade schools used to tell: A father and his son break into a field filled with vines. Exploiting the owner's absence, the father starts picking clusters of grapes. The son warns him not to do it, but the father curses him, then tells him either to eat some or shut up. No one is there to see them, the father says. But then the boy shocks his father by saying, "But God is watching us, Father!'

Muhammad was still standing hesitantly by the door when, just like a child, he said "But God is watching us, Father!'

Gertrude could not help bursting into laughter. "What's the matter with you?" she said. "Do you want to enter heaven all by yourself?"

It was hopeless trying to convince the two women. He felt like a snail being pulled out of the security of its shell.

"Nature knows no sin, so why should we be compelled to commit any?"

Deep in his subconscious there lurked a vague fear, the normal reaction of a Muslim who does not regularly worship, "a non-practicing Muslim" as people say. In spite of everything, he did not remain faithful to his childhood self; no doubt, the child that he had been betrayed him!

While Muhammad inserted himself into the communal bed between the two different female bodies, Gertrude kept repeating her homily. "My friend," she said, "the world is not as you imagine it to be. Everything is inevitable: what you like and don't like; what pleases you and what doesn't; what you think good and what you think bad. I am well aware that you are always good-natured and simple, but you must realize that the Lord God alone is not enough; if he is, then why did God have to create the Devil as well?"

Alice nodded her agreement. "True enough," she said, leaning on her elbow. "We aspire toward God, but at the same time we run after the Devil, seeing neither one nor the other. It's all a matter of conviction and desire. Isn't that so, Gerty?" She opened her eyes wider as she stared at her companion. "As you can see," she went on, "we aspire to love, and yet we hate. We aspire to tolerance, but we loathe and are roused to anger. We aspire to tenderness, but we are still cruel. We aspire to extend our hand, and yet all we show is jealousy!"

Gertrude reached over to pick up her notepad, while Alice continued with her moment of enlightenment, something that rarely showed with her.

"You're right," Gertrude interrupted her, "that we always aspire to the heavens, and yet we still hanker for the dust of earth!"

For several seconds Muhammad was somewhere else; he may have still been weighing up his situation and working out how he had come to be willingly involved in a kind of perversion. Deep down, he kept asking himself why he could not object or make clear how uncomfortable he felt. How could he discard his childhood so easily?

Gertrude seemed supremely happy, like Karkar birds—flesh and grass at one and the same time, its talons relishing what it desired, just as it desired. The three of them rehearsed again the original trip to Tangier and their first meeting with Muhammad. There was a good deal of laughter and a lot of jokes that were difficult to transfer from one language to another. Gertrude especially knew what Tangier meant, and so did Muhammad. This was a golden opportunity to go over all the details again with Alice there.

"What a night that was, Mo," Gertrude said, "in that room upstairs in the Hotel Villa de France, on the southern coast of the Mediterranean. I'd traveled a long way—one wave clothing me, the other stripping off my garments!"

Like Alice, Muhammad was listening to what Gertrude was saying as though he were watching a scenario in which he had no part to play.

"You and I," Gertrude said, "had no pity on each other until you dived into my pond. After that, your breaths were all mine!

What a night that was, Mo!"

The young American woman had emerged from the end of the nineteenth century to visit Tangier at the beginning of the twentieth. At the time Tangier looked like an organized urban spectacle, sloping down from lofty heights toward the sea. Its white houses and high walls were in ruins, and the city was surrounded by a wide, dirty trench. The kasbah on the top was what caught your attention first, it and the seven minarets. Apart from two streets leading down to the sea, there were only dark, narrow, winding alleys which were climbed with steps and stone staircases. Whenever a visitor approached houses and dwellings, it was to find that they were extremely low. Needless to say, this description did not fit the residences of the three foreign delegations, those of France, Spain, and England, and the dozens of consulates, mansions surrounded by well-constructed walls and with high balconies and large windows.

The three of them spent the entire night exchanging memories and recalling as much as they could about Tangier: nine international powers in a daily contest by way of a mere handful of consuls; three separate postal authorities who never stopped working; four currencies in daily use; exchanges; smugglers; spies of every kind; port workers; Jewish, Muslim, and Spanish prostitutes; homosexuals of every conceivable nationality; Indians in banks; Spaniards in the building trade—you could watch them hanging on wooden perches high up, covered in cement dust and sand; places high up and low down.

As Gertrude climbed up a slope with sweat on her face, Muhammad teased her. "Just stretch your arm out a bit," he said, "and you'll be able to touch the European shore. Take a look; that's Spain shining over there!"

Alice kept on talking about how poor people were, whereas Muhammad told her that she was talking only about the unemployed. The city was actually full of energy and life, and the vigorous way that Muslims and Jews were functioning in the local market was there for anyone to observe.

They all remembered arriving at the Tangier port and burst into laughter, especially when they remembered how one of the porters had almost dropped Gertrude off his back as he was going down the boat's gangplank and doing his best to get her clear of the water that inundated the low dock where they had arrived. Muhammad said that the problem now was the final settlement. When he had left, they had been in the process of completing the important parts of port construction. They seem to have consigned matters to the Tangier International Company. That may have explained how they came to bring in the engineer Gauthrouet from Tunisia; he was the head of port construction and interests there. Since, as you know—Muhammad told them—Tangier was under international administration, the project involved Britain, Germany, Spain, and Austria, although the largest portion went to France, which had by now also become the "protective" party for Morocco.

"Good heavens, Muhammad," Gertrude commented. "You know a whole lot about your country! Where did you find it all out?"

"Anyone who really loves his country, Gerty," Muhammad responded in a broken voice, as he rubbed his head, "has to be involved in the details!" Muhammad asked her another question. "Do you remember, Gerty, how panicked you were about riding a mule in Tangier?"

"No," she replied, "certainly not. It wasn't the mule, it was the trip involved. You expected me to ride a mule to that other city a long way from Tangier. What's its name?"

"Tetouan," he replied.

She then made it clear that she could remember that trip, one that Matisse deeply regretted not taking. It was hard and tiring and took a whole day, which explains how she came to avoid repeating the experience.

Matisse had arrived in Tangier in late January that year, in good time for the rain. He found himself confronted with the color grey that covered everywhere and everything; that made him unwilling to do anything. While he was waiting for shining light and bright color to return, he was advised to take a trip to Tetouan. It was his only trip outside Tangier, and he came back with no memorable impressions. The poor man yearned for the beginning of March, the appropriate time for the kind of weather he had been promised. Gertrude kept repeating to Muhammad—almost in a whisper—what Matisse himself had told her and kept telling other people: "It's the East that has saved us!"

"Me too," Gertrude said in a distracted moment. "The East saved me. Tangier, Tangier. Ah Mo, what wonderful days those were!"

Muhammad told her about his first encounter with Matisse in Tangier.

He used to visit him in his room, no. 35 at the Hotel Villa de France, amid the fascinating natural finery of the garden of the Englishman, Mr. Brooks. From his window high up, Matisse could look out on Tangier, in all its brightness, glow, openness, and tolerance. It had yet to grow really old. The gleaming white and the pure blue hues afforded a dazzling scene for his bespectacled eyes. Whenever he went out, he would wander around in his Moroccan gandora and slippers making sketches. It is true that at first the rain in Tangier kept him away from scenes of nature and the city itself, but that is what led him to focus on faces. However, no sooner had the springtime daylight made itself felt than he discovered his own internal light.

Gertrude now went back to her recollections. That visit to Tangier was a signal event in Matisse's life. It was his friend Albert Marquet who had advised him to go. It was then, she went on, that I myself understood the meaning of the quest for a different light and another sun. Matisse was eager to get away from the optics of old; oh, for that brilliant, pure Mediterranean blue, the washed blue that made vision come coursing forth—that overwhelming celebration of joy, or, as Matisse himself expressed it to me and others at the time, "the sheer joy in the universe's repose when a human being manages to locate its position!"

Gertrude then carried on talking about her associations with that first night, and with the subsequent ten nights she spent in Tangier. She had no idea what she would have done, had she not made that trip to Tangier, the port, the hotel, the big room overlooking the trees, the light, the sea, not to mention this "little Moroccan"! And with that she turned and looked at Muhammad.

"You were a wolf!" she said. "You knew exactly when to pluck the apple off the tree and drink the lake water. I was your rustic shepherdess. I shall never forget your face, your touch, your voice, your clothes, and your nakedness. In particular I'll never forget your mouth: how it touched, bit, muttered, panted, spoke, and did not speak, saying nothing. Ever since Tangier I have given thanks to the heavens; it is as though it was in Tangier that I cut my umbilical cord."

As Alice watched and listened in silence, she was obviously burning on hot coals, as though a tape recording of their time in Tangier were rolling before her eyes for the first time. At this transcendent moment, Gertrude was eager for Muhammad to hear her fulsome encomia for Tangier.

"Tangier brought me back to life again," she said. "I was worried about my body, scared in fact. I was beginning to have some heart murmurs, too. Days were going by too slowly. Every morning, every evening, I checked on my face, my eyes, my cheeks, my lips, my forehead, my whole body in fact, for fear that time was marching in my direction and my body was about to dry out. But then Tangier suddenly loomed on my horizon, and I came over here to change my life. I have no idea which kindly, generous wind it was that brought me here, but many thanks to Matisse for his advice!"

Once again she recalled the climactic night with Muhammad in her room in Tangier (and she almost stood up on the bed to show how panic-stricken Muhammad actually was at the time).

"Did anything awful happen?" the poor man asked her in would-be shock.

"No, it was nothing. Just a matter of virginity, but I've got rid of it now!"

As she said that, she was trying her sarcastic best to recall how the Moroccan had been so panic-stricken. He had grabbed her hand and started kissing it.

"Forgive me," he said, "I had no idea that you were still…"

Gertrude chuckled as she recalled how she had made fun of the whole thing. "I know what you're thinking," she had said. "Relax! I'm feeling liberated!"

Muhammad had been even more alarmed when he spotted the blood on the white sheets.

"I've done wrong, I've sinned," he said. "I've compromised your honor."

"No, it's nothing to do with honor," Gertrude had shocked him by saying. "Do you realize that in America we say that it's men who invented the idea of virginity! Honor is something completely different."

Muhammad could still remember his own reaction at the time and what he had said to her: "I feel as though I've wounded my own flesh. You didn't tell me; you didn't warn me."

As far as Muhammad was concerned, on that night long ago his behavior had involved a transient whim, a fleeting encounter between a man and woman. That at least had been his initial expectation, but, ever since that blood-stained night, the American woman had come to possess him. He still had the feeling that what he had lived was a kind of dream, one in which he had touched a body made of lead crystal and chipped off a small, quavering piece of it.

"You did wrong, you didn't tell me!"

"Oh," she sighed, affected either by the pain she was feeling or the unexpected moistness, "I don't know how I can have let myself do what I've just done!" But a moment later she went on, "But I had a good time!" She paused for a second to catch her breath, then used an embroidered handkerchief to mop her brow. "I won't hide it from you," she went on confidently. "It's only now that I've got rid of an ancient frustration!"

That night of memories in L'Ain lasted until early morning; it was only when the cock crowed and the first shafts of light came through the cracks in the window that they became aware of the time. Gertrude suggested that they get a bit of sleep.

"This American woman certainly knows how to make her body vibrate," Muhammad thought to himself as he laid his head on the pillow. "She has this special gift. Only she can drink a double gulp of wine at one go. Not only that, but she's kinky as well!"

11. GOD DOES NOT LOVE ME

A dank Paris morning that weighs heavily on the soul. Muhammad says that he does not like Paris this way. Someone like him who hails from southern climes is like a person sliding down from the solar disk who finds it hard to adjust to thick clouds or to be content with a dim, frigid light.

He heard the maidservant, Léonie, giving a rapid verdict to Alice: "Today it'll rain for sure."

The old buzzard was standing in the hallway, looking like the head of household. "No, it won't," the old buzzard replied to reassure her. "it'll just be a quick passing shower."

He was still brushing his hair in the mirror.

"Maybe we'll take a stroll along the Seine," she said, turning toward him as usual, "past all the second-hand booksellers!"

"No," he told her explicitly (as was his wont). "Today doesn't look good for the Seine. I'm thinking of visiting my friend Bernard in the gypsies' suburb. I haven't been there for quite a while."

Bernard, that tiny white hand that had offered him so much warmth and clasped his sagging shoulder so he would not feel too lonely. He was also thinking about his other gypsy friends, of course, even though the whole idea did not please Alice.

He stood there, looking at Léonie. She seemed almost ageless: freckles on her face, honey-colored eyes, and red hair—a fully mature woman. People seeing her for the first time would find it hard to decide whether she was a young woman or a precocious teenager. She used to burst into laughter and loved jokes and teases; nor was she the slightest bit shy about mouthing uncouth words and certain distinctly ambiguous expressions. He noticed that her body was an open invitation, and he may well have offered up a silent prayer of thanks to the heavens for this particular gift that confirmed the possibility of a policy that would bring heaven and earth closer together! All of a sudden he became aware that he was acting distracted and was worried in case his eyes had strayed too far or his gaze had revealed too much. Ever since he had entered this house, he had been anxious to appear as upright as possible and was still anxious to convey the impression that he was not going to trample down the shadow he loved, the one he had traveled through so much space and time to join up with in Paris.

In recent months, ever since they had returned to Paris from L'Ain, Muhammad had been noticing that his own special portion of body had begun to diminish. The luscious body that had previously been so generously available and submissive was now off limits; door keys had proliferated; boxes and chests were always locked; even empty suitcases were firmly locked. It was not normal. To him it seemed that some kind of block had slunk its way into his life with Gertrude. He did not ask anyone why he had become a stranger among strangers so very suddenly. Then he started asking himself why it was that, every time he went up to his rooftop room, he found the sky so low, almost touching his very fingertips in sympathy, and, whenever he went downstairs, it was to find the floor slippery, like some precipice where it was not safe to step, as though the time was not actually the right time, and the love of old was no longer as ripe as it used to be.

He took a short stroll on the roof next to his room. By now the flock of pigeons had grown used to him; they would peck away at the scraps he left for them by the flower pots—a daily spectacle that amused him and lightened his sense of alienation and loneliness. Down below he made sure to move cautiously: no step or word out of place, only answering if spoken to, and never starting a conversation himself.

It was back in Paris that he must have realized how profound is the sense of isolation that can invade your soul and pervade the very bases of your inner self, like the drip of freezing rain—the kind of isolation that you feel even though you are living with other people, one that keeps you awake at night as you try to negotiate with your insomnia.

Gertrude had turned into another woman, always in a bad mood and continually blaming him. "What does your common sense tell you, Mo?" she would say. "Why are you always plying me with stupid, skeptical questions?"

He realized that she had started to get aggravated by his silly doubts which, no doubt, someone was volunteering to communicate to her. With his transparent and penetrating spirit, he had obviously gone too far in his surmises regarding the portrait that Picasso had done of her. He obviously had not been aware of the limits of jealousy and possession, while Gertrude herself was crazy about the portrait and preoccupied with it. She was now essentially basing her whole life on the painting and kept changing its location: sometimes it was on the studio wall, at others in the reception hall, and at still others in the living room over the woodstove. Most of the time, however, it was in her bedroom; she wanted it near her all the time, like a mirror.

There were a number of paintings or drawings of Gertrude, and several sculptures of her head, but it was the Picasso portrait that was closest to her heart. Muhammad actually preferred the portrait that Vallotton did of her; there were no cubist, experimental, or other adjustments to her face; she was wearing her velvet, purple-colored dress, a blue-beaded necklace, and a red belt; her hands were exposed and a little bit open. Muhammad was also fond of the bronze head of Gertrude by Lipchitz; it looked like a Greek bust and showed her with determined features and her forehead crowned with a garland of hair. Muhammad mentioned to me that Berman had also done a portrait of Gertrude, but she did not like it, even though she showed it to everyone who visited the apartment, just like everything else.

"I had to make you understand…from the very beginning," she yelled at him.

This was a kind of cruelty he had not encountered before, although he had sometimes felt it in other forms, but he had decided to look away and postpone any real understanding of what it meant. At the time he did not realize what he was supposed to be picking up, but he felt nevertheless that he was beginning to lose his self-esteem, that sense of security that had been part of his life ever since he had entered this apartment.

I realize that that was the exact moment when he decided that, swallowing hard, he had to leave for good, but he still hesitated. In one of his recollections he told me that he made the decision, but kept going back on it. He kept thinking about leaving, but then changed his mind and tried his best to forget it as quickly as possible, something that required him to eradicate his own sense of self. He was not aware, it seemed, of the secret of the amazing attraction that made everything about this American woman so fascinating, drew him in, and bound him to her. Not only that, but he also did not understand the misgivings that lurked in the soul of the American woman, in her behavior and her moods.

As he was standing on the threshold by the front door of the apartment, he heard Alice's voice talking to the maidservant: "Rien de rien! Does the crayfish emerge from the sea in order to dry out on the sand, and then go back to its water in the evening?"

Alice heard Gertrude asking her to bring the Cézanne painting, "Portrait of Madame Cézanne with a fan," which was hanging on a wall in the hall. Alice brushed some dust off the painting with her hand and blew on the edge of the frame, then took the painting off the wall.

"Do you want to write about it?" she asked.

Gertrude stood up to adjust the painting over her desk. "I want to examine Madame Cézanne's face," she said. "I'm hoping to be able to transfer the work into story form. If only I could brings Cézanne's spirit into my own soul!"

With a hand gesture Gertrude waved her away so she could concentrate on writing, but Alice stayed where she was by the door.

"What now?" Gertrude grumbled.

"Didn't I tell you, Gerty?"

"What, exactly? I'm asking you!"

"Everything's clear now. The Moroccan has married a gypsy woman, for sure."

"Where did you get hold of that idiocy, Alice?" Gertrude yelled at her once again. "We're not seeing anything untoward about him."

"He's got crafty eyes," the buzzard went on, as though talking to herself.

The remark seemed to get Gertrude really worked up. "Don't get me wrong, Alice," she said in a different tone of voice. "I know what I'm doing; I know what I want. Please, I'm no longer ashamed of my own emotions. Let me love and hate whomever I choose. Please don't try to orchestrate my feelings the way you want to…"

Alice just stayed there licking her lips, as though she had suddenly developed a thirst or her saliva had completely dried up.

"Please, Alice," Gertrude added in anger after a moment's pause, "don't foist your psychological problems on me."

Alice responded as though she had been doused with a pail of cold water. "Do you want me to go away, Gerty, and leave the house? Are you that fed up with me, and I haven't understood?"

Gertrude now became even more annoyed. "Please, Alice," she yelled. "Don't put words into my mouth!"

Alice now went to her room in tears. The servants were all standing there in the hall watching the scene from close up. A few moments later they saw Gertrude trail Alice up the stairs.

Léonie, the new maidservant who was not a little curious, moved closer to the door and listened to the two women. "I'm just like you," Gertrude was saying. "I don't trust his eyes either. I realize that he has a look that is scary...but he has amazing bodily strength. You understand! The way he strokes, that magic touch...just like this—" And she snaps the fingers of her right hand. "That's how life's pleasures come to be, that fleeting sensation that can't be named. You understand, don't you? Oh, my God!"

Gertrude had started wiping away Alice's tears and lowering her voice. "Have no fear, my love, I only have feelings for you. With him it's just flesh in contact, but I'm still empty. With you, it's all fullness, believe me! There's absolutely no one who can take your place, my darling, my precious wife! I'm not hiding anything from you. For some time now we haven't touched, he and I. My body is tired of his; I'm not jumping like a frog anymore!"

Léonie just stood there listening as Gertrude swore to Alice to convince her that she was no longer making love with the Moroccan; she was just pretending.

"With him it's all a game of pretend at this point. But with you, my little lamb, you're always wonderful, closer to me. I love you, love you, love you..."

Looking out on the gypsy suburb, Muhammad was in the process of recovering his lost happiness. It felt as though he had contracted a weird disease and come there in quest of a cure. He had no idea where his sense of calm radiated from or how it was that he could actually find himself in this disseminated chaos among the open spaces of the gypsies—those strange faces and features! Some of them had cube-shaped heads, others had square-looking faces, and still others had deep-set eyes. There was a good deal of fascinating beauty to behold as well. Among the first things to attract Muhammad were the colorful shirts they wore, the thick chains on their necks and on men's chests, and the black and brown leather belts with large, ugly metal clasps.

Bernard chose to correct Muhammad's spontaneous impression over a first glass of wine.

"It's not chaos you're seeing here in the gypsy suburb. What you see is actually order by the very millimeter, something that not everyone can see. That's why they call it 'chaos'!" Bernard went on to ask Muhammad if he had thought about lightening the burden of those haughty looks that seemed to be counting his every breath at Rue de Fleurus.

"My friend," he said, "maybe that's not your place anymore!"

"Forget all about Gertrude," Gonzalo told him, "and that portrait that you dust off every evening. Forget painting and painters, the whole lot. Come over here and change the whole rhythm of your life."

Moldovan remained silent but nodded his head to express his agreement with the idea.

"Come here every evening," said Helena. "Why every evening, you ask? So you can stay and enjoy what you really love. We've many, many songs that we've brought with us together with all the dust; we've collected them all via wagons and horses along the many tracks of our travels…voices emerging from the earth's very belly…the dead have given us the tunes!"

Gonzalo invited Muhammad to stay till evening and told him he would introduce him to his "princess," someone he was bringing to spend the evening with them all. "I must have spoken to you about her before, Mo, haven't I? Her name's Anaïs—Anaïs Nin. Do you remember?"

Muhammad nodded his head to accept the invitation, although he did not say a word. During his Parisian exile he had become an expert in expressing himself more often through silence.

Muhammad noticed that Helena seemed particularly interested in him and kept staring at him. He shook himself out of his reverie when he heard her talking to him. "Are you over there, Mo," she asked him, "still perched in your rooftop room?"

"No, I'm not," he replied in response to her gentle teasing. "I'm right here."

She pulled up a wooden box and sat right in front of him. "I realize that you're suffering over there. We gypsies can intuit those nasty situations. When someone feels like a lonely bird, he'll take any old nest under a plaster roof or in a wall cavity and cry to himself." She stood up and looked straight into his eyes. "How can any person suffer alone," she asked, "and still be a human being?"

As he listened to her, his gaze was fixed on her rose-patterned dress. Oh my, these gypsies! How far they traveled, how they managed to sleep in the exposed nakedness of life—in the wind, beneath the sun, in rain and frost! But they never stopped traveling, like moving towers constantly in motion within the firmaments of existence!

The five of them moved to Gonzalo's place, which was just a short distance from Bernard's. His Peruvian décor was obvious enough, and it seemed that Gonzalo had a strong and developing interest in esthetics even though the house was only a modest wood and tin structure. There were some of Gonzalo's own paintings, quite discordant: Catholic icons, dolls, bits of embroidered cloth in the Latin American style, tourist pictures of Peru, Cuba, Chile, Bolivia, and other South American countries—almost as though he were an amateur postcard collector. The company all sat on multicolored chairs or leaned back on couches.

"By the way," said Gonzalo, looking at Muhammad, "I've just met our American friend, Miller…the writer Henry Miller."

Muhammad immediately perked up. He had become passionately interested in the topic of Miller even since he had attended a debate between Gonzalo and Moldovan in Bernard's house.

"He's a really nice person." Gonzalo went on," even though he's a lousy gringo. His facial features give you the impression that he's Chinese. You should know that he doesn't like Gertrude at all. I met him recently at Anaïs's salon, along with his wife, June. Anaïs holds her own literary salon in Louveciennes, no. 2b Rue Montbuisson (but I'm sure you already know that)."

"How come you hate an American like yourself?" Anaïs had jokingly asked Miller that night.

"I'm not even sure that's what she is," he replied, without even pausing for thought. And he went on sarcastically, "The two of us are not alike in anything. She's even managed to pollute our common American language with her phony cubist pretenses [*cubisme de la merde*]. If my life allows me, I think I'm going to learn hieroglyphics, so I can use it for my writing. Then I won't have to be constantly fenced in by this mob of people who live and survive on public relations…"

"Everything you say is absolutely true, Gonzalo," Moldovan interrupted. "Miller loves crazy writers, as he calls them. He's a gypsy, just like us! For example, he really likes Blaise Cendrars; he says he's a street kid, just like him!"

Muhammad looked away again. He stared at Helena, following her as she moved around inside Gonzalo's house: thick black hair coursing over her shoulders and a tight full bosom. The sudden thought may have struck him that her body was the only thing behaving spontaneously, the body that wanted only to smell the scent of another body. One short sentence would be all that was needed to ignite an electric spark. At that point he became aware of the way the people all around him were staring; he adjusted his gaze, moving his hand across his eyes as though to remove some invisible insect.

Helena had a broad, enigmatic smile, and Muhammad could not tell whether it was intended specifically for him or rather was one of those dancing expressions used by women to make people feel happy at weddings and parties while in most cases actually concealing their pain. At a certain point, however, it became clear to him that there was a flickering gleam in her eye that was talking to him. She gave him the best glass ("Take it for my sake"), and offered him the most comfortable couch ("Come over and sit here, for my sake").

Conversation about Gertrude and Muhammad continued, and, while everyone was drinking and the bottles were doing the rounds, Muhammad kept emptying his bag of sorrows for his friends. "Every time I ask her something," he said, "she responds with a gesture or a nod. Just recently, we were taking a stroll together, taking the dog for its daily walk. I was asking her about a perfectly routine and simple thing. Gertrude pointed at the dog. 'This wonderful, loyal creature is the only one who can answer you,' she said."

Muhammad told them all that he could not explain why their conversation was not like the way it had been before; there was no love interest. He said that he could excuse her for that because he was well aware of the burden of reproach that was being heaped upon her. That applied particularly to Alice, who would lose no opportunity—any opportunity—to scold Gertrude for "her weird relationship with that Moroccan."

Gonzalo confirmed Muhammad's hunch. "That's true," he said. "I've heard some of the Stein family's French friends commenting that 'Gertrude has a lover with no social standing'!"

"I'm sorry to have to tell you that, Mo," Gonzalo added, clasping his shoulder as he did so.

"No, no, no!" Muhammad said, grabbing his hand. "It's no fault of yours. You're my friend."

From time to time Gonzalo would stand up, anticipating the arrival of Anaïs by bus. From his vantage point by the window he turned round, glass in hand, and continued his words of caution to Muhammad. "Believe me, Mo," he said, "there's no place for you there anymore. The last time I met Alice at the press, she kept on questioning me about you and checking on this suburb. I told her my most sincere feelings of appreciation toward you and sang your praises—but you deserve them in any case. She did not believe me. She thinks you have a secret wife here among the gypsies. I even swore by all the holy fathers of the church, but she still did not believe me. I've no idea who it is has filled her head with this nonsense. She told me that Gertrude no longer trusts the Moroccan. I told her that he was not lying in any way about his relationship with us gypsies. I told her to believe me, but she said that Gertrude might be convinced that it was all a lie, but she would probably not be all that sympathetic when things seemed so unspecific. I noticed that Alice was not listening to what I was saying; she was absolutely uninterested in either hearing or understanding."

When Anaïs came in, she was bursting with energy. She looked young, bright, and soft, a pliable entity, just like water. She was wearing a long red dress, gloves, and a black hat, and looked just like a princess emerging from a children's storybook. She had brought a box of chocolates with her and was carrying a colored umbrella and a small notebook with a patterned leather cover. She greeted the assembled company with a kiss on the cheek, and Gonzalo quickly left his spot on the couch and started fussing over her. Everyone raised their glasses in another toast of welcome. In fact, everyone knew Miss Anaïs already, as she did them, except, of course, for the Moroccan who was seeing her for the first time. She knew the district well too, and often came to visit her mulatto friend.

"I see you're not saying anything," she told Bernard. "That's not normal."

"I've nothing left to say, Anaïs," he replied. "My life's in ruins. If it were not for friends here, I would not have recovered. Thanks for your concern, and thanks too for your generous presents. You're wonderful."

"Bernard's always like that," Moldovan butted in. "He only talks when he has to."

Gonzalo now asked her how things were going with that banking-type (by which he meant her husband, with whom her relationship was in trouble). She told him that they were probably about to separate.

"So that's why your eyes have such an anxious look," Bernard commented.

"What's important," she replied with a maidenly blush, "is that I can still see through them well enough!"

"What she means," Gonzalo said with a laugh, "is that she can see me, no one else. For my sake she keeps her lips tight shut…this way, like two cherry pits."

That made everyone laugh. People sensed that the music was about to start.

"Moldovan, gypsy chieftain!" Gonzalo shouted, "Get your hands working, my friend. Get on with it. You're like a racing hound that's no longer a puppy. We don't want to lose our bet."

With that, he started singing and clapping. Those gypsies certainly know how to set the night alight!

When Anaïs had first set eyes on Gonzalo at the press, bent over his work as a typesetter, she had been bowled over by his lithe frame, dark honey-colored body, and crafty childish grin, which showed all over his face and not just on his lips. Whenever she went to the press to see about the production of her book, she made a point of getting close to him. Then she gave him a sneak invitation to a musical soirée to celebrate her move to her new home. She told him that a Tahitian troupe was going to provide the music for the party. "Come and spend a wonderful night with some of our friends," she said.

It was a wild night; everyone sang and danced. Gonzalo was the tallest person there, the Indian descended from the Incas, with the profound and ambiguous stare.

"Where do you get so much energy?" he asked Anaïs as their bodies brushed. "Anyone seeing you for the first time would be put off by both you and your voice."

Anaïs in turn was struck by his soft, gentle voice, with its penetrating quality and Spanish lilt. She asked him to talk to her only in Spanish. "In Spanish," she told him, "I hear words with my entire body, not just my ears!"

Gonzalo was fascinated by Anaïs's writings. He started putting her books under his pillow so he could read them over and over again before he went to sleep and when he woke up. Her lovely little book *House of Incest* particularly won him over, while she was taken with Gonzalo's bare arms and their brown skin. Love, ambiguity, stories, and Indian lore brought them together, and he was soon getting rid of his almost dumb wife, Hilba, to chase after Anaïs. He could never stop extolling his new position by her side. "You have reawakened my self-esteem again," he said. "I had almost turned into a roving drunkard."

He started taking her with him to the gypsy suburb, "the garbage-pickers' village" as she had first called it. Once there, Gonzalo could not stand up in his friend Jango's wagon because he was too tall. It was there too that Anaïs fell in love with the gypsies, their rapacious eyes and savage glances, and came to appreciate their guitar music that spoke to the dead while they invoked spirits with their arms.

Anaïs had just purchased a wagon for Gonzalo from Jango. She had been attracted by the idea of making love in a wagon like gypsy women, but he also had a wooden home there.

"Here I can write with relish," Anaïs said.

"And here I can paint," said Gonzalo.

The gentle miss could come whenever she wished to share love, write, sing, dance, and enjoy the spectacle of the garbage-pickers as they returned with their incredible daily spoils from Paris's garbage. She could also enjoy the gypsies themselves as they lit oil lamps and cooked dinner in the open; the fortune-tellers as they counted the money they had made that day; the thieves dividing up their day's spoils; and children rambunctiously playing their games as darkness descended. They looked like pieces of ruddy cloth jostled by the wind!

Among all the clamor, music, and singing, with cigarette smoke everywhere and a small clamorous crowd rapidly forming a wide circle to include neighbors, Gonzalo carried on his conversation with Muhammad about the coming revolution, strikes, workers, and his elegant "princess."

"Just look at Anaïs, Mo!" he said. "There's my mermaid bride. How passionate and generous she is, almost sick with passion and lecherous with it. Do you follow me? She's the one who chose me, my friend. No one can choose Anaïs for himself. When she falls in love, she's the one who makes the choice—isn't that true, darling?" he asked, but she could not make out his voice clearly enough. "We've made a pact: she'll never mention me in her diary. I want to remain under wraps." He turned to look at Anaïs again. "Ha! We've agreed: don't mention me in any book of yours, please, or else Monsieur Jean-Gabriel Daragnès will fire me. Anaïs, you know that strange printer, don't you? He hand-makes his expensive books and works longer hours every day than his own employees. You know him very well as a book craftsman. He will never allow any of his workers to be forward with his customers, so what do you think about one of them having an affair with a female customer? He has a furious temper, and it's become even worse since he has had medical problems with his prostate."

"This situation won't last long, darling," Anaïs interrupted. "I'm going to open a private press for you, and then you won't be working at someone else's place. You'll be directing your own, and I'll work there with you so I can learn from you."

The mulatto boy's eyes gleamed, and he started kissing her face and hands over and over again. "Anaïs," he said, "you're giving me a second birth. You've taught me how to love poetry and books. I was close to death, but you've restored me to life again. You've given me desire and love. You've taken on all my problems, all my follies and those of that damned woman, my wife [Hilba], or rather who used to be my wife. You've kindled inside me the essence of drawing, and you'll be refashioning me as a creative artist whereas before I was merely an emigrant laborer wandering amid the ruins of the world and the trash of politics and politicians!"

"Rest assured, Gonzalo," Anaïs told him, her hand clasping his shoulder, "you'll be free of all kinds of worry. I too plan to write about you as I wish. I shall never betray my own diary. I'm not going to deprive my diaries of your coal-black eyes and this gorgeous black gypsy hair."

She stretched out her hand to bury it in Gonzalo's hair while he started kissing her hand again.

"You're a strong woman, my darling," he told her, "very strong, delicate, and gentle like a waterfall cascading over me from high in the Andes Mountains. I love you, oh how I love you…"

At this point Muhammad asked her a question. "Do you go to Monsieur Daragnès's print shop a lot?"

"No, not really," Anaïs replied. "He produced one of my books with great efficiency. Actually, I made his acquaintance via an article in the magazine *Le portique*, which talked about his valuable work and his artistic and technical skills. I read the magazine a lot, and so do book lovers. It was there that I met Gonzalo for the first time; he managed to bewitch me with his Indian chants. He was the one who told me that Gertrude and her friend Alice frequent that press, so I stopped going there for that reason. The things I've heard about your friend disturb me. In fact, I've met Gertrude once—I don't remember where exactly. It may have been at Sylvia Beach's bookstore, at the reception for Tzvetaeva or Neruda, or the gathering we organized to honor Rilke. I can't remember now, but I didn't like her. I got the impression that she insists on imposing her will and personality on everyone around her!"

It was Muhammad's opinion that Gertrude was a good person, someone with the feelings of a child who had never grown up, but that all the hyperbole and rumor created a false image of her.

"Come over and see us at Rue de Fleurus," he told Anaïs. "I can introduce you to her. You'll like her a lot. Come whenever you want, although Gertrude generally doesn't like people visiting after five o'clock in the evening. But then why do we need to postpone things? We can go together tomorrow morning if you like."

"That's very kind of you, sir," Anaïs replied. "I'd love to see the pictures that everyone talks about, but I'm uneasy about the idea. I don't want to cause any problems…"

"What problems do you mean?" Muhammad interrupted. "Gertrude will be happy to see you. She loves having people around her and getting to know the whole world. Don't worry!"

When the singing and music were at their height, Helena came over, held out her arms toward Muhammad, and invited him to dance. She tried dragging him from his seat, but he kept resisting, claiming that his legs never did what he wanted. But eventually he put his inhibitions aside and stood up to dance. Helena went back and accompanied Anaïs to the small dance floor. She dressed her in gypsy garb while another gypsy woman put a long, colored shawl around her neck. Everyone clapped in delight at the heavenly visage that had joined the gypsy tribe. It was obvious that everyone there had come to adore her.

This gypsy Anaïs returned to her place and spread out her dress to look at the decorative flower-pattern. She talked to Bernard and Muhammad about her sense of elation at the moment. "Wow, how wonderful this life is!" she said. "Just look at this music that brings sparks out of your blood. That gypsy boa, Helena, is really something. Heaven help anyone who falls in love with her!"

Noticing how distracted Muhammad was, she gave a golden smile, but he was not looking at her while she was talking. She could not talk to anyone who was not looking at her. "I see you keep lowering your eyes," she said. "It's as though you're not seeing what you're supposed to see!"

"Oh, I can see all right," he said, overcoming his drunkenness and opening his eyes wide. "I can see. There's magic here and magic there. In which direction am I supposed to be looking?"

Next day, as they were on their way to the Stein family residence, Muhammad told Anaïs that Gertrude would undoubtedly be glad to see her and to make her acquaintance.

"Are you certain?" Anaïs asked.

"More than certain," he replied, full of self-confidence.

He walked beside her along the street, feeling almost as though he were carrying an angel on his shoulders. He told her about the dozens of visitors, tourists, art lovers, journalists, and art-school students who visited Gertrude's apartment every evening and the other folk who used to frequent the Saturday salon. Anaïs started telling the young Moroccan about her life; he asked questions and she would answer: about her Spanish-Cuban father and her Franco-Danish mother, her birth in Neuilly near Paris, her parents' divorce, her travels with her mother and brothers to New York, her marriage, and the beginnings of the breakdown with her husband, who had brought her back to Paris; and about her initial efforts at writing.

"I started writing when I was ten or eleven," she said. "I began with letters to my father. Perhaps you can't understand how fascinated I was by my father. I loved him a lot…that sort of forbidden love. Do you understand?"

It was Gertrude herself who opened the door when Muhammad rang the bell on the studio side. It was as if she were ready to perform a role on the stage: she scarcely poked her head outside and looked up and down, first at Muhammad, then at Anaïs who was standing right behind him. She looked as though she were fully prepared for a scene she herself had fully prepared; all she was waiting for was Muhammad to come back from his trip to the gypsy suburb.

"Hi, Gerty," Muhammad said. "This is a friend of our friend, Gonzalo, the writer Anaïs Nin. Maybe you know her already; you've certainly heard of her. She's come with me to visit the studio and look at your art collection…"

"This isn't a public gallery, sir," she interrupted him in a very gruff fashion. "If you don't mind, this is a private residence."

"Are you having a joke on us, Gerty?" Muhammad asked, trying his best to smile.

"No," she replied with unexpected vehemence, "I'm deadly serious."

Muhammad was so shocked that he was completely tongue-tied.

"I was about to go out and take the dog for his daily walk," Gertrude went on after a moment's silence. "Let's take a stroll together, and we can chat, if the lady doesn't mind, that is!"

He just stood there looking at her, his head raised because she was still staring at him from above. Her gaze looked vague and distant; her coloring had changed from brilliant red to a wan pallor. It was a face that made him recoil even before he heard her harsh words.

That particular nasty situation was to remain with Muhammad for the rest of his life! He would describe it, talk about it, and discuss it till the very end. "In a flash," he used to say, "you find yourself trying to understand—just yourself—how a particular feeling can extinguish a woman's bloom and how you are supposed to manage to absorb such a crushing blow. Do you allow the woman who has come with you, Anaïs, to reel in shock, while you creep inside, head lowered like a castrated dog that has made his master angry? Or do you instead take a walk with her, you on the left and her dog on the right so you can try to remedy the situation or at least understand why? Or maybe you escort Anaïs to the end of the street, apologize, and then go back?"

Gertrude thrust the dog leash ahead of her and locked the door.

"Come on," she said, "I'm going to talk a walk along the Luxembourg Gardens wall."

For the two hundred meters between the apartment and the gardens, she walked without saying a single word, dragging the dog Basket along behind her. Muhammad was walking by her side, not knowing what he was supposed to say, while Anaïs walked behind the two of them, clicking her fingers and humming a tune which was either French or Spanish—Muhammad could not tell which. She was obviously trying to give the impression that she had no part to play in this tense situation.

Once in a while Muhammad raised his head and turned round to look at Anaïs, as though gasping for air. He was sweating all over and felt that his heart had turned red with embarrassment, not just his face. Whenever he talked about this cruel moment more recently, back in Tangier, he would say that he had felt as though he had lost all self-esteem, lost his own self in fact.

"In a trice," he said, "I was no longer the person I'd been. I started feeling as though I'd been assaulted."

Anaïs stopped for a moment, and Muhammad did too.

"Come on," Gertrude said. "Don't bother about a woman who doesn't know how to think or behave outside her own self."

"But at least she has a brain which she can use!" said Anaïs as she changed direction and started moving away.

"I don't think her brains are in her head like other people's brains!"

Anaïs laughed, thanked Muhammad for being so kind, and moved off toward Boulevard Raspail and Rue Boulevard du Montparnasse.

Muhammad simply stood there watching as Anaïs disappeared down a side street. He decided not to catch up with Gertrude and went back to the apartment. That face, the one that had possessed him for years, the one that still glowed in his life, had now been totally erased.

As a narrator I have to try to imagine what that sudden, awful moment that kept his tongue tied was really like. In the flash of an eye, the door is slammed in your face while you are on your way back to the house, the one that you have started to feel is your own—indeed to call it that. Let us imagine that you are heading for the place you are familiar with and have got to know well (and you have a major figure like Anaïs with you), and yet it feels as if you are walking along a road in the dark, which is the wrong way. It must take your breath away, and there is no going back. Anyone who does that has already decided to make a clean break with things.

We have to imagine as well that Gertrude had told everyone in the apartment not to open the door. She was going to be the one to do it, so that, when the lodger returned from the gypsy suburb, she would teach him a lesson. She may even have stood in front of the mirror to practice her new cruel role. She hears the bell, and, standing on a small table to look a bit taller, opens the door a little and very slowly. She then looks out and says in a cool, dry tone, "This is a private residence, sir, not a public gallery or museum!" Muhammad's face turns pale, as does that of the woman facing him. Each one of them has his or her reasons. Muhammad is feeling utterly mortified and confused; he is sweating profusely, but then suddenly he feels cold. Ouch! The whole thing happens so quickly, like a light going out, a wall clock stopping, or a sudden passing storm before it is enveloped in cloud and fog!

Going up to his rooftop room, he started collecting his clothes and shoes and put everything in a suitcase; his papers he put in his briefcase. Once that was done, he collapsed weeping on the bed. It was some time later in Tangier that he could recollect his devastated feelings. "I felt," he said, "like a soldier with a dishonorable discharge!"

Gertrude must have thought hard about all this; she was not the kind of woman to behave this way. I would venture to suggest that she knew what she was doing and knew what she wanted. She had organized a completely new horizon for her life, one that would last forever: to live without a man; to eat, drink, sleep, wake up, and travel—all with no man, and to enjoy herself!

"So that pig of a woman has dumped me!" he told himself.

In fact he grabbed hold of his suitcase and briefcase and made up his mind to leave, but then he put them back on the bed again. He was not sure of himself and hesitated: should he up and leave, or find some kind of excuse as he usually did? After a short, while he left his suitcase and briefcase and tiptoed downstairs to see how things were down below. Gertrude had come back, and he heard her asking the servants about him. He stood there for a moment to listen. Alice was stubbing out her cigarette in the ashtray and staring skeptically at Gertrude.

"Please let me try to understand, Gerty," she said. "I'm trying to work out whether he was the one you intended to get at, or the woman who was with him, or both of them? Didn't you bear in mind that that particular woman is a friend of the man involved in the strike, the one who never stops doing things for us on a daily basis?"

"Oof!" was Gertrude's response with a sigh. "I don't know. I just don't know."

For several moments he stayed where he was, and did not go down all the way. Going back upstairs, he grabbed his things and looked round at the room for a moment. If I don't leave now, he told himself, it'll be too late. This time he could think of no excuses for either Gertrude or himself.

"But why this way?" he asked himself. "Why does anyone lose their moral stance, so suddenly and with no warning?"

The servants stood there thunderstruck as they watched him carrying his cases. Léonie and the Cambodian servant in particular had been deeply upset by what had happened; they both had tears in their eyes. How much he would have liked to listen to them put this incident with Gertrude into a different light. The two women were sitting together by the big table in the middle of the apartment, silently observing him as he walked around, saying farewell to the rooms and looking at the paintings in the studio. Finally he stopped in front of Gertrude's portrait and looked at it as though seeing it for the very first time. "Goodbye," he said in a loud voice.

"When you leave," he heard Gertrude say, "close the door behind you. Please never come back here again."

With that he left and never looked back, although out of the corner of his eye he could spot the flock of pigeons behind him. In fact, he may have seen the shadows of tiny wings on the ground reflected in the sun's frigid days, but then maybe he did not see anything at all. But he could still remember the gentle smile on his lips, a smile of gratitude to the cooing birds, the rustle of wings shading life!

The ever-patient coachman who was driving the omnibus raised his voice to goad his twin horses on their way toward Austerlitz. Muhammad grabbed hold of his suitcase and briefcase so that neither would fall off the side of the bus. He kept looking at the buildings, bars, restaurants, and outdoor cafés, at the crowds of people passing by, his head in the clouds amid a strip of fleeting images. He was planning to take the train to Marseille and seemed in a hurry, as though he could not stand any more of Paris, any more time, faces, images, memories. He was anxious to travel that very day so that neither Gonzalo, Bernard, Moldovan, Helena, nor any of the other people whom he loved and who loved him could catch up with him and stop him from leaving.

As he was trying to load his things into the train carriage, the suitcase fell out of his hands, but he picked it up quickly. However, the briefcase hit the platform and fell open. Notes and various papers all spilled on the ground.

"Oh God!" he yelled. "Why don't you love me?"

He bent over to pick everything up, and a railway-man helped him, putting his hand on his hat to make sure the wind did not blow it away while he picked up pieces of paper with his other hand.

"Thank you, sir," Muhammad said. "Thank you very much. You railway workers in this country are wonderful. I know that very well! I've loved you all, I've loved Bernard…"

Once the train started moving, Muhammad felt that Paris had turned its back on him, so he sat in the compartment with his back to it. On his way to the south of France, he watched green meadows under the cold evening sun, red-tiled roofs spread across the countryside, all of which he was leaving behind him. He felt tears welling up as though to mourn his own self, and surrendered to a series of random thoughts. Can love's flower really fade, he wondered. But, he went on, I have to confess, if only to myself, that that pig of a woman had started to get angry in recent months. I didn't pay enough attention—as though it didn't concern me. Maybe this foul mood of hers concerned me precisely; I was the cause, and I didn't even notice. I sensed a kind of malevolence, but I couldn't be bothered. I didn't allow myself to get aggravated. That's the way I am. I always look for the good side in people's intentions. What am I supposed to do? That's the way I am; I behave like a fool or a simpleton. I open my eyes, but don't see anything; I hear and block my ears!

The train compartment was big but full of passengers, so, even though Muhammad tried several times to close his eyes and get some sleep, he failed. Sleep seemed to evade him. He was obviously angry, in fact furious; he could almost feel himself cracking like a glass tumbler. The hum of the iron wheels on the train tracks never stopped, and every so often the whistle sounded. All that made sleeping difficult, if not impossible. It may be that his agony was not quite that bad, but I have come to know Muhammad very well in more recent times, especially his brittle temperament, so I feel entitled to go so far as to exaggerate the effect of this final journey of his, a human being in his exile-train, expelled from his paradise, and on his way back to the earth down below!

All of a sudden he could not control himself any longer.

"No, no, no, no!" he yelled inside the compartment. "O God, not here, not here!"

All the other passengers stared in amazement at this Arab man who was expressing his fury in their own language, as though he were standing in front of them stark naked. None of them knew for sure whether he was really crazy, or merely in a state of utter despair. A monk in his clerical garb who was sitting in a far corner of the compartment volunteered to go over and talk to him; he seemed to be a man of faith who was confident in his role and encouraging in his counsel. He tried calming Muhammad down as gently and kindly as he could.

"Come on, my son," he said, "sit down for a while. Relax and seek solace in the One who can relieve your pain… 'Yet the Lord longs to be gracious to you; therefore He will rise up to show you compassion. For the Lord is a God of justice. Blessed are all who wait for him [Isaiah 30:18]?'" By now he had managed to get Muhammad back to his seat and calm him down somewhat. "God exists everywhere, at every moment, inside us and all around us, and yet we cannot see Him. We do not wish to see Him, my son. 'O God, be gracious unto us.' The Lord is here. Change your vision and gaze into the depths, and you will see Him!"

"I cannot see anything, Father," Muhammad replied, staring at the man of faith. "All is darkness in my eyes."

"Ah, my son, be not afraid! There is light inside you. Follow the path, and in a while you will see everything clearly."

As the man of the church returned to his seat, Muhammad put one hand over the other and let his gaze wander far off into the distance. He was like a dead person, someone whose only need at this point was a hand to close his eyes.

12. THE FINAL WALL

I have to think again, in fact to think all the time, about the significance of a friend's gift, the privilege of having him die in your arms.

I had put off getting involved in his life for a long time. I was the first and only person to be there at his death. Now many years have passed since Muhammad's death; I still regard the feeling as a starting point, although I do not know whether to express it now or later on. Maybe I should not be talking about it at all. There are certain insignificant ideas that should remain unexpressed, like a shadow or internal light buried deep in the heart. Even so, I can say that I have decided to start where he finished, like some kind of living fetus emerging from the womb of a dead body!

Right up to today I can still recall the creases in his crushed countenance as if I were looking straight at him now. I can see him alone and silent, his life a tissue of pain.

It was a strange sort of pain. He told me once that for him everything hurt; even the water used to wash him shared his pain. In saying that, he may have been recalling what Lamartine said in one of his poems about water, that "sad element" that "weeps with the entire world."

The pain he felt kept renewing itself, every single time he remembered an event, touched something, or looked at a picture, newspaper, magazine, or television. One thing I was sure of was that he had surrounded himself with a whole forest of memories and could not get rid of them. He never forgot those distant times in Paris and would always recall that city—its skies, its faces, its smells, its colors, its special flavor. He would talk about every single moment in the city, as though he were still living there and had never left. Many of the images and scenes he talked about issued from his eyes, and I would suggest that they were what furnished the light that he was using to see.

He had compressed his entire life into a single instant, and it had come to an end in a flash. While living in a single location, he had now become far distant from it. With regard to a single woman, he would recall the large circular face in every luminous moment before it suddenly vanished: in a glass of wine, for example, although its taste had abruptly turned bitter on his tongue. He would stare at the glass and see it was empty except for the dregs at the very bottom.

In imaginings, dreams, and fiction everything is simple and possible, and so Gertrude kept paying him visits, trying to apologize and be humble.

"Believe me, Mo," he would hear her say. "The voice that you heard was not mine. It wasn't me saying what it said and doing what it did. I love you. Please forgive me!"

He would push her image away and move on. She would catch up with him, move to the other side and stand in his path so he had to look at her, face to face. "When you left," she went on, "I didn't sleep that night. I couldn't even lie down on my own bed. I spent the entire night crying. Believe me, Mo, I love you. I made a mistake!"

Things actually work in the opposite way, of course. In reality there are things in life that are neither simple nor possible. Muhammad used to wake up to the sound of a vacuum crashing around deep inside him. Everything had changed; in effect, everything had come to an end. No longer could Gertrude sing her favorite song again: "I knew that the night that took you would bring you back to me. It's wonderful to wait for the ones we love!" He would keep hearing a single sentence here and there, one of a series of echoes from an entire record of cruel phrases that he had to swallow so as not to ruin the relationship.

"Luigi the barber told me…"

"Don't believe a bald barber," she interrupted without even letting him finish. "He doesn't respect the hair on your head. It would be better if he had some respect for what's inside your head, assuming, of course, that there is something!"

"Gerty," he said, "I'd like to ask you…"

"I can only answer," she replied curtly, "if you let me have the full essence of the question!"

There would follow the echo of her voice far away, sitting on her bed and asking him what the weather was like.

"It's cloudy today," he would say, to which her response would be, "Never mind; I'll get up and then the sun will shine on the world!"

She used to stand by the door of his room like an immovable mountain, looking arrogant and disgusted. "The day'll come," she said, "when Americans put my face on dollar bills!"

My face was close to the lighted candle on the dining table inside the Entrecôtes Restaurant in Rabat.

"What an exceptional woman!" I heard Lydia say, "Like a modern Sappho, mixing wine and love while rumors swirl around her, and winning."

"She didn't win," I say. "She lost him!" I hold my hand up for a moment. "Wait a minute and let me tell you the rest of the details first…"

He had confessed to me that his sense of humiliation was not just because she had got rid of him and he had left her apartment. It was more than that. He had just received a package from Paris. When he opened it, he found his pictures with Gertrude in Paris.

She had cut her face out of every single picture. Apparently this was to be an official announcement of the beginning of the end.

"That pig of a woman has thrown me out not just of her apartment but her entire life!"

He would keep on saying that to the very end of his life, photographs reduced by half or even more, destroyed by the scissors of oblivion!

I am trying to get Lydia to grasp the meaning of anger for a man who has been rejected. I do not think that the problems resided in the normal end to a relationship between a man and a woman, but rather that, after a man has shared body and soul with a woman, she suddenly shoves him away with a single sentence: "When you go out, don't forget to close the door behind you!" Those may be simple words for a woman to say, but for a man they are cruel and deeply wounding, words that stay with him for the rest of his life!

It was Lydia's opinion that Muhammad may have had enough time to think about things differently, but he did not wait to work it all out. In response I told her that, when things like that happen, it is only later that you start thinking about them; most of the time it is too late. Even so, I agreed with her in general. It felt as though I was remembering the way Muhammad talked about his hesitation before finally leaving his room on the roof and about his panic while crossing the Mediterranean by boat between Marseille and Tangier. He heard another passenger sitting beside him say, "So, brother, you're going back to your own country!" To this Muhammad replied, "To tell you the truth, I'm going back to reality!"

It was when the boat was close to Tangier and Muhammad was staring at the blue water under the sunny sky that he finally lost control and burst into tears. As he told me once, he did not know whether his mistake was emigrating to France or coming back home!

I have no idea how to count the number of hours I have spent with Lydia in Rabat restaurants and at her home. How many evenings have seen her leading me to her bed, and how many dawns have found me waking up in her arms. I think we both share the same level of emotion in our relationship and the same degree of caution as well, the same distance as demanded by common sense, the same quiver in the voice—almost like a frog in the throat—that tells everything. But her touch on my cheek is amazing, and the look that transfixes me makes me feel drowsy; I can only look back at her with dreamy eyes. Then comes that voice of hers.

"Be careful now. You may hurt the feelings of the rhino between your hands!"

I say nothing and change the theme so as not to hurt potentially sensitive feelings.

Lydia's voice haunts me all the time now. Even when she is not with me, her voice is there, that richly nuanced sound that I cannot describe exactly. I have started having powerful feelings for her, but some obscure sensation keeps holding them back.

I resumed. By now I was used to her moods and started thinking seriously about our relationship. It is her conception that only marriage can be the proper course of action for this secret, voiceless communion.

"So where are you," she asks, "with that lousy marriage of yours?"

In fact I have never told her that my marriage is lousy; she was the one who called it that so she could move on quickly to the conclusions she wished to draw. To a certain extent my marriage may have been tedious and problematic, but it was never a burden on me. Maybe lots of people have the same feeling about their marriages, but they do not come to hasty conclusions or remarry every single day. But that kind of talk never satisfied Lydia. As soon as I said that my family life was quite ordinary and did not suggest that there were going to be any explosions any time soon, her gaze would falter with disarming speed; I would watch as the light went out and the shrouded barrier that causes so much hurt to the oppressed horizons of lonely women would loom, one that can be breached only with an embrace and the retention of a little bit of hope in opportunities to come.

When we went back to her house, I was searching for the appropriate words. My companion was clearly not completely in agreement with her own self. I had no desire to lie to her and give her false hopes. Yes, there was genuine love, to be sure, but it kept holding back. There were actually twin desires rolled up into one, two bodies blending into one, but I had yet to be fully convinced of the pattern of this love. I had a strange fear, something like starlings scared of low-level traps or a hawk shot while hovering high in the sky.

She was looking straight at me. "One more glass, and I'm going to kiss you, you stubborn, spoiled Moroccan! Don't rush us to bed tonight. Don't you realize that bed is the most dangerous place in the whole world? That's what statistics show. I'm sure you've read about it in newspapers. About 92 percent of people die in bed!"

She laughed as she said that, stretching it out as much as she could. I noticed that Lydia was wearing a light spring top that did not cover her shoulders, and it looked as though she had taken off her brassiere as well. She put her hand in mine and intertwined our fingers. "And now," she told me, "I can give you the good news. We've had a positive response today from Washington about your trip to America. They've accepted our recommendation and agreed to all our selections and proposals regarding New York City, the Metropolitan, San Francisco, and the Alcatraz prison. So, as you can see, now you can complete the picture and finish your book about your friend as you wish. You'll get to see Gertrude's face directly in Picasso's portrait in that wonderful museum in New York. You'll see everything you need to see in order to write your book."

I told her how delighted I was and how much I looked forward to traveling. Her face lit up, and she looked thrilled by my reaction. With that we went back to our ardent relationship; she was eager, and I was as well.

As we were hugging each other, the shadow of a guard passed the salon's window at the back. The thin white curtain covered the windows, but it did nothing to conceal what was going on inside. No doubt, the guard did not see us (Did he really not see us?) Fingers crept under the night shirt toward the waist. She felt a stirring lower down.

"Wow, your hand's cold!"

She started to moan, softly and intermittently, that soft feeling, no doubt, that suddenly courses through the body when limbs talk to each other and soul responds to soul. A kind of electric current, a part of the brain that collects signals coming from a hand close to the pool; an amazing response from heart, liver, or soul; a sudden jolt to the nervous system; an ultimate state of detachment for the entire body; a spreading warmth; pores oozing perspiration. This time it was the shadow of a maidservant that passed by, clearly visible as she went over to the dog kennel (maybe taking the animal its dinner). For sure the servant did not see anything through the glass because our breathing had made it fog over, but she was already familiar with our habit of eating in one of Rabat's restaurants and then coming home late. Sigh after sigh after sigh, my hand resting on the honey of the bronze-colored body while her fingers had started slipping into the distant clouds. Lydia was no longer here, but up there on high as though carried on the wings of a cloud or as though a gently flowing river was leading her to the source of life itself like a drowned person.

Sometimes I get the impression that a bed can turn into a floating water surface; it moistens the soul so that it manages to relax. Sometimes too heaven can lower itself a little so as to re-cline naked on an affectionate, submissive surface. They exchange breaths and everything else…ah, ah, ah!

As usual, Lydia keeps up the pressure, using short sentences. "Why do you make your ideas so stilted?"

She wants me to be "realistic," as she puts it. The whole idea makes me laugh. Truth to tell, I have always behaved spontane-ously. That is the way I am. It is hard for me to remake myself. I speak with a habitual informality; I say what I think. I can't con-vert my daily life for presentation on a stage where I'm required to change masks and play a variety of roles with other people.

"You need another way of understanding things," she tells me. "You need to change your point of view!"

What she wants me to do is to change my skin, almost to turn into an opportunist. Who knows, maybe that's the way they all are. In that dull American embassy that looks just like a military barracks their major ambition is to succeed in their tasks and develop their administrative careers. A successful professional career is their perpetual goal. It seems that Lydia wants me to change my life-direction so as to face the embassy, up there on the hill overlooking the Abu Riqraq valley, a place where I can admire in all due humility the stars and stripes fluttering overhead where everyone can see it.

We both now went back to our herd, as the saying has it, and Gertrude wheedled her way in between us again. Lydia talked to me about the Metropolitan, that incredible museum exhibiting more than a million objects and paintings (can you imagine?), stretching over a broad area of a hundred and thirty thousand square meters (can you believe it?), and visited each year by about five million people (can you imagine?). She then started talking about the Gertrude portrait.

"At last you'll be able to see the actual portrait, the one you've loved only through pictures and books. You'll be able to have your picture taken alongside it if the guards will let you. I realize that they watch things like hawks over there and have to be extremely cautious, but I think they'll allow someone like you to do it as an official visitor sponsored by the State Department. You'll usually be accompanied by an official from Public Relations. Ah, what a wonderful place that is!"

Lydia noticed that, now that associations with Gertrude had provided the necessary stimulus, I was focusing on the minutest details of Gertrude's body. Lydia did not like the idea of my posing still more questions and expressing doubts about Gertrude as a dominant female.

"I don't know a lot about your profession as a writer," she said, "but I'd still like you to preserve Gertrude's status as a great woman. Don't try thrusting the camel through the eye of the needle and out again. True enough, she may have had her personal faults, but maybe she could not tolerate differences."

I nodded my head to give Lydia some reassurance and said nothing for a while. Needless to say, I was aware that I was writing about a woman via memory, not imagination. I had no intention of impugning her memory. What I was trying to explain to my girlfriend was that I was planning to reorganize that memory and other things. Gertrude had ideas about everything, wrote about everything, and did everything. I could not see how it would be possible to rewrite her selectively, instinctively, or ideally. I was not going to make things up, but neither did I wish to be the kind of historian who indulges in fancy digressions.

Lydia gave me a fixed look but said nothing, as though she was not convinced by my enthusiasm. Just then she turned her head and body toward me, as though a flash of light had gleamed deep down inside her. "Please give careful thought to the subject of your book. Have you ever asked yourself why a woman like Gertrude left her own country and looked for an alternative? Call it flight, call it renunciation, call it what you like. Whatever it was, it obviously was not a trip in search of sexual experience, whatever her temperament may have been. You need to think about Hemingway's situation, Miller, Fitzgerald, Paul Bowles, Burroughs, Ginsberg, Kerouac, Bokovsky, and many, many others. You're not asking why they fled, left the country, and attacked it. Be serious, I beg you; don't make light of their reasons. I already shared this conviction with you when we were at the Le Julien restaurant. Do you remember? These great people did not come to Europe, and some of them did not spend time in your country, merely in order to offer their backsides or in search of cocaine as some of your utterly irresponsible and tasteless writers have suggested."

While Lydia carried on reciting this litany of instructions, I remained silent.

"Please," she said, "don't rob the genuine past for the sake of a phony present. Get more serious."

This elevated tone she was using shocked me to the core. When I looked at her to verify that she meant what she was saying, her eyes looked completely sincere. I had never expected her to utter such severe words. Maybe she had always been that way, but I had preferred the softer side. Such bitterness may have been lurking inside her all the time, concealed in those recesses containing love, sympathy, and kindness; but now they had come to the surface in verbal form. Even so, I said nothing, preferring to listen and reflect. That did not stop me from telling myself that she could be right, but that her way of expressing it was wrong. Lydia paused for a while, but then continued in the same vein, although there was a certain amount of suppressed disappointment as well.

"Please don't make a mistake in your opinions and your writing," she told me. "When we go far away to make love with other people, it isn't because the men in our country are eunuchs or because the real he-men only exist in your country. There are men from Tangier who have spent time in America and behaved just like women over there; I am aware that you know that very well. Tennessee Williams has written about the shape of their backsides in his memoirs with a great deal of supercilious sarcasm, something that marks his particular style. I'm sure you're aware of that. There's no real difference between here and there. We can locate the phallus and its opposite; sex is a human trait with no nationality. Here I am right in front of you; in giving you my body, I'm not a whore. Quite the contrary, I'm living my life as I wish, spreading light deep inside me and behaving like any female human being. Please," Lydia said, to bring the night to a close. "Don't rob a great woman like Gertrude of her life's significance simply because she's dead now or happened one day to have a disagreement with a friend of yours."

She wanted me to spend the night with her, but I put on my coat and left. I did not like her tone of voice, although I respected the clarity of her vision. At the door I said farewell to the guard. "Good night, Abu Rahhuw!"

He was wide awake. He had a glass of tea by his side, along with a transistor radio so he could listen as usual to the news on the hour and the nighttime program. I thanked him and walked away, hoping that I could find a taxi on the street. I was still bearing in mind the things Lydia had told me and thinking about Muhammad and Gertrude...and then about Lydia herself and me.

"You're supposed to realize when you've become a routine part of a relationship or when it's time to withdraw. It's better to separate again before we're struck by the volcano!"

On my way home I thought about the trip to America. Lydia was still insistent that it was crucial for me to travel there to find out about Gertrude's country, along with the culture and society.

"You need to write about things you know, not things you don't," she told me.

That managed to convince me, even though I did not totally believe her.

Ever since I had decided to see this game through to its conclusion, I had made up my mind to learn, investigate, and find out things. From Lydia I had come to realize that writing a book could not rely on memory alone. What a friend had told us was not enough; I had to consult books and other people, to listen to those who had also shared a friendship with Muhammad in case they reminded me of something I had forgotten or through talking to them I stumbled on a detail about him that had escaped my notice. As far as possible, I needed to visit all the places where he had been. I had thought of visiting Paris, the Rue de Fleurus, Rue Madame, the Luxembourg Gardens, the Basilica of Saint Sulpice, Rue de Vaugirard, Boulevard du Montparnasse, Boulevard Raspail, Rue Saint Marseille, Gare Austerlitz…and other places. Lydia had added New York to the list, the Metropolitan Museum, and Gertrude's portrait. I was very enthusiastic. The book was still just for Muhammad, but it was now my personal project; I had to produce it for my own sake as well. When it came to that famous, wonderful, cursed portrait which had so disrupted my friend's life, I would make it the first thing I went to see after my arrival in New York. As soon as I was settled in, I would rush to see it. But I would not just be seeing it; I would touch it, smell its paint, and use my vision to erase it, to make a copy to take away with me, in my memory's gaze and deep inside me: its colors, its lines, its light and shade, the smell of the wood frame, and its fabric. I would note down its exact position in the exhibit, how other people looked at it, how they drew close and then moved away. Were they able to take a picture of it or have their own picture taken with it? Was it attractive enough to make it possible to draw the attention of people all around it; by which I mean, did it still have a life of its own, especially now that both painter and model had moved on forever?

Oh dear, if only Muhammad had thought about it seriously and at the proper time, he could have written the book of his life as he should have written it. Everything was close to hand and within his purview, inside his very self. Even today I cannot really understand why he could not do it. Sometimes I tell myself that he may have thought the whole thing fairly simple at first, especially since people often tell themselves that writing only involves composing your life adventure: to live life, remember it all, describe it on paper, and that's it! But, of course, the basis of the enterprise is the adventure of writing itself, that vision that helps you remember, imagine, organize, describe, and invent things; that you know where and how to begin and when and how to bring things to an end. Writing involves style; the writer is the style, in fact; or, even more than that, "the style is the man himself," to quote that eighteenth-century French academic, the Comte de Buffon.

Muhammad dug deep into the recesses of his memory, to the furthest point possible, and came back to us—as we sat in the Café Paris—with minute details about events, names, and aspects of the life he had led. We were not particularly attentive, nor did he record everything he recalled. It was as though he were escorting us to his secret gardens far away and allowing us to pass through the fence and go inside. However, we did not look at the same flowers as he did nor in the way he chose to look at them. A thick curtain hung between us and his buried memories. At this point I could not recall very much, even those few expressions that I wrote down eagerly with a view to writing but that did not seem particularly helpful when it came to producing something worthwhile.

It is really a shame that we never train ourselves to write diaries at the time things are happening. As a result, when we decide to write about our lives, it is almost impossible to do so; we have to rely on vague, faulty, and even distorted memories. That leads in turn to lies, forgeries, and recalibration of details. Truth to tell, life involves being with other people. When it is right in front of us and before our very eyes, we lose interest in it because of sheer habit, almost as if it is not our life or it is all happening in our absence. When we decide to write about it, we have to approach it from afar, like a past we are trying to recover or, let's say, like a process of forgetting that presents itself in a fragmentary and disjointed form.

Life is a question of details, continuous details that give life meaning and additional value, tiny, fleeting details whose enormous value only time can confirm. We lose a great deal when we discover that we have not recorded all those details and that forgetfulness is now our partner, sharing all details and non-details with our memory. That, in a word, was Muhammad's special fault, the painful shortcoming that colored his entire life, something he did his best to conceal from other people and even from himself. As is the case with all of us, he never bothered about details at the time. It is not a little odd that people suppose that their profession involves ignoring details because they are not important. The profession involves gestures, but they are never collected.

It is only now that I recall his boisterous laugh as we walked together along the Tangier shoreline. He used to tell me about the glory days at the Hotel Villa de France where Gertrude and Alice stayed (and Matisse before them); about the Procuré Général's office, the seat of the French Consul where Delacroix stayed in 1830; and the Bar Central where Saint-Saens had been inspired to write some of his music (and especially "Danse macabre"). We walked slowly, exchanging jokes, laughter, and memories, before locating a spot at the Café La Pergola.

"Maybe the only mistake I made in Paris," he told me jokingly, "was that I hesitated about marrying Gertrude when the opportunity was there." He laughed so hard at that that his eyes teared up. "But," he went on, "I came back to Tangier and left her like a virgin!"

With that he suddenly got to his feet, clasping his arms to his chest as though doing a congregational prayer, and started reciting Baudelaire, much of whose poetry he had memorized by heart and whose short prose poems in *Le Spleen de Paris* he adored: "'A woman always wanted to be a man. 'You're not a man. Ah, if only I were a man! Among the two us, I am the man! [*Vous n'êtes pas un homme. Ah, si j'étais un homme! De nos deux, c'est moi qui suis l'homme!*].'" ["Portrait de maîtresses," no. 42]

He quoted the lines relying on his memory, reciting them in an almost Sufi fashion, as though for him memory were an open book hidden behind a veil. In the poem in question four men are talking in turn about their experiences with women. The first of them talks about the "mediocrity" of women, while the second wishes that his behavior had not been a mistake—but for that, he says, he would have married his beloved. Muhammad ground out the words with his teeth as though stomping a cigarette butt with his shoes: "'Sometimes I regret it all. I should have married her. [*Quelques fois je la regrette. J'aurais dû l'épouser.*]'"

As Muhammad recited this poem, I could envision him as the person in the poem itself, as though he could see Baudelaire sitting in the café with three other men. A wonderful piece of luck had come his way, but he had made a mistake and never compromised. The beautiful woman had gone away and married someone else to produce six offspring like the children in fairy stories. "'Very well, dear friend. The bride is as much a virgin as your mistress was. Nothing has changed about this person! [*Eh bien! mon cher ami, l'épouse est encore aussi vierge que l'était votre maîtresse. Rien n'était changé dans cette personne!*]'"

He kept talking about the background to this poem, one he felt deeply and, one might say, suffered. I took note of the way his voice crumbled.

"My friend," he told me, "I have to confess. Trust me. The topic of women in conjunction with men is always an impossible subject. There can be no sure answers! Even in the best of circumstances all you get are a few indications that may need to be combined before you can glean a tiny bit from them. Failing that, you have to forget about confessions.... In fact, you may not understand anything at all!" His tone of voice sounded like that of a lonely man. "I was there…and that's that. Now I'm here, and that's that, too!"

With that he took his seat again and looked out to sea. He said nothing more, nor did I. As I looked over at him, his gaze was far away somewhere. The thin thread of terminal shadow had started to appear, that wavering condition that starts ever so slowly to wend its way into the internal makeup of people advanced in age.

"Poetry has always helped me," he said. "In Baudelaire, Mallarmé, and Rimbaud I can always find things to describe my situation. I often ask myself why we bother to write when other people have already written everything that we need! Even so, other people's poetry will never take you as far as you need to go. It touches your particular situation, then leaves and moves on to other people's situations. Even now I have never found a poem stored in my memory that can really engage with my former malleability with Gertrude. That pig of a woman was stronger than I, and I only realized what was happening to me when it was too late. In that relationship I was impelled by genuine feelings that were both sincere and trusting, whereas what it seems I was being asked to do was to live on the basis of wanton feelings and behave as though I were convinced by them. I did not do that; needless to say, I would not have done so even if I had realized the way things were going to turn out. I have to admit all this now, not because of some ethical posture on my part, nor to salve my conscience, but simply for some instinctive sense to which I cannot even give a name!"

Paris had gradually started to fade in his vision; it no longer possessed that fabulous quality that had stayed with him through all the years he had spent in Tangier since his return from exile. By now it had turned into a foggy kind of image, just as images tend to be cloudy in the eyes of someone who has slept badly.

I do not know if I have the right to suggest that in Paris he had in fact lost his soul.

After his return to Tangier he was never anything but a ruin, always distracted, as though in a deep slumber. He would stagger his way along the streets as though balancing on a suspended wire. At the end his equilibrium gave way, as he told me on many occasions. In Tangier he no longer had a regular routine as he had before. Even Tangier itself had changed a lot from the way it had been; as though he had left it as a young man and returned later to find that it had lost its virginity and turned into a whore. The bride had grown old before her time. At that period his own relationship with the city had turned sour, and he could no longer recognize the primary features that identified his own life's city—and maybe the features of his own identity as well!

Even though he had actually stopped drinking, he looked drunk all the time, tottering as he walked and slurring his words. All around him empty spaces extended into the distance. He and the city by the sea embarked upon a savage, silent feud, never even exchanging pleasant sentiments, each never sensing any need on the part of the other. Tangier felt standoffish and ungrateful, more antagonistic toward him, like a cat eating one of its own kittens. He seemed discontented, aggravated, disgusted, as though he were being pulled down in a riptide whose forces of give and take he could not see. He became much more touchy, more angry, more morose, as if he had lost his store of memories, his entire past.

By now he was really old. His hair was white, as was his rounded beard. His face glowed with his wounded sentiments and a flood of suppressed anger. A glimmer of something akin to death began to show itself. At the time he was still insisting that he was going to write his life. He had tried to start by writing down details he had forgotten, but his memory had failed him; he had even tried to start actually writing as best he could, but that had failed too. As is usual with us folk from the Middle East, he kept putting things off, imagining that time was not actually slipping away and that he still had plenty of time to produce his book. He only finally resorted to me when, as he told me, he discovered that his life was indeed fading away, day by day, hour by hour, minute by minute, second by second. But by that time he was already a shadow of his former self, overtaken by weakness and self-paralysis.

I gave him my word. At first it was merely a passing phrase, but it gradually turned into a commitment. So here I am writing the book now, both for him and for me. I would be lying if I said that I'm writing it for other people as well.

We are not doing wrong when we write things that others can write, the kind of people who simply have things to say, so they lose out on the sheer joy of writing and life itself and forfeit the precious gift of simplicity. At base, when we write, we do it only through other people. The writer is like a storyteller, relating his tales in the public domain to a small passing group of listeners. There he stands, straddling eras while the story comes to him from some point in the past and runs through his body to some other period. The writer writes what he lives, what he reads, what he hears; he writes what others have written before him. There has never existed a writer who starts from a complete vacuum in order to be able to write. Every writer is other writers, other people, other books, other lives, and so on…

Whenever we write what we write, we are in one way or another simply rewriting something that has been written before, as though we are revealing the secret alphabet of the book of the world lurking on our pages, which we assume to be blank; as though we are living again the lives led by many others before us, reenvisioning the same acts, roles, and events that happened before us. That is why, when we write a fresh sentence, we usually ask ourselves where we have read it before. If we draw a new face in a poem or painting, we ask the same question: where did I see that face before? Like life itself, writing is a continuity of elements that are constantly repeated, and we are in constant need of the signposts on the road so that we can recall the steps we have taken. We need those elements from the past that come to us and indeed the ones that are to come from the future as well, so that we can remember and then write, forget and then write, imagine and then write. It is as though we do not actually repeat what others have already written but rather live a kind of life that others have lived. In writing, destinies often come together, since it is possible for a person to swim in the same river that others have swum in before. For that reason people do not die as long as they have things to write, remember, or restore them to life in some other guise.

A week has passed since the last night at Lydia's house.

To tell the truth, I had no idea why I found it necessary to get so angry about a point of view that, upon reflection, had its justifications. I realized that I might have been too hasty in my reactions. What worried me in particular was the idea that Muhammad's former stance might have got the better of me, which led me to behave in such a negative way. Once in a while the motives of other people will infiltrate us without our even being aware of it, at which point we will chase after a shadow, a trace, or a scent, abandoning a beautiful place or a wonderful moment, especially when people we love are involved. Regret comes later. And that is the way it was with me, regretting that night as I made my way home after enjoying Lydia's kisses.

That proved to be a nasty night for me; I felt a chill running through my body like a tomb covered in green moss, buried in ocean depths.

A kind telephone call from Lydia came to my aid. She called to wish me a happy birthday; she was the only one who remembered. I myself had forgotten it for years. She was teasing me as though nothing had happened, and, in spite of everything, I needed to hear her voice. No sooner had I finished talking to her in my office at the newspaper and put the receiver back in its place than her personal messenger arrived with a bouquet of red roses along with a tiny neat card saying "Happy Birthday and Many Happy Returns! I hope you'll get in touch with our office to complete the procedures for your trip to the United States—signed L.A."

I called her again. "You didn't tell me you'd sent me a bouquet of roses," I said. "Now you've done me two favors!"

Over the telephone she laughed her usual laugh tinged with that lovely soft twang. "My dear sir," she said, "I can distinguish between the demands of work and those of friendship!"

With that we exchanged some small talk and agreed to meet again soon. (Can I actually do it?)

I got in touch again with my friend Mustafa al-Sallami and told him that I was going to New York. He told me that he had known about it from the beginning and was happy to accept the suggestion that I make the trip. Mustafa was a highly cultured and attentive person, but he was no longer the way he had been when we were both adolescents; his current image in no way reflected his earlier one. He had turned into a veritable lexicon of religious terms and phrases that were perpetually on his tongue. You would see him walking distractedly, his beard turned white before its time. The prayer mark on his forehead and an august air of piety added about ten years to his age.

In spite of the best efforts of time and age, I never lost my affection for him. I believe that he too kept renewing his feelings of friendship for me, even though he would not allow me to take him back to memories of earlier days. In my opinion he provides a good example of the shrinking of certain initiatives in our country. I do not wish, of course, to question his commitment, but I do not know how it is possible for a gentle, open personality, bursting with joie de vivre to be converted into someone completely different—and all attached to the same body and the same name; someone over-cautious, always preparing for death, the punishment of the tomb, and the next world, and meanwhile dealing with the world with a generous dose of vague intuition.

Si Mustafa escorted me to a back office in the American Embassy building, then left. Lydia was waiting for me at the entrance to a large portico; once inside the office, she remained standing, while I sat down opposite some of her assistants—Suzanne, Angelina, and Dominique—who proceeded to provide me with information about my trip to New York and other American cities and states. The visit was to last for a month.

"It's good that you've chosen May for the trip," Lydia told me.

"It's the best spring month over there," Dominique added, with a lively expression on her pretty face.

"But spring's short," Lydia went on, "and summer comes charging in during the second half of the season. That's the way it always is in New York."

"Ah well, you're going to visit my own city," Angelina said as she congratulated me on the trip. "It's where I was born. Good luck to you in the 'Big Apple'! My mind and heart are both there. Say hello to its wonderful districts, Little Italy and Brooklyn Bridge, both of which I adore!"

The various procedures came to an end, and I learned everything about the trip and the travel plan: Casablanca–Amsterdam–New York. I would be spending five days in that city, one that was always on its feet, night and day; then I would go on to

Seattle, Santa Fe in New Mexico, San Francisco, Boston, and Washington, DC. Everything was clear, precise, and carefully prepared. I did not pause for a moment, but immediately started thinking about the Metropolitan Museum; more precisely, about the shape and size of Gertrude's portrait.

"Hah," said Lydia, "where have you gone? I see you've started the trip. Are you in New York already?"

I looked straight at her. She was still standing right in front of me, although by now her gaze had slipped a bit. "You're right," I told her. "I was on my way into the Metropolitan!"

I have no idea how or why I suddenly imagined Lydia as a thievish character in Henri Barbus's novel *Hell*, gradually making off with parts of me through a small aperture in my interior wall. As she gave me a look that was almost as good as having sex, I felt as if she were in charge of my soul.

I had already arrived in New York when I thought about her again out of a feeling of gratitude for everything she had done for me. I sensed a good deal of happiness in our relationship. Actually, a rapid and difficult heartbeat does not necessarily imply love; some relationships can never tolerate adjustments, however favorable the circumstances. There are obviously a large number of factors that make life possible, but there are just as many others that make it difficult. I realize that writers write, poets emote, singers sing, and actors act, and all so that possibilities may vanquish difficulties. That said, even when people are full of conviction, most of the time they still have no idea what to do with their feelings. But I am prepared to admit to being corrupted by reality. Whenever I fail to find someone on whom to unleash my psychological wounds, I always burst into tears. If people offer to do me a favor and give me emotional support, I consistently refuse to accept any sympathy.

I found a small, suitable place for myself in the Madison

Hotel. It is always difficult to sleep on your first night in New York; in fact there are any number of reasons for not sleeping on any of the other nights as well. Even when I was feeling exhausted from all the walking around, I tossed and turned in bed trying to find a way of falling asleep.

"Tomorrow I'm going to the Metropolitan Museum. I plan to spend the whole day there."

New York is indeed a real city, one that gives you the best possible example of the sheer power with which mankind can interfere in nature so as to reform the world. It felt as though I were walking in a completely open movie scenario, with films, scenes, images, and numerous faces coalescing; as though Martin Scorsese, Francis Coppola, Blake Edwards, or Sergio Leone were sitting in some lofty spot, directing this amazing world from behind their cameras. I stare in amazement at the Yellow Cabs and immediately see the image of Robert De Niro armed and in uniform in "Taxi Driver" ("You talkin' to me?").

The weather was humid, the sun in New York seemed very close, and the temperature was so hot that I felt as though I had washed in salt. This was a city on the fly, with any number of surprises, as though I had come to the realization here in New York, amidst the forest of cement, iron, and glass, that we usually look at all the ironies and differences around us with a good deal of surprise and curiosity. That is because we all carry within us a bucolic tendency of long standing or else a deep-seated instinctive urge without the need for that to imply a state of innocence. I opened my eyes and was astonished; I closed them again and carried on walking so I would not be dazzled, or lose my way, or capitulate. I had not come here to capitulate, nor was my journey a quest for fortune. I came from another kind of system. For me money was neither a dream nor a fantasy, but simply a means of working—nothing more. So why this vortex that makes the void a way of shaping our life?

Long, endless streets, moving swiftly on their way to the distant horizon. From the outset I felt that the day was too short for the Manhattan streets; it was only at night that this street could lead me to the Metropolitan. In New York I became aware of the meaning of carrying the burden of your own self, as I made my way along the street teeming with people, listening to all the voices around me and others further away—including especially Muhammad's voice, which had started echoing in my ear as softly as a tassel's rustle. Here in New York, amid the bustle of colorful crowds and the cacophony of voices, I was able to a certain extent to remember my own self, even though, like everyone else, I was being dragged along the street, thirsty and dry-lipped, doing my best to find bits of shade, wall by wall, corner by corner. On the way I kept thinking of Anaïs Nin talking about New York.

"I was walking with a friend of mine"—and she mentioned the name to Muhammad, but he had forgotten it). "'Let's run, Anaïs,' he told me. 'If we run fast, we won't have to see how ugly New York really is!'"

As I strolled around this elemental city, I did not see any ugliness. I continued on my way. After passing dozens of alleyways, streets, and sidewalks, I climbed the marble steps to the Metropolitan Museum. I had seen it so often in films and read so much about it in poems and novels that I now felt that New York was an old friend of mine. I was impressed by the fantastic museum rising like a Greek temple over Olympus.

Mrs. Deborah Roth, the Public Relations official at the museum took me to her office on the top floor. "Our museum was built along with the first skyscrapers at the end of the nineteenth century," she told me. "It was part of an artistic renaissance in our city at that time. It was begun at the same time as Carnegie Hall, the New York Botanical Garden, and the Statue of Liberty."

I listened carefully to Mrs. Roth. She had dark blonde hair and was neatly dressed in a light green dress. She was close to sixty. She offered me a cup of coffee and went on to tell me that she was very sorry to convey two pieces of bad news at the start of my visit; she nevertheless hoped that it would be fruitful. I remained silent, doing my best to put on a resolute front as she moved her hands, obviously trying to lighten the atmosphere as much as possible. There was however no connection between her hand gestures and the bad news I had to hear.

"The first piece of news has to do with the museum director, Mr. Bill Lieberman," she told me, "who apologizes profusely because he has an urgent matter to attend to and thus cannot welcome you in person. He has left you this catalogue of some of the objects found in the museum."

She handed me a beautiful book, and I read a tiny business card attached to the outside cover: "Dear Mr. Hasan, I'm sorry to miss you. This catalogue contains a special file of pictures of Alice Toklas. I do hope that we can meet some time soon."

"But, Madam, the appointment was arranged over two months ago," I said, bursting into a sweat,. "from over there in Rabat and here in Washington."

"That's true, sir," she replied calmly, "but it was something unavoidable."

So what was the other news, I wondered. I was turning over the pages of the expensive book, looking at some of the museum's collection of paintings from the 1895–1950 period in Paris. The svelte lady now started to tell me that this month the Gertrude portrait was currently not in the museum either. What? What was that she just said?

"As you've just heard, sir, we've sent that painting to the National Museum in London for a Picasso-Matisse exhibit there. I'm sure you've read about it in the press. You surely know that Gertrude lived close to those two great artists in Paris and owned a number of their works. She wrote books and articles about them both…and so on. I have to tell you, of course, that our museum has a cooperative exchange with the London museum; our administration cannot ignore the agreement. I'm sure you understand."

For a few moments I sat there stunned, while the woman stood there assessing from my facial expression the impact of what she had just told me.

"However, sir, the portrait will be coming back at the end of this month. After London, the exhibit is going to Paris, then Amsterdam, then St. Petersburg, but in accordance with our exchange agreement the Gertrude portrait is only on exhibit in London. If you're planning to stay till the beginning of next month, you'll be able to see the portrait as soon as we get it back!"

It was almost as though this woman, Deborah Roth, had been practicing the process of giving me this dreadful news, because she handed me a large envelope, telling me that it contained three detailed scientific studies on the Gertrude portrait. She then asked me if I wished to visit any particular wings of the museum and told me that she was ready to accompany me.

I thanked her for being so kind, then asked her if she was from England or had at least some origins there. She asked me why.

"I have the impression that you're from there," I replied immediately. "Cool blood seems to run in your veins, and you have the calm features of an English woman!"

I asked her simply to take me to the place where the Gertrude portrait was normally hung.

"Of course, I'll be glad to," she replied, and we went back to the elevator.

On the first floor Deborah walked a little way beside me, then pointed to a brown wall at the back of the huge hall of modern art. I stretched out my hand to thank this mature American woman, whose green dress and thin stature made her look like the Statue of Liberty. I stared at the long brown wall. There may well have been other paintings hanging there and indeed there may have been one in the place where Gertrude's portrait normally hung until it came back, but for me the wall was completely empty. I was feeling really upset because I felt the whole trip had been wasted; actually it had been over right from the outset. As I made for the exit, I looked down at my hand; it was empty and sweaty. But the delay in writing the book about Muhammad was not my hand's fault. Instead, what was needed was to produce a hand that was mature enough to be able to write, to prepare a body that was in tune with spirit and memory, and maybe with the imaginaire as well. In fact, basic primary material was required for the act of writing: a little gratification, patience, research, attention, modesty, and silence…and a lot of talent!

As I left the museum, I counted the steps like a child playing on the stairs of the neighbors' building: four steps, then a small walkway, then eight more steps beyond which was a small horizontal space on which hordes of visitors and tourists were sitting, then four more steps. As I went down, I was counting and looking at each step, one by one. Each one was made of carefully carved grey marble, just like Roman stones—twenty-eight steps in all. Once I reached the sidewalk, I started walking along with the crowds of other people and watched the street artists and people selling pictures and mementos made of wood and wire, crafted by skillful hands like those of the Chinese.

I stopped for a moment at the corner. New York taxis are so eye-catching with their bright yellow color; there seem to be more of them than of private cars. Images of Muhammad now keep flashing before my eyes and deep inside me. We are sharing our raucous laughter of old and exchanging the same old gentle conversation on the sidewalk by the Café Paris in Tangier. I watch as passersby rush to beat the clock; faces, expressions, colors, languages from every continent. I have read a lot about Babel, but here it is on the street, in Manhattan, here in New York. I laugh, and a passerby stares at me in amazement. I point my finger at Muhammad, and he does the same to me. I give him a military salute in the same old way. My tricky question surprises him.

"So, Abu Muhammad," I say, "is all this craziness for the sake of a fat, masculine woman? Ha, ha, ha…!"

"And what about you?" he replies. "What kind of luck did you have in the end?"

"Shut up, you!" I say. "My American woman was quieter, nicer, and prettier. But my feelings are closed and unreliable. I'm a disaster!"

Seeing his image in front of me on Fifth Avenue, I admitted the truth to him. In a flash it occurred to me that I would eventually be turning away from this book project. Whereas I had always assumed that things were simple in novels, it was exactly the opposite; I would need to suffer through Muhammad's book in order to be able to write it. As I kept recalling his tiniest gesture, he stayed in front of me all the time. Once I started writing, no one and nothing distracted me. In fact, my dear Lydia Altman was an enormous help; if it were not for her, and her fingers on the piano keys and the soft parts of my body, her loving voice as she sang Bessie Smith's song, "My house fell down, and I can't live there no more…" How that song manages to go beyond the limits of mere tears: a song about a disaster, a fierce storm that turns the sky dark, then arrives to rip off the door, destroy the house, and drown everything. I loved that song too; it came to project a disruption of another kind, a musical message that allowed Lydia to cry. I would wipe away her tears, clasp her naked shoulders, grab her moist hand, lead her into the other room, and turn out the light.

No sooner had the subway arrived than I got on and threw myself into the first available seat. I felt happily tired and immediately realized that I was happy with myself, full of an invigorating internal sense of peace. I took out the novel *The Sound and the Fury* again and told myself I would pick up from the place where I had bent over the page that morning. I love Faulkner, that amazing American writer, who demands that you like him in spite of his occasional long, tiring sentences. I started reading, listening to Compson repeating what he had heard from his father:

> *Don't spend all your breath trying to conquer it [time].*
> *Because no battle*
> *is ever won, he said. They are not even fought. The field only*
> *reveals to man*
> *his own folly and despair, and victory is an illusion of*
> *philosophers and fools.*

On one of the underground subway branch lines I had a strange feeling, as though I were on my way to some extra-terrestrial place. Maybe I was just tired or had had a surfeit of scenes from this cinema of scientific imagination, or else the shape and structure of the subway train with its silver color, screeching noise, and rapid pulsing rhythm like a space ship. I no longer knew whether I was still looking in the subway glass or my eyelids had drooped in a pleasant kind of nap. But I see Muhammad's face once again, seemingly drawn in the mist right in front of me. There he is, enmeshed in my gaze, squeezed between the passengers on the silver subway train which is even now transporting me out of the ground. I see him too in the distant shadow, in the dark green grass, lying on his back. Gertrude has thrown herself on top of him, her ample bosom exposed—a fully ripe apple that has fallen off its lofty branch to offer thanks to the earth. I see her get up and move away like a hyena leaving its prey. Then I spot Bakhta, descending on his shoulder like a white bird, as though she is rousing him from a snooze; I see them next like two shadows, linking and unifying in the light of his gaze, then disappearing. Then everything vanishes, and I come to myself, walking distractedly along Madison Avenue on my way back to the hotel, with my own fears preceding me. The image of Muhammad almost gleams underneath that dark cloud, seemingly suspended on high from the universe's ceiling. I almost hear his voice at the end, the very end—I mean, the sound of his regret and dejection, or something else I do not even know: the sound of his death, if you will.

"I hereby consign to you my trust. You have given me your word. Fine. You have to write the book of my life. Treat it as your own book, and score a victory for your brother!"

So that is what I have done; I have written it. And here is its final set of proofs.

DESTINIES
(A SHORT GUIDE)

GERTRUDE STEIN

[Note: The name "Stein" is pronounced the German way: "Shtein."]

Gertrude died recently at the American Hospital in Paris of colon cancer. She had had an operation which did not spare her life.

One of the doctors stated that she had woken up immediately after the operation. They heard her ask, "What's the answer?" (Granted, the pain may not have let things be all that clear.) Then she sank back into her unconscious state, which proved to be terminal.

Days before her death, she had composed her will, in which she bequeathed her valuable art collection to the new Guggenheim Art Museum in New York. The famous portrait of her by Picasso was given to the Metropolitan Museum in the same city.

She left nothing to Alice B. Toklas.

[*Encyclopedia Americana*, Vol. 25, o. 673]

ALICE TOKLAS

Alice stayed on her own in Paris, forgotten, in the new apartment, 5 Rue Christine. She had lived with Gertrude for thirty-eight years: two bodies in one, two spirits blending into one, their flesh and breathing intermingled. When Gertrude died, Alice virtually died as well. She remained a mere shadow, like a corpse walking around the rooms in the empty apartment.

Once in a while she would respond to friends' letters. Among them was a letter of condolence that came from Muhammad, who was living in Tangier at the time. She replied briefly but politely, not forgetting to include in the letter a sad reference to herself: "It is my fate now," she wrote, "to live alone."

PICASSO

Picasso could not stand Gertrude's domination for long. He stopped agreeing with her about anything, and she reciprocated the sentiment. The relationship cooled, and the split lasted for an entire year. They met only by chance at Adrienne Monnier's home.

"How are you?" he asked her. "You should come and visit me!"

"No," she replied. "I'll never come, and that's definite!"

He turned to Alice who was standing next to her. "Is she serious?" he asked.

"If Gertrude replies that way," Alice told him, "what it means is that that's the only response you'll get!"

They encountered each other again at an art opening. Picasso came up to Gertrude in the hall and grabbed her by the shoulder. "Enough," he said. "From now on, this enmity must stop."

"Agreed!" she replied, and they hugged each other.

"Now," Picasso continued, "when shall I see you?"

"I'm afraid we're both busy," Gertrude replied, "but come at the end of the week and we'll have dinner together."

"No," he interrupted, "I'll come by tomorrow, but I won't stay for dinner."

And indeed he did come by the next day.

In his last visit to Gertrude, Picasso was totally shocked when he saw that Gertrude had cut her hair short, thus getting rid of her enduring feminine hair garland.

"Now the portrait doesn't look like you at all," he told her. "You've destroyed my work!"

People say that that was his last visit to the apartment at 27 Rue de Fleurus.

ANAÏS NIN

She adamantly refused to meet Gertrude ever again. In her renowned diaries she writes: "I met Gertrude only once. I did not like her because she insisted on imposing her own dominant personality on me and everyone around her."

Nin was the lover of Gonzalo, Henry Miller, Antoine Artaud (before he went mad), and many other men. She started running away from love when she discovered over and over again that (as she put it) she "kept falling into traps," and "she always felt bewitched and enslaved."

Even so, when of necessity she separated from Gonzalo, a young man named Pablo entered her life immediately ("and in an enjoyable fashion," as she recorded in her diaries).

GONZALO

Gonzalo was not successful in directing the small press that Anaïs set up for him. He spent too much time on political activity among the workers and émigrés from Latin America. He had elaborate dreams about revolution everywhere and was always ready to sacrifice his life for the cause. Anaïs said that "he had an unrivalable bodily courage, but it was one devoted to death rather than life."

No one has ever claimed that he became a poet or that he achieved much success as an artist either.

In her diaries Anaïs records that "I started to feel constricted by the pressure of work in the press. I could no longer put an end to Gonzalo's problems." In another part of the diaries, she notes: "Things are getting more complicated at the press. Gonzalo has caused a number of problems, breaking promises, not meeting deadlines for production of books, and not keeping up the accounts…"

Gonzalo returned to his homeland. His projects faltered, and his relationship with Anaïs was completed severed. It was the Peruvian consulate in Paris that finally gave him the ticket to go home.

BERNARD, THE FRENCH FRIEND

His mother died a short while after Muhammad's departure from Paris. He continued to take care of his invalid sister for some ten years until she too departed on her eternal journey.

Muhammad told me that he finally settled in a rest home in a Paris suburb. The two friends continued to correspond with each other by letter and congratulatory cards.

"My loyal friendship with him never faltered," Muhammad told me once.

LYDIA ALTMAN

After serving her country in a number of posts both within and outside America, she eventually became her country's Consul General in France.

She visited the Père Lachaise cemetery in Paris and put a bouquet of flowers on Gertrude's grave.

To all intents and purposes I lost contact with Lydia, although she did occasionally send me postcards or courtesy letters. The last one may have included a picture of Gertrude's grave with a bouquet of flowers on it.

That bouquet became one of Lydia's regular Parisian customs.

THE FORD, GERTRUDE'S CAR

The last Ford car (called "Aunt Godiva"), after having a number of French owners, finished up with an Italian who belonged to an association of antique car enthusiasts in Assisi, near Perugia.

I saw it during a car show. I had received a generous invitation from my friend Francesco Picchi and his wife, Rosanna, to spend time in their lovely, cozy wooden house in Gualdo Tadino, that tiny city that I loved so much.

I was astonished to discover that they were raising a male and female wolf inside their home.

"Wolves don't do any harm," Francesco told me. "It's human beings that hurt wolves. People get scared of the pictures of wolves they've made up in their imaginations."

I immediately expressed a desire to raise a pair of my own wolves, but I no longer have any faith in the loyalty of dogs!

OTHER PEOPLE

MOLDOVAN

He managed to set up a nightclub on a back street off Boulevard du Montparnasse in Paris. People also told me he had acquired a fast-food place on Rue Notre Dame des Champs.

HELENA

She linked up with a young gypsy from the Roma and left with him for parts unknown. No traces of her remain. Muhammad always remembered her with relish. "With her," Muhammad told me once in his characteristically simple way, "there was night and no morning." By which I assume he meant that night took her away and, when morning broke, she was no longer there.

THE NARRATOR

I have now given up the newspaper career; I was fired by a dreadful newspaper that suddenly adopted a thoroughly vague and ambiguous editorial direction. I "failed" (meaning actually that I refused) to fall in behind the newspaper's editor, a highly regarded politician who was himself very fond of "falling in" behind virtually everybody and presented himself as a leader even though he was in essence a has-been.

I still compose poetry with a passion, although I have lost the pleasure derived from getting published. I no longer like the readership.

ABOUT THE AUTHOR

Born in 1960, **Hassan Najmi**, Moroccan poet, novelist, journalist, and educator, is a major figure in the cultural life of his country. Between 1998 and 2005 he was twice elected as president of the Moroccan Writers Union, and in 2007 his prominent role as a poet was recognized by his election as president of the Moroccan "House of Poetry." In addition to his activities as a littérateur, he has occupied many administrative positions in the cultural sector and journalism. In 2006 he was awarded a doctoral degree in Arabic literature by Muhammad the Fifth University in Rabat.

ABOUT THE TRANSLATOR

In 2011 **Roger Allen** retired from his position as Professor of Arabic and Comparative Literature at the University of Pennsylvania. The author of many books and articles on the Arabic literary tradition (including *The Arabic Novel* [Syracuse University Press, 1995] and *The Arabic Literary Heritage* [Cambridge University Press, 1998]), he has also published a large number of translations of modern Arabic fiction, by authors including Naguib Mahfouz, Yusuf Idris, Hanan al-Shaykh, `Abd al-Rahman Munif, Salim Himmich, and Ahmad al-Tawfiq. In 2012 he was awarded the Saif Ghobash Banipal Prize for his translation of Himmich's novel *A Muslim Suicide*.